# Joe and the Governor

## A Novel
## Bill Cronin

Printed in the United States of America

ISBN: 978-0-9908381-5-9

Library of Congress Cataloging-In-Publication Data

Library of Congress Control Number 2016910503

*Dedication*

To my wife Linda, the person I write for.

# 1

I've often stood on Whitehead Street across the road from Ernest Hemingway's Home and Museum and tried to imagine the scope of Hemingway's career. One of the most complex men ever to take a number-two lead pencil to paper, Hemingway wrote seven novels, six collections of short stories, two works of non-fiction and collected the Pulitzer and Nobel prizes. But, my reason for gawking at his home had nothing to do with his inspiring career.

I wanted to understand what led Hemingway to buy this house. It wasn't a large structure. Even by the standards of 1931, it wasn't ostentatious. Why here? Why this particular spot? I was here in Key West to find a place of my own. I already knew I wanted something quiet and secluded. My home in Mount Dora, Florida had a separate, detached building I used as a studio that had suited my purposes. I was curious about Hemingway's and whether examining it would offer something I hadn't considered.

From my research, I knew of several reasons he selected Key West. First, the Florida Straights between Key West and Cuba was home to the best sport fishing in the world. Fishing drew Hemingway to Key West in 1928, a place to unwind from seven years as an ex-patriot in Paris. In 1931, he and his wife Pauline purchased the abandoned, neglected Whitehead Street mansion amid the great depression. They bought it for taxes owed—a mere eight-thousand dollars. For a perspective, if they had purchased the home today, they would have paid one-hundred-twenty-eight-thousand for property worth more than a million dollars. On just over an acre of ground, the location offered privacy. The three thousand square feet building was large enough to handle his growing family and provided space for frequent guests. Numerous French doors opened onto the wrap-around verandas on both floors. They provided adequate ventilation to combat Key West's stifling heat and humidity. While all these were positive considerations, what I think attracted Hemingway to this particular spot was the detached two-story building to the rear of the property. A garage took up the bottom floor. Tattered servant's quarters occupied the second, which he had converted to a studio. Hemingway needed a workroom away from distractions. At the time, he'd been writing the manuscript for *Death in the Afternoon* and a place to write, I thought, would've been foremost in his mind. In time, Hemingway had a bridge constructed from his second story veranda, near his bedroom, to the second story workroom above the garage.

As I stood and observed the Hemingway grounds, what stood out was an ill-constructed, six-foot high, redbrick wall. It surrounded the property on three sides. In 1935, Hemingway hired Toby Bruce, a family friend and woodworker from Piggott, Arkansas to build it. Having no experience as a bricklayer, Bruce's inexperience was evident in the meandering lines of the out-of-level bricks. A tour company in Key West had added Hemingway's abode to their circuit. Hemingway had built the wall to keep the curious from wandering about his yard. It took Bruce an entire summer to construct the barrier. While city leaders viewed the structure as an eyesore, Hemingway was well pleased. Bruce may have been a novice, but the wall still stands after more than sixty years and several hurricanes.

I hadn't considered a fence for security. In Mount Dora, FL, five hours to the north, my home sat on a lake in a suburban setting two miles from the city center. Not once, in all the years I'd lived and written there, did I have any issues with invasive tourists. When I compared my career to Hemingway's, the commercial success of my novels and movies had exceeded his. I'd written more novels, and my gross sales had been greater than his even adjusting for the differences in value of the dollar from the 1930s and 40s to 1996. Yet, even in the early stages of his career, he was such an icon he had to construct a wall to keep out curious fans. It was humbling. While my work had enjoyed commercial success, I knew nothing I'd written could compete with Hemingway's two literary prizes.

I'd been fortunate. I'd spent my life doing what I love to do; write novels. I had no pretentions about what I had written. I picked genre fiction and topics designed to appeal to the masses. While I'd considered writing a more literary work, the need to make a living predominated. In that endeavor, I had done well. I wanted to write a book like, *The Old Man and the Sea*, something noteworthy. I'd always been in awe of the simplicity of the subject matter of Hemingway's most praised work. But, I had yet to find a subject whose theme rose to the level of compelling greatness. I'd just refreshed my contract with Reynolds & Ryan Publishing. I'd negotiated and received wider latitude in what I wrote, and they'd agreed to buy three non-genre books of my choosing. I'd hoped to pursue a topic of substance, a serious attempt at literature. The "what" had eluded me. As with so many of my books, the ideas for them often came in serendipitous fashion. My attempt at prize winning literature would have to wait. I had matters more pressing. I needed to decide if I was going to move to Key West. If I was serious about the move, I needed to find a home that met my needs.

Three months ago, following the completion of my last novel, I'd announced at a party thrown by my half-sister Billie that I'd intended to sell my house in Mount Dora and move to Key West. At the time, there were several factors pushing me in that direction. Then it seemed like a stellar idea. Standing across the street from Hemingway's, I was having second thoughts.

First, I'd just gone through a divorce after an eight-year marriage to Emily. A three-year writing dry spell caused by severe depression sent me to an emotional bottom. The spiral downward didn't wear well on Emily. Complicating matters, Emily was my manager and editor, a job she still held. During my bout with depression, Emily sought the solace of my best friend, Bob Decker, who was also going through a rough patch in his marriage. The mutual commiseration evolved into an affair, which Emily kept secret until the ink was dry on our divorce papers. Two weeks before she would marry Decker, she took me out to a public place and confessed her affair. She said she kept it a secret because she didn't think I was emotionally stable enough to handle such difficult news. She made it clear she liked working for me and wanted to continue in the role of manager and editor. At that point, I needed Emily's skills. While writing novels takes skill, the editing and revision process takes a mediocre work and transforms it into something noteworthy. She was more than a line or copy editor. She analyzed each draft for content, guiding my revisions and she drove me to raise the level of my writing. Emily and I were a good team. The work we produced was successful. Then, I was in no position to fire her. But I didn't have to be in the same town with her and Decker either. There were too many memories of Emily in my home in Mount Dora. Even though I still had to work with her, I didn't want to be around her.

Second, my half-sister Billie lived in Key West. Within the last year, we had reunited. I hadn't seen her in thirty years. She owned a restaurant in Key West, The Mangrove, on the corner of Duval Street and Olivia Street, a block from Hemingway's house. My father had just recently passed away while my divorce from Emily was in the process. Aside from my aunt Glory Jean, my mother's sister, who lived in Savannah, Billie was my only living relative. Following Emily's news, I needed that familial connection. When my depression reached rock bottom, I'd come to Key West to find my sister and to attempt to reconcile our relationship.

Third, when I was fourteen, Billie was instrumental in introducing me to Jody Holland, the first girl I ever kissed and loved. Tragedy struck Jody's family and cut our budding romance short in a disturbing way. At the same time, I was searching for Billie, Jody had moved to Key West and wandered into Billie's restaurant and recognized

Billie immediately. They became instant friends. When I came to Key West looking for Billie, she reconnected me with Jody. It was Jody and Billie who helped me work my way out of my depression and put me on the road to writing again.

In the months following, my relationship with Emily imploded. Jody and I found the chemistry that drew us together as kids produced the same reaction more than thirty years later. I was in love with her and, as time progressed, it expanded and grew more comfortable. She owned a successful business in Key West and had deep roots there. If I wanted to be with her, I needed to make the move.

In light of all these factors, moving to Key West seemed natural. In fact, as I stood across from Hemingway's, I couldn't think of one rational reason for not making the move. Still, I was hesitant. Billie, Jody and I had emotional scars. We all had childhood events that had wounded us and had eaten away at the edges of our happiness. We'd built our emotional foundations on shifting sand.

Our mother abandoned Billie when she was a small child, and again when she was eighteen. It wasn't until Billie had met Alexandra that she'd been able to move past childhood events and stitch a meaningful life together.

In 1961, Jody's mother had suffered from postpartum psychosis and shot four of her brothers and sisters and her father. She'd shot Jody, too, but had only inflicted a grazing wound to her head. The courts committed Jody's mother to a mental institution where they incarcerated her for ten years. Three months ago, Jody and her mother reunited after thirty years. Jody's mother, Helen, was staying in Key West while she and Jody attended joint counseling to work through the emotional damage created so long ago.

We were all wounded souls. We were all needy. But it was my relationship with Jody that gave me pause. I had no idea how counseling would affect our relationship. I was hesitant to make such a huge life investment in Key West until I'd more time to see how my relationship with Jody worked out.

I dodged passing cars, crossed Whitehead Street and aimed down Olivia Street, walking past the crooked brick wall and past Hemingway's studio on my way to Billie's restaurant.

Behind The Mangrove, a driveway served as a pad for a dumpster and a place where trucks delivered food and supplies. There was a man dressed in soiled clothes sitting on a fruit crate. I wouldn't have taken notice except the restaurant hadn't opened yet, and he seemed out of place. As I walked past the drive, the man with an unshaven face looked up at me with clear blue eyes and smiled. I nodded and continued down to the corner of Duval Street and Olivia Street, turned right and approached the front gate. Billie had converted an old two-story home into a restaurant. The front yard of the house was a brick-paved, courtyard and outdoor dining area. Two towering banyan trees shaded it. The corner lot was bound by a white picket fence with an entry gate on Duval. At the entrance, a tall white, wooden podium served as a host station. A sign read, "Closed." I unlocked the gate and ambled past teak wood tables covered by forest green canvas umbrellas to the old home, which sat to the back of the lot.

Billie redesigned the house into a kitchen and indoor dining area. When you came through the front door, bathrooms were to the left, a café door to the kitchen was straight ahead and to the right a dining room that had been the living room of the large home. A stairway hugged the wall and led to a second floor, which provided storage and an office for Billie. Behind it, where the old dining room had been, Billie had converted it to a private dining area for large parties or meetings. Billie was in the kitchen, talking with her chef, Molly Flynn.

I'd just returned to Key West from Mount Dora the night before. I stayed at Billie's home last night, and she had invited me to have brunch with her this morning.

When I approached the café doors that separated the kitchen from the front door, Billie turned away from Molly and looked at me. In contrast to her flyaway, rusty, red hair, her brilliant green eyes dominated her round face.

She pushed the doors apart, hugged me, stood back, looked at me and said, "You look rested. And warm! Look at you, you're dripping wet."

"I was standing in the sun looking over Hemingway's museum. It's a lot more humid in the middle of July than it was when I was here in April."

"They don't call it the mold capital for nothing. But, I love it. All the snowbirds are gone, and except for the cruise ships, we locals have the island all to ourselves."

"Before I forget it, when I was walking up Olivia, I noticed a man milling about behind your restaurant."

Billie led me into the empty dining room. They had set the table for two. We sat across from one another.

"It must be Joe. Homeless guy?"

I nodded.

"Joe and I have an arrangement. I let him pitch a tent in the back behind the dumpster in exchange for him keeping the yard picked up and keeping others from rummaging through my dumpster. We have a real homeless problem in Key West. People were going through my trash after I closed the restaurant. By itself, that wasn't a problem, but they were pulling garbage out of the dumpster and throwing it on the ground, leaving a mess. Joe offered to help."

"Do you pay him?"

"No. He won't take money from me. I offered to feed him but he won't have it. The only thing he wants is a safe place to sleep at night. The shelters are full, and the chances of finding a place where he won't be robbed or mugged are slim."

"So does he just hang around all day?"

"No. Not at all. He packs his belongings in the morning, puts them into a shed I have in the back and goes off for places unknown during the day. But here is the strange thing. One day a week, he gets all cleaned up, puts on clean clothes, comes into the restaurant through the front gate and has a meal, like a regular customer. He insists on paying the bill. And he leaves a generous tip for the servers."

"What do you know about him?"

11

"Nothing. He never talks about himself. He deflects every personal question I ask him. But, Jack, he's one of the most intelligent people I've ever talked to. He's a mystery, that one. Every time I talk to him, I think about you. He seems like an awesome character for a book. You should meet him—talk to him."

"I'd like that."

Like I said. Sometimes ideas for stories come to you in serendipitous ways.

# 2

When I'd arrived late last night, Billie and Alex had already gone to bed. Billie left the back door unlocked and I'd gone up to her guest room. Both Billie and Alex had already gone before I got up.

The chef brought us eggs benedict, a plate of cantaloupe to share and a decanter of coffee.

Once we settled into our meal I asked, "So tell me, how's In-Vitro going?"

When I was here in April, Billie announced she and Alex were going to try to have a baby. Billie, in her early fifties, had already gone through menopause, but she wanted to carry the baby. IVF was their only option. Billie had already been to see a fertility doctor in Miami for an initial consultation when I was here last.

"The clinic performed all the tests. The docs gave me a green light. The biggest snag is a legal one. Using eggs and sperm from donors is more complicated than I thought. It is almost like a legal adoption, where the donors agree to give up legal ownership and custody of their eggs and sperm. We're all set to go, procedure wise. I just want to meet with Cynthia before I sign all the papers. I want to understand what I'm getting into."

Cynthia Pike was her attorney and friend.

"Sounds complicated." When she told me she was considering IVF, I'd never thought about the legal issues.

"The fertility clinic says it isn't complicated. All the sperm and egg donors sign forms and give up all their rights of custody. We have to file court papers to become legal parents of the fertilized eggs or embryos. But the docs want me to sign a form that holds them harmless if at some point the egg or sperm donors want to sue for custody. Sometimes, that can happen. Alex and I felt like we needed Cynthia to go over all this with us before we press ahead."

"What kind of tests did they have to do?"

"They had to determine if I was healthy enough to carry a baby for nine months. I'm fifty-two, Jack. I'm no spring chicken. They had to examine all my female plumbing and perform a mock embryo transfer, which is too personal to go into detail. But they just want to make sure they don't encounter any issues during the procedure.

"After the legal issues, Alex and I have some tough decisions. For example, the most important decision is how many embryos do we want to implant?"

"I don't understand. Why would you consider more than one?"

"Jack, they drain your bank account every time they perform this procedure. Implanting more than one embryo increases the chances of a successful pregnancy. But it also means I could have twins or triplets depending on the number of embryos we choose to implant."

"Doesn't that increase the risk of health complications?"

"Yes, but the fertility docs assure me I'm healthy enough to handle a multiple pregnancy."

"Are you and Alex prepared for something like that? I mean, you have this restaurant to take care of. Could you handle the stress of more than one child?"

"I don't know, Jack. Alex and I are working through that now. I think I'm more concerned about the prospect of not having a child. This is very important to me." Billie gave emphasis to the word "very." "I want to be able to give a youngster the childhood I never had. This is about me, as much as it is about having a baby."

When I thought about the loveless childhood Billie had had, abandoned by my mother as a toddler and abandoned by her uncaring natural father, I could empathize. This would mean she would have a teenage child when she was in her late sixties. I wanted to raise it as an issue for her to consider, but thought better of it.

"So how is Alex feeling about this? She was against this, wasn't she?"

"Yes. You helped us work through it, Jack, and I appreciate it. After you left here in April, Alex and I went to see my doctors. When they explained to Alex the tests they would do to insure I was healthy enough for the procedure, it alleviated her concerns. Now that the docs have done all the exams, she's good. The legal issues are another matter. She's troubled about the problems that could come up. Our meeting with Cynthia is pretty important."

"So what comes next?"

"It's a simple process for me, since I'm using donated eggs and sperm. I go into the doctor's office, and they inject embryos into my uterus. This is nothing more than might happen in a routine pelvic exam. If I were younger, and using my own eggs, the docs would treat me with synthetic hormones to stimulate the ovaries to produce more than one egg. After fourteen days, they'd give me more medication to help the eggs mature. I would receive more medications to prevent the body from releasing the developed eggs too soon. Whether a woman uses her own eggs, or donated eggs, they give you progesterone supplements to make the lining of the uterus more receptive to implantation.

"If I'd been using my own eggs, the Doc would retrieve them. From that point on, the procedure is the same whether I have eggs or use a donor. First, the clinic would fertilize the egg. After about six days, they perform genetic tests to ensure the embryo is healthy and there are no birth defects. The Doc implants the embryo and checks the progress of the pregnancy. Of course, there's no assurance I'll get pregnant on the first try. Although the fertility clinic plays up their success rate, they also are honest that they may have to make several attempts before I get pregnant. Because of my age, the chances of more than one attempt are higher, and there's more of a risk of delivering a pre-mature baby, or in the worst case, I have a miscarriage. They'll give me medications to prevent this, but there's still that chance."

"When do you meet with Pike?"

"We meet in a day or two when Alex returns. I was hoping you'd come with Alex and me. I'd like you to be there. You may think of something to ask her Alex and I haven't thought of."

"I'm concerned about being a fifth-wheel with Alex."

"Alex suggested it, Jack."

"I appreciate you wanting to include me, but this is personal, Billie. This is something you and Alex should do."

We chatted while we ate and finished our meal. We refilled our coffee cups.

Billie asked, "Did you put your house up for sale in Mount Dora?"

"No. I know I said I was going to do that, but I decided I'd hold off for now."

"Getting cold feet about moving here, Jack?"

"No, not yet anyway. I thought it might be wise to try to find a place first and live here a while before I severed ties with Central Florida. Homes are so expensive here, I'm wondering whether it would be wise to rent before I buy."

"Tell me about it. I bought our house through a foreclosure sale. Today the taxable value is over a million and the taxes are killing us. We paid half that amount just six years ago. The problem is land to build new homes is scarce. Because of a shortage of water and sewer facilities in the keys, the government limits building permits. Jody paid more for her little cracker house than Alex and I paid for ours. It's nuts."

"It's hot in the summer in Mount Dora, but nothing compared to the heat and humidity you have here."

"For six months, it's paradise here. And we're currently in the wrong six months."

"Yeah, and then the Conch Republic morphs into hell on earth."

"Thank God for the cruise ships or we would starve. So what kind of a house are you looking for? You know you're welcome to stay at our house as long as you like. And Jody would be ecstatic if you moved in with her."

"I'm not ready for that yet, Billie. Besides, what I need is a place to write that's free of distractions."

"You're welcome to one of our bedrooms. We have three that just collect dust."

"I appreciate your offer, but in Mount Dora, I have a separate building for my studio. The previous owners had it built as a guesthouse with its own kitchenette and bath. I need something like that, here. And it needs to be private and quiet."

"And my house won't do?"

"Interruptions and distractions are the kiss of death to a writer. As good as my focus and concentration skills are, I need seclusion. All Mrs. Berger would have to do is fire up the vacuum cleaner she runs twice a week and she'd ruin my day of writing."

"She's not the quietest person on the planet."

"And Jody's place is just too small. There's no place to write except on her back patio, and there's too much ambient noise there."

"If you're looking for something on the Island to buy, that could be expensive."

"With real estate prices going up so quick here, it sounds like a good place to invest."

"But you're hesitant. I thought you wanted to get away from Emily. She's still working for you isn't she?"

"For now. I do want to get away from her. It's just too close, especially with her married to my best friend. The problem isn't just the house in

Mount Dora. She still works for me. Before I can do anything about that, I need to find another editor and manager. And I don't want to do anything until I make up my mind about Key West."

"I thought you decided to move here. It's Jody isn't it? You're not sure about Jody?"

"Jody needs space right now, Billie. She has her mother here, they're in counseling right now and, well, there's no telling how all this will affect her."

"I think you're wrong about her needing space. While you've been away, she's been missing you something awful. The woman is in love, Jack. She needs you. All this turmoil with her mom has dredged up long suppressed feelings. She's struggling."

"I know Billie. I talk to her everyday on the phone. And it's upsetting to listen to her go through it."

"Is that what's bothering you?"

"I don't know. I want to help her, but what can I do? I feel helpless."

"You still feel the same about her?"

"Yes."

"I think all she needs right now is you to be there for her. I don't think she wants or needs anything but your love and support."

"I know."

"She's anxious to see you, too. I think she was a little disappointed about not having breakfast with us."

"She was a little upset I didn't stay with her last night."

"Something's going on Jack. What is it?"

"Billie, I've just recovered from a significant depression of my own. No sooner do I have my life back together; my publisher fires me. Emily divorces me, my father passes away and I find out Emily had been having an affair with my best friend. On top of that, Jody and I went digging into her past, the reunion with her mother and it's all a little much. I'm hesitant to wade into another emotional quagmire."

"We haven't mentioned all my junk; almost losing my restaurant and issues over having a child."

"It isn't that Billie. It is the sum of all of it. I needed a break."

"Is that why it took you three months to return to the Keys?

"Part of the reason . . . okay, yes it was the reason."

"Then why are you thinking about a move here?" There was a wounded quality to Billie's voice. A sarcastic tone.

"For starters, I love you. You're pretty much the only family I have. And I'm in love with Jody. I want to be here."

"I don't want to be a burden to you, Jack."

I regretted the turn in our conversation. "Billie, you're misunderstanding me."

Billie lifted her elbows off the table and pushed back into her chair. "Doesn't sound like it to me."

"You aren't my concern, Billie. I'm not worried about you. It's Jody. She's looking for a commitment from me, one I'm unwilling to make until I see how everything goes with her mother."

"I thought you saw Jody and her mother going through counseling as a positive step."

"It is."

"You said you admired her courage and wisdom in hitting her issues with her mother head on."

"Yes, I did. And I still feel that way. I do admire her. It demonstrates a lot of character. But I guarantee the process she's going through with her mother will change her."

"Yes, there could be changes. But do you think that part of Jody, the part you fell in love with as a boy and now again after all these years as a man, will have changed? She's one of the finest people I've ever known and she's in love with you. Yes, she's dealing with some significant emotional issues. You can't experience what she went through without collateral damage. But, she's dealing with it, facing it. You were a mess when you first came to Key West, and Jody jumped in that hole you were in and helped you dig yourself out. She didn't hesitate."

"I know, Billie. I know. I'm grateful to her and to you. You both saved my life. And I'm not having second thoughts about her. I just want to go slow. I just want to make sure it's a relationship that can endure."

"It's endured for over thirty years, Jack. I don't know how much more enduring it can be."

"You're right." I threw up my hands. "You're right. I'm worrying for nothing."

"You should go find, Jody. But, tonight's the night Joe usually comes and has dinner. There're no ships in town, so tonight will be slow. Why don't you and Jody come and have dinner with me. I want you to meet this guy."

I agreed.

# 3

Ninety degrees plus ninety percent humidity equal miserable. Even though I'd dressed for the heat in shorts, a light T-shirt and flip-flops, my clothes stuck to my skin. Jody's art gallery was halfway down Duval Street between Billie's restaurant and the Pier House. It was nearing noon, and the foot traffic on the sidewalk was light. The smell of the sea filled the air. The sun was relentless and a shade elusive.

The Pegasus Art Gallery logo in gold leaf was emblazoned on the glass entry door. Jody had filled the plate glass window with several watercolors featuring a local artist. An electronic bell chimed as I opened the door to enter. Jody was sitting behind a small table that doubled as a stand for her cash register and a work surface. She looked up from her work, saw it was me, bolted from the chair, crossed the short distance between us and threw her arms around me. I returned her hug with enthusiasm. She kissed me on the mouth.

"Mmmmm, have I missed those." And she kissed me again, longer and deeper. She pulled back. "Yes, indeed I have." Her eyes beamed; a smile spread across her thin face.

"You look marvelous, Jody." And she did. As I was holding her, the conversation I'd just had about commitment with Billie echoed. In her arms, those feelings seemed silly and melted away. I pulled away from her. "I'm soaked. I'm going to mess up your clothes. And I smell like last year's laundry."

"We need to get you out of those clothes, then." She winked at me. "I think we should close up for lunch, go to my house, and we'll run your clothes through the dryer. And maybe while we're waiting we can think of something to do. A shower perhaps?"

And that's what we did. Afterwards, we sat on her small deck behind her conch-style house and she and I caught up. The lunch-hour stretched into two hours.

I asked her, "Don't you need to get back to the gallery?"

"Okay. Let me see. I haven't seen you in three months. You're in my house and you're sitting on my porch. I was thinking that as soon as we finish our lemonade, we could find our way back to my bed. So why would I want to go back to the gallery? Unless of course you want me to go?"

I smiled at her. This was typical Jody, a playful, unabashed tease.

We spent the afternoon, napping, playing and catching up. An hour before dusk, we dressed and walked the short distance to the Pier House sunset deck. We selected a table with an unobstructed view of the setting sun. We ordered Margaritas and then sat close together watching silhouetted boats of every description motor past the deck.

Jody volunteered. "My mother and I are meeting twice a week now."

I'd wanted to ask how the counseling sessions were going with her mother. I'd learned with Jody, on this particular subject, it was best not to pry. Over the past three months, we'd talked on the phone every day. I took the position that when she was ready to talk about her mother, she would. It had been a couple of weeks since she'd brought the topic up. She'd already told me a month ago they'd increased their joint counseling sessions to twice a week.

"Oh? How is that going?"

"If Dr. Carnes asks me one more time about how I feel about something, I'm going to scream."

"So, how are you feeling about all this?" I drew out the word feeling and smiled.

Jody punched me on the arm.

I asked, "Has it accomplished anything?"

"When we started meeting with Dr. Carnes, I'd no idea what to expect. In our first meeting, Dr. Carnes asked my mother to share what was in her heart. That took up the entire first session."

"What did she say?"

"Same thing she told us when we first met with her. She knows what she did was wrong; she was out of her mind when she did it. While she feels horrible about what happened, she's adamant it was not her fault."

"Your reaction?"

"Mentally, I understand it. I know she was sick. I understand it in my mind. Deep down, all I feel is rage. And, after three months of counseling, I still feel that way."

"Has there been any progress?"

"Yes. I can be in the same room with her. And our sessions are more like guided conversations. I know this is going to sound strange, but I'm beginning to see the anger I feel isn't connected to her. I'm beginning to see her as a person instead of a convenient bull's eye for my angst. The rage I feel is much broader than my mother. I haven't said this to Dr. Carnes, but I can separate my mother from that anger."

"How?"

"First, I understand the anger problem is my issue, not my mother's. She was the catalyst, the first-mover. My anger comes from my inability to deal with what happened to my family, not my mother. My anger goes beyond her."

"So who's the target of your anger?"

"I don't know, Jack. I'm still trying to sort it out. When we first met with my mother, she equated the tragedy of our family to a natural disaster. Hurricane Andrew was the example she used that stuck with me. I remember my anger as I watched the news coverage of the people that monster storm had killed. I remember the anger I felt that something so horrible and senseless could happen to the innocent."

"You know, Jody. I remember reacting the same way."

"Good. Now magnify that a hundred times and you approach how I'm feeling." Jody drew out the word feeling for emphasis.

"So you're angry at God?"

"Yes . . . No . . . I don't know. I'm angry at what I don't understand. But I agree with what my mother said to us three months ago. Tragedies occur all the time. Fate takes the lives of the innocent. And there's no one left standing to take the blame. I want someone to be responsible. I want to hurl my anger at someone. I want to hurt someone over what happened to my family. When I look at my mother, and what she's been through, I know she's not to blame. She was a victim, too."

"Sounds like a lot of progress to me."

"I suppose. A mixture of good and bad. The good news for my mother is she gets the target taken off her chest. The bad news is I don't know where to place the blame. I still have the anger. My life was simple before we started counseling. I hated my mother for what she did. Now it isn't simple any more. Now I still have the anger, but I don't know where to direct it. Here is the interesting part, Jack. I don't want to give up that anger. It has become a part of me. And while I may be able to forgive my mother, I'm concerned my desire to protect and sustain my anger is the real monster hiding under the bed."

"It seems to me your recognition of the problem is more than half the battle. Have you shared any of this in counseling?"

"No. I wanted to talk to you about it in person, first. I'll be honest. When I make that confession, and let my mother off the hook, the dynamics of the counseling will shift its focus to my issues. Do you remember the first time we met with my mother, we had this little exchange about why she wanted to see me. I assumed she wanted my forgiveness. If you recall, she said she didn't want or need my pardon. She had come to help me deal with the emotional damage created by what she'd done. I understand that now. She's not my problem and my mother has known it all along. My issue is that I haven't dealt with what happened to me in the correct way. The irony is I have an emotional illness that's the cause of my angst, not my mother. Once I let the cat out of the bag, I'll have Dr. Carnes and my mother pressing me to deal with it. The focus moves off my mother and what she did, to me."

"And how do you feel about that?" I again dragged out the word feel into three or four syllables, and feigned a broad smile.

"I feeeeel like Dr. Carnes and my mom have me hog tied and they're dragging me toward mental health. I know I need to do this; everything in me is fighting against it. Do you think I'm crazy, Jack?"

"Quite the opposite. Even on my best days during my long bout with depression, I was not thinking as clearly as you are. I'm so impressed with your analysis and the conclusions you're coming to. You've a keen intelligence I find attractive."

"Thanks, you're kind to say that. But right now I don't feel like I have it together. So . . . you're only attracted to my intellect?" A hint of a smile broke at the corners of her mouth.

I said, "So you think what we did this afternoon was a meeting of the minds."

"Yeah, something like that." Her light brown eyes sparkled.

"Have you and your mother gotten together outside of counseling since I left for Mount Dora?"

"No. She's invited me several times to have a meal with her, but I declined. Until I'd sorted out my relationship with her, I didn't want to add any complications. I told her you were coming into town and she suggested you and I get together with her. She likes you, Jack. She always has."

"So you're okay with that?"

"If you're with me, yes. I think I'm ready. I need to share all this with her and Dr. Carnes tomorrow when we get together. I'll suggest we get together at Billie's for dinner. I'm not ready to invite her to my house."

"Billie wants us to come to dinner tonight. She wants me to meet this homeless guy named Joe."

"Billie has been talking about this guy for a couple of weeks now. I've seen him hanging around the restaurant."

"He gets cleaned up once a week and becomes a paying customer. Billie thinks this guy would be a good character for one of my books."

"Billie has an enormous heart, Jack. I just hope she knows what she's getting into."

# 4

Jody and I finished our drinks at the Pier House. I went to Billie's to shower and change clothes. Jody and I agreed we'd meet at the restaurant.

I got there early and found Billie in the kitchen assembling dishes and preparing them for delivery to the tables.

"Hey, Jack." She looked up at me a little frazzled. "I'll be so glad when we remodel the kitchen and we have more space in here. This is a joke." She looked around at the cramped quarters.

"When will they start construction?"

When I left in April, Billie was working with a commercial kitchen designer to remodel the bottom floor of the old house into something state-of-the-art.

"Next week, thank God." She moved closer to me and whispered, "If it had been up to me, I'd have it done by now. But my chef, Molly, bless her heart, has worked and reworked the design to the point I finally had to tell her to stop. Even now, after the architect submitted the blueprints to the city for approval, she still wants to tweak this or change that. Anyway, the city issued the building permit and the contractor begins work soon."

"By the way, Jody is coming. I hope you don't mind."

"I already counted on you inviting her. How's counseling going with her mother? Every time I ask her anything about it she deflects my question."

"Well. They're making phenomenal progress, or I should say Jody is."

"Now that you've spent more time with her, are you still apprehensive?"

"No, those concerns melted away this afternoon."

"And what happened this afternoon?"

I didn't say a word. I just smiled.

Billie nodded; a Cheshire cat grin on her face.

We both enjoyed the intimacy of the moment, then, she said, "I have the private dining room set up for us. Go find a seat and I'll have Gwen bring you a pitcher of Margaritas and some appetizers."

Except for colorful oil paintings that hung from the walls, the room was stark white, with dark stained hardwood floors.

Just as I took my seat at a long table for six, a small, trim woman placed a pitcher of Margaritas filled with crushed ice on the table.

"Hi, I'm Gwen. I'm going to be taking care of you."

"Hi, Gwen." I extended my hand.

With enthusiasm, she shook it and said, "You're Billie's brother, right?"

"Yes. Have you worked here long?"

"Been here since she opened. I love it here. I love your sister. She's the best boss; more than a boss."

"Thank you for telling me. I'm sure it would please her to know how you feel."

"She knows. I tell her all the time. As soon as the others begin to show up I'll look in on you."

"Thanks, Gwen." She left me with an empty room to collect my thoughts.

I replayed the conversation I had with Billie about Jody. When I was with her, it felt as natural as breathing. As I contemplated our afternoon together, we were so compatible in every way. My apprehension about a commitment to her while I was away in Mount Dora seemed irrational.

Billie appeared at the door with the man I saw earlier behind her restaurant. He was at least six feet tall, trim but not athletic looking, sporting a beard with flecks of gray at his chin. His hair was long but pulled into a ponytail. He wore leather open-toed sandals like Birkenstocks, khaki shorts, and a Hog's Breath Saloon T-shirt that said, "Hog's Breath is better than no breath at all."

Joe had a dark tan. His thin face was almost Christ-like. It was his glacier blue eyes, which stood out and impressed. They were clear, confident, penetrating eyes; not those of a drug addict, or alcoholic.

Billie escorted Joe to the table.

I stood.

"This is my brother, Jack McNamara."

Joe extended his hand. "Hi, Jack. I'm Joe."

His handshake was firm, and his eyes never left mine during the introduction.

"Joe, you sit here." Billie gestured toward the chair opposite from me. "I'll leave the two of you to get acquainted while I clean up a little. I'll join you in a minute."

Billie left and the silence was only momentary as Joe and I sat and adjusted our chairs.

"I'm a huge fan, Jack. I've read all your books. I can't believe we're having a drink together." Joe helped himself to the Margarita pitcher.

"Well it's always nice to meet a fan."

"Billie tells me you're moving to Key West." He unfurled the white napkin on the table and with a flourish laid it across his lap. Then he took a sip of his drink.

"That's the plan so far."

"Sounds like there are caveats."

"Well, it depends on whether I can find a place to buy."

"The nice thing about my current status is I don't have those kinds of worries. What kind of place are you looking for?"

I said, "I've been wrestling with that question since I got here last night. I think the major consideration is finding a house with a detached studio where I can write in privacy and seclusion. I have that in my current home in Mount Dora. I'd like to find something similar here."

"A clean well-lighted place." A reference to one of Hemingway's stories.

"You're a Hemingway fan, I take it."

"More of a fan of his writing, than his lifestyle. Here is a man who could put some words on paper, yet the town here idolizes the alcoholic version of Hemingway as carouser and barfly."

"Yes, I agree," I said, "The image of a Nobel laureate and town drunk aren't compatible are they?"

"I take it from the sheer volume of the books you've written you have few outside interests beyond your work."

He impressed me with his deductive reasoning. "On occasion, I like to take my boat out on the lake and fish for bass. Except for that, which seldom happens, writing is my singular vice."

"What project are you working on now?"

"I'm between books at the moment. I have some ideas, but nothing I'm ready to share yet."

Joe took another sip from his drink and put his elbows on the table. "After all the books you've written, how do you come up with ideas for stories?"

"That's an excellent question, Joe, a question for which I have no logical answer. They just come to me. Sometimes they're no more than an embryo that requires thought to build it into something substantive. Other times, complete stories come to me in just a few minutes."

"So do you follow an outline?"

"I know this will sound contrary to what you learned in creative writing class, but I can't begin to write a story until I've worked out the entire plot in my head. If I can't see the whole story, front to end, I can't write it. Sometimes an idea has to stay with me for a while until it develops in full. I call it marinating. Once the story is in my brain, I can write it. The outline is in my head, not on paper."

"So you think a written outline is too confining?"

"You can't pin down the creative process in writing. You can't nail down characters either. They have to be who they are. When your outline is rigid and over thought, you deprive your characters the ability to express themselves. I create a series of scenes that will carry the book from beginning to end. And even then, they aren't hard and fast."

"Are you married?"

"Divorced. Recently divorced."

"Same here."

Before I had the opportunity to inquire further, Jody appeared at the doorway in a pale yellow, sleeveless, short summer dress, with white, spaghetti sandals. She wore her blond hair up in a French twist.

I introduced her to Joe. They shook hands and exchanged greetings. Jody took a seat next to me. I poured Jody a Margarita.

I had hoped to question Joe further, but before I had the opportunity, he was already in the question-asking mode with Jody. What did she do? Where did she come from? What did she like about Key West? How did she get into the art gallery business? He was clever and kept the spotlight off himself. Jody finally turned the table on Joe and cut him off from his fact-finding mission.

"So, Is Joe your real name? It just doesn't seem to fit you."

Jody surprised me by asking Joe such a direct question.

The surprised look on his face told me he hadn't expected the question, either. He looked around as though he were deciding to leave or stay.

"It is one of my names."

"What's your real name?"

Just as Joe was about to answer Jody's question, Billie appeared at the door with Cynthia Pike, her attorney. We exchanged greetings. Billie introduced Pike to Joe. We all sat down. Gwen delivered another pitcher of Margaritas along with tortilla chips, salsa and cheese dip.

Billie said, "Cynthia just popped in to see me and I invited to her eat with us. I hope no one minds."

Pike said, "In fact, Joe, you were the man I was hoping to talk to. Billie has told me about you several times. From everything she said, I think you'd be perfect."

"Perfect for what?" Joe sounded suspicious.

"The attorney general for the state of Florida was in my law office yesterday on another matter. He told me the governor was scheduled to be in Key West next week to give a speech on the homeless problem in the state. He's giving his talk here in Key West, because our fair city has the highest percentage of homeless persons to total population of any city in the state."

"What does that have to do with me?" Joe's eyes narrowed and he sat back in his chair.

"The governor has a plan to deal with the problem, and the AG would like to have a spokesperson to represent the homeless; an advocate if you will."

Joe looked uncomfortable. "Key West has at least half a dozen agencies that deal with the homeless. They'd be better advocates than me, Ms. Pike."

"Solving the homeless problem in this state is a complicated issue made more complex by politics. Most of the agencies you speak of receive funding from the state. A change could be adverse to them. The AG is looking for someone who has no political stake, someone who's knowledgeable about the plight of the homeless. Someone like you, Joe."

"I appreciate you thinking about me, Ms. Pike, but I've no desire whatsoever to be a part of that. I don't want the saddle of the woes of the community on me. I've enough trouble taking care of my own day-to-day needs."

"The AG will pay you which might help with some of those day-to-day."

Joe fidgeted in his chair. "It's just out of the question."

"Billie describes you as intelligent, articulate and gracious. We have a horrific homeless problem in Key West, Joe, which is only getting worse. Every time the state gets involved, there're always unintended, negative consequences. We need a fresh set of eyes on this problem, a new perspective. The AG will be back here in a few days. Would you at least consider meeting with him and hearing him out."

Joe said, "With all due respect, Ms. Pike, that won't happen."

Pike said, "You have until Monday noon, to change your mind. I hope you will."

Uncomfortable silence fell upon the table until Billie served dinner. It was surf and turf; a filet and Florida lobster.

Joe said little for the rest of the meal. He thanked Billie for the dinner, said goodbye to each guest with sincerity and left at the first appropriate opportunity. On his way out, he said to me. "We need to talk. Alone." He gave me the name of a restaurant and asked me to have breakfast with him at seven-thirty in the morning. I agreed.

As the chef prepared our dessert, we chatted about Pike's offer to Joe.

"Well that was awkward," I said.

Jody said, "Billie, what do you know about this guy?"

"Not a lot. He doesn't offer much about himself."

Jody said, "Well, we know Joe's name is a fake. That tells me he's hiding something. Doesn't that concern you a little?"

"I'm sorry you didn't have the opportunity to talk with him much. He's a good man. Yes, I suspect he's dealing with something in his life. Aren't we all? From the exchanges I've had with him, I like him. For example, I know when I talk to Gwen, Joe, or whatever his name is, will have tried to pay for his meal or leave Gwen a nice tip. It shows character to me. I'm impressed by that."

"I'm worried about your safety, Billie. I think you need to be cautious here. I understand your desire to help him. But . . ."

Billie cut Jody off. "I appreciate your apprehension. I've been careful. And, until I know more about him, I'll continue to be watchful."

I was going to tell Billie and Jody about meeting Joe in the morning, but decided against it. I didn't want to raise Jody's concern. Ditto with Billie.

Jody and I left Billie's and I walked her home. She asked me to stay with her and I did. Before we went to sleep, Jody said to me, "Jack, there's something off about this guy Joe. He's too smart, too . . . whatever. He's more out-of-circulation than homeless. Everything about this guy tells me he's a dozen pay grades above a guy living on the street."

As I drifted off to sleep thinking about the potential mysteries surrounding Joe, the writer in me conjured up all kinds of nefarious scenarios. Only Joe knew the truth. I hoped to learn what it was in the morning.

# 5

I walked from Jody's and, even at this early hour, it was eighty degrees and the humidity was a least ninety percent. Sweat poured off me by the time I reached the breakfast joint Joe had picked. It was a few blocks from Billie's restaurant off Duvall. Hanging from a pole parallel to the ground was an antique neon sign. The fish was solid blue with the name The Marlin over it, flashing in red. The building looked like it was an old gas station from the 1930s with a drive under carport and a concrete island where two gas pumps were once located. A local artist had painted the exterior walls with fishing themed murals. Inside, there was a twelve-seat counter, and a dozen four-top tables crammed into the small room. Soft sixties music played in the background, and as I came through the door it rang a chime and the wait staff greeted me in unison with, "Good morning." Fishing paraphernalia adorned the walls, antique ceiling fans whirled and the place was clean. Plate glass windows surrounded the dining room on three sides.

Joe sat at one of the window tables, a steaming cup of coffee stationed in front of him.

If yesterday was the cleaned up version of Joe, this morning was the unkempt version. He'd combed his hair, but his soiled T-shirt looked like it hadn't seen an iron since it was new. His tangled beard added to his frazzled appearance.

As I approached the table, Joe stood and extended a hand. I shook it and we both took our seats. Before we had the opportunity to begin a conversation, the server brought a cup of coffee and set it in front of me.

I asked the server, "How did you know I wanted coffee?"

She smiled, "You looked like a coffee kinda guy." She winked at me.

"I'm serious. How did you know?"

"Ninety percent of the people who come through that door drink coffee. The odds were in my favor." She smiled and headed off to refill coffee cups at all the other tables before she returned to the kitchen.

Joe dove right in. "Thanks for coming this morning. I need your help with Billie."

"Alright. Good Morning, Joe."

"I'm sorry, forgive my manners, Jack. Good morning to you." He raked the curls of his dark brown hair with his fingers.

Joe was in his mid to late thirties. He sat forward in his seat with his elbows on the table. He was an intense man on a mission.

He said, "About last night. I know Billie is trying to help me, but it's the kind of help I don't need."

"You're referring to the AG thing."

"Yes."

"I got the impression she was hearing about the AG for the first time."

"Yes, Jack. It's just an example. She's always trying to help me."

"And why is that a problem? She likes you and wants to help."

"People are homeless for many reasons. There are addicts living on the bottom and the mentally ill who've fallen through the cracks. Both of these groups need help, but they won't take it. Some are down-and-outers who need and want help and then there are those who live on the street by choice. They don't want to work, they don't want responsibility and there's something attractive about living free of encumbrances. There are those who want to disappear and live in anonymity; who want to live unnoticed. That would be me."

"You seem well educated, sure of yourself and clear headed. What're you running from?"

"I don't want to go into it. All I'll say is I'm not a criminal. Beyond that, I want to remain anonymous, I don't want anyone to find me or be part of anything that will raise my visibility."

"So what is your real name, Joe?"

"I've gone by several names. Joe is the current name. That's all you need to know about me."

"So you're afraid Billie's efforts to help will raise your visibility?"

"That's part of it. I like Billie a lot. She's all heart and a fine person. She wants to help me. Her idea of help is improving my lot in life. All her solutions involve me plugging back into society. When I do, I might as well announce to the world where I am. That can't happen. I'm beginning to get concerned that even befriending Billie was a mistake, because she talks about me to others."

"So why do you want my help?"

"You need to talk to her. Make her understand that the best way she can help me is not to help me."

"I think it would be best if you told her yourself. She's pretty perceptive."

"That's why I'm talking to you now. I've talked with her but she ignores me. I haven't been as blunt with her as I've been with you because I don't want to hurt her feelings. If I can't get her to back off, I'm going to find somewhere else to go. She has no idea what a gift it is to be able to camp out behind the restaurant. Pike is right. The homeless problem in Key West is out of control. The homeless swamp the shelters, soup kitchens and all the parks and beaches. Crime among the homeless is rampant. Being able to stay behind The Mangrove is a safe haven. She's helping me more than she knows."

"How do you survive? Billie says you come in once a week and order a meal as a paying customer. Nothing on her menu is inexpensive."

"I work in Garrison Bight doing repair work on vessels moored there. The elements are tough on finishes and hardware and need constant maintenance. What I charge is half what a regular boatyard would bill, so I've plenty of work. It's all cash under the table."

"Why don't you rent an apartment somewhere?"

"They want information I don't want to provide. I know there are places who rent without asking questions, but those are the first places they'll look. I can't afford to take that risk."

"So you're running from the police?"

"If it were the police I were running from, I wouldn't worry. Look, Jack, I appreciate your interest, but the less you know about me the better—for me at least. I'd like to leave it there."

"How should I explain this to Billie?"

"You're the man with the words. The message should be she's helping me more than she knows, by letting me camp out behind the restaurant. Beyond that, her help could cause me a problem. I help her by providing after-hours security. We help one another. That's as far as I can go. And that's as far as I want her to go."

"I understand. I'll talk to her."

"Thanks, Jack."

"I'm curious about something. Will you indulge me?"

"Depends on the topic."

"How big an issue is homelessness in the Keys?"

"It's a huge problem."

"Are there solutions?"

"For certain segments of the homeless population, there are solutions, but they require hard work and money. And there are solutions that make it worse. What most government programs try to do is apply a one-size-fits-all solution to fix everything. And the issue is more complicated."

"Can you give me an example?"

"Let's begin with the vagabond class, those who don't want to work, and enjoy the lifestyle of free meals, free housing, and panhandling for money. South Florida and Key West are especially attractive locales because of the weather. The trouble is freeloaders clog the soup kitchens, and ministries that provide places to sleep. They freeload because government makes it possible for them to game the system. This class of homeless has a mentality I don't understand at all. They've no incentive to work and we reward their lack of motivation by sustaining them."

"Can't the system screen these people out?"

"There's no incentive for them to do it. Quite the opposite. Organizations that serve the homeless are numbers driven. Once established and organized the people who work for them and run them begin to depend on the organization for their own livelihood. The only way to sustain these organizations is to have homeless people they can serve. The state and private food banks base their funding on the size of the homeless shelters and the numbers of people who use those facilities. Organizations that depend on funding for survival will oppose any changes. Despite the complexities, this issue is fixable."

"How? It would seem to me to be a problem no one wants."

"You put your finger on it. Today, addressing mental health issues is different than it was just ten years ago. Today there are drugs to treat most mental illnesses. In conjunction with outpatient counseling, the opportunity exists to move these unfortunate creatures off the street and put them back into society. It just takes money, organization and commitment."

"And the will to do it! What about those who're unwilling to undergo treatment? Can we force these people?"

"Yes. Most states have Baker Act type laws with which to institutionalize those whose mental illness can't be treated. Because the pendulum on dealing with the mentally ill has swung away from institutionalization, today authorities are reluctant to take this approach.

"Then there are those suffering from drug addiction and alcoholism. With this group, comes the most crime. If you dig down into crime statistics, the majority of burglaries, muggings, and petty theft, are caused by drug and alcohol addiction. Drug and alcohol treatment is a lot cheaper than the cost to incarcerate."

"And what about the people who're just down on their luck and they need a little help?"

"These folks are the easiest to help. They want to work and be productive. They just need a chance. Once we remove all the freeloaders from the system, there are existing programs designed to help people who want help."

"Sounds complicated."

"It is complicated. Take a hospital for example. They deal with a conglomeration of health issues many of which are life and death. When you go to the emergency room, a triage nurse or doctor screens each patient and designs treatment. Then the hospital calls in specialists to treat a patient's particular health issue. We need a triage approach to the homeless, an organization funded by the state and private sources to screen the homeless, determine the issue creating it, find the resources to correct it, and provide vouchers to pay for it. The state should demand that able-bodied homeless work to earn vouchers for food and shelter and any other services they need. Laws should be stiffened against panhandling, and vagrancy and the state should compensate local police departments for the additional officers needed to enforce these laws.

"All the incentives to freeload should be removed. The mentally ill should be forced to get treatment, and make it impossible for the addicted to ignore their addiction. Short term help should be provided to those who've had a bad run of luck and need a temporary helping hand."

"Your expertise in this area didn't come from being homeless, Joe. Your assessment of the problem comes from the policy level, as one who's studied the problem."

"I have some experience in a previous life, Jack, that's all I can say."

"Don't you find it a little providential, that the AG connection found his way to your doorstep given your experience? You're qualified for the role he wants you to play."

"Now you know why I was so uncomfortable last night. It occurred to me it was more than coincidental; that someone may have discovered my whereabouts. And it was a ploy to draw me out into the open. I know my reaction sounds paranoid."

I said, "Now I understand. I've no idea what you're running from, Joe. But it has to be something powerful."

"Jack, you've no idea."

# 6

Joe and I finished our breakfast. He drilled me about writing novels and all the intricacies involved in getting a book published. When I asked the server for the check, she told me Joe had already taken care of it. When I looked at him, he said, "I have connections."

We both left at the same time, we shook hands and I said, "I'd like to do this again, Joe."

He agreed.

I stood outside the restaurant and watched as Joe aimed for the marina at Garrison Bight and I contemplated how I'd spend the rest of the day. I had talked to a Realtor on the phone before leaving for Key West. She was one of Billie's regular customers. I told her I needed help finding a home on the island. She told me to give her a call when I got into town, but 8:30 a.m. was still too early.

I'd left Jody's before she had awakened. I decided to walk to her gallery and explain my mysterious departure. It concerned me that when I told her with whom I'd had breakfast, she might be angry I didn't tell her this last night as we walked home.

I turned right and walked down a deserted Duvall Street. Most retail businesses opened between nine and ten o'clock. There were some signs of life in a shop here, or an office there, but no businesses were open. I mulled my conversation with Joe and became more intrigued with him. There's so much research in fiction writing you'd fail as a writer without a natural curiosity. I had it in abundance. The mystery surrounding Joe hooked me. Try as I might, I couldn't shake it.

As I neared the gallery, I thought about Joe's assessment of the homeless problem and his ideas for a solution. He sounded like he knew what he was talking about, but I'd no idea if what he was telling me was true. I decided after I visited with Jody, I would call on a couple of homeless organizations in Key West and get their opinion. Perhaps I'd stop by city hall and verify the size of the problem.

When I reached the door to her shop, the closed sign hung in the window and the interior was dark. I glanced at my watch and it was ten minutes to nine. I looked down the street toward the Pier House. A block away, I recognized Jody walking in my direction. As she came closer, I could have sworn she put more sway into her hips for my benefit.

She reached into her purse hanging off her shoulder, pulled out a wad of keys and said, "Well there he is, the disappearing man."

"I had to meet someone for breakfast, and I didn't want to wake you."

She worked the key in the lock, "So are you going to keep your breakfast mate a mystery?" Jody pushed through the door, flipped on a light switch and I followed her in.

"I had breakfast with Joe, the homeless guy from Billie's last night."

"Is that what that little exchange was all about just as he was leaving last night? Well, are you going to let me in on it, or do I have to humble myself and ask?"

"You were right. Joe isn't his name. And Billie was right about Joe, too. He's a man of character caught up in something he swears isn't criminal."

"Did he tell you what it is?"

"No."

"Did you find out who he is?"

"No."

"Did you learn anything at all from him?"

"He wanted to meet with me to intercede with Billie. Billie is trying to help him and it concerns him her help might compromise him."

"You mean he's hiding from something and he's concerned her meddling will expose him?

"Exactly."

"So you don't know anything more about him than you did last night."

"Yes I do. I've learned he's somewhat of an expert on the homeless. It is ironic he's trying to keep a low profile and in walks Pike who's just met with the attorney general and wants Joe to advocate for the homeless. He thought Billie had compromised his identity."

Jody said, "Now I understand why he was acting so squirrelly."

"For Joe, it was a little close to home."

"So why doesn't Joe, or whoever he is, talk to Billie himself. Why does he need to drag you into this?"

"He said he'd talked to her and she just ignored him. He likes Billie, wants to stay but if he can't get her to back off, he'll have to find somewhere else to go. His main concern is he doesn't want to hurt her feelings or her to feel he's ungrateful for what she's trying to do."

"So he could be a rogue spy for the Russian government for all you know and the Russians are looking for him."

"You're right, I don't know. From the language he uses and his obvious advanced education, he had a connection with the government or someone working with them. His understanding of the homeless problem was quite remarkable. Of course, it could be one major snow job. He could have taken cues from Pike last night and fabricated the whole thing."

Jody was wearing a pale blue, sleeveless, one-piece dress, which hugged her chest and hips. She caught me looking at her.

She looked down at the dress, "You like my dress?"

"I like the way you fill it."

"Good. That's why I bought it. But, you're trying to distract me."

I followed the lines of her body with my eyes from her knees to her chin. "I could say the same thing."

63

"You need to stop or I'll close up the shop and drag you back to my house."

"Maybe I'll just lock the door."

She looked at me as though giving it serious consideration. "I'd love that, but I open in five minutes."

I said, "Back to Joe. I'm going to call on some of the homeless shelters and try to verify what he said to me. He said many homeless suffer from mental illness. They suffer from treatable disorders but they lack the money for medication, treatment and counseling. My own near fatal brush with depression, your mother's experience and the emotional damage you and I have both gone through have made me sensitive to the mentally ill. When I think of the plight of those on the street who're suffering mentally, I feel like I should be doing something. Meeting Joe, whether he's feeding me a line of bull or not, helped me see where there's a significant need."

"Alright. So maybe I'll wait until after you do your homeless research before I drag you home and rip your clothes off."

I hugged her, "I love being with you." I embraced her in silence then remembered the Realtor. "I almost forgot. I'm going to try to meet with a real estate agent today. I assume you want to go with me."

"Are you using Florence Keen, Billie's friend?"

"Yes, I called her before I left Mount Dora. She asked me what I was looking for, but I couldn't tell her. Yesterday while I was standing outside of Hemingway's house, my thoughts crystallized."

"I have to meet with Dr. Carnes and my mother during the lunch hour, but after our meeting, of course I want to go. All you'll care about is a place to write. You need a woman's eye, Jack. My eye. So what is it you want?"

"Hemingway's house. Not his house exactly, but one like his."

"You're aware of how expensive real estate is here?"

"I think so."

"Cause, if you want a house like Hemingway's, on the island, you're going to need a Brinks armored truck to haul the money to the closing."

"I don't want to worry about the money right now. I'd like to try to find the right house, if it even exists."

"This is going to be fun," Jody said. She paused a moment. "Do you mind if we meet with my mother for dinner?"

"Great. Let's do it."

I walked to Billie's house on Whitehead Street and enlisted Mrs. Berger's help finding a current telephone directory. I called around to various charities. The consensus was that Harvest House, and Jacob's Ladder, both providing shelter to the homeless, were the largest. In Harvest House's case, they also operated the largest soup kitchen on the Island. While there were other organizations, these two had been in Key West the longest, and reputed to be well run.

I spent the afternoon interviewing the managers and came away with a similar analysis of the homeless problem as described by Joe earlier in the day. Harvest House and Jacob's Ladder had parochial views on solutions to the problem with each of their organizations playing a pivotal role. They felt the system was adequate to handle the problem. They just needed more money and less interference from the state. Neither one of them expressed the goal of eliminating the problem. Their view was more reactive to the need, rather than proactive. I used the opportunity to delve into the plight of the mentally ill. Both organizations raised the issue that many of their mentally ill refused any sort of intervention. They said there were programs available to help them but getting them to avail themselves of the help was another matter. They painted the same picture of those suffering from addiction. Help was there, it was getting the addicted to take advantage of it. Neither organization saw themselves as enabling either the mentally challenged or the addicted to avoid the help they needed. Neither suggested using the police or the legal system to force people suffering from these disorders to seek help.

There was nothing I learned which contradicted what Joe told me earlier this morning. He was either the real deal, or one of the most perceptive con men I'd ever run across.

On my way back to Billie's, Jody called me to announce that we were to have dinner with her mother at Billie's at 7 p.m. I told Jody I'd finally called the Realtor and set up a meeting for the next day at 10 a.m. to begin our search for a home. She said she'd find someone to watch the store.

# 7

It was a Friday night and patrons jammed The Mangrove. Jody and Helen Holland found me at the bar. Helen and I exchanged hugs and she felt small and frail. Billie wended her way through the crowded courtyard to the bar. Jody introduced her mother to Billie. Then Billie led us to a table Jody had reserved earlier in the day. Billie made a fuss over Jody's mother, assuring her she was welcome at any time. One of the servers came up to Billie and said the chef needed her. She excused herself, encouraged us to enjoy ourselves and she followed the server toward the kitchen.

I smiled at Helen. She smiled back. I looked at Jody, waiting for her or Helen to start the conversation. They both began to speak at the same time. We all chuckled.

"Let me save both of you," I said. "Jody, let's start with you. How are the counseling sessions going?"

"That's what we wanted to talk to you about. I believe we had a breakthrough of sorts."

Helen, in her seventies, looked thin and gaunt. Her straight dyed black hair hung to her chin. At just under five feet tall, bent over from what I assumed was Osteoporosis; she looked like she needed a child's booster chair.

Jody continued, "I told Dr. Carnes I felt like I could separate my mother from my anger. I told her I could accept that we're both victims of a terrible tragedy. That I no longer held her responsible for what happened."

I looked at Helen. Tears streamed down the heavy make up on her cheeks.

Jody looked at me and nodded toward her mother. I reached across the table and took Helen's tiny, bony hands into mine.

Jody said, "Mom, look at me."

Helen lifted her eyes to meet Jody's.

"I didn't want to say this in front of Dr. Carnes, because it is much too personal. But I want you to know I forgive you for what happened." Jody got up from her seat, walked around behind Helen Holland, bent over and wrapped her arms around her mother's neck. "We both went through something horrible and we've both suffered enough for it. I'm sorry I carried this grudge for so long, Mom. Will you forgive me?"

Helen pulled her hands from mine, patted Jody's arms still wrapped around her and said. "You've done nothing to deserve forgiveness, Jody. You had every right to feel the way you did. Your forgiveness is the answer to a lifelong prayer. I can't begin to describe how valuable it is to me."

Jody kissed the top of her mother's head, patted her on her small shoulders and returned to her seat.

"I'm still angry, though," Jody said.

Helen said, "Jody, you watched your father and four of your brothers and sisters die at the hands of your mother. Even soldiers who suffer from PTSD, don't have the deep emotional attachments to their adversaries that you had to your family. You were so young and impressionable. No one could have gone through what you did and not suffered from deep wounds. I'm astounded that you've made so much progress with Dr. Carnes in just less than three months."

"Why am I so angry?"

"I'm over simplifying, but it was your way of coping with what happened to you. You took an overwhelming event and shaped it into something you could handle. While you've internalized some of it by blaming yourself for what happened, you directed the force of your anger outward at me. It was a way of defending yourself against the horrors of what happened to you."

"Will I ever get rid of it?"

"Yes, for the most part. Dr. Carnes can help you, Jody. It will take time, but, yes, I think you can get rid of most of it."

"Does this mean you won't be in my counseling sessions any longer?"

"That's up to Dr. Carnes. I don't want to second-guess her. I've no plans to leave Key West until you tell me you're on the mend. My infrequent presence in your sessions may be beneficial. I'm also hoping we could build on our relationship. I have so much love to give you if you'll permit it."

"Helen, can I ask a question?" I said.

"Of course."

"When I look at Jody, I don't see anger. Next to you, she's one of the most gracious people I've ever known. I've never known her to have a temper or show any outward signs of an anger problem."

"The problem is she repressed it, Jack. She shoved it down deep. Those feelings need to come out."

Helen said, "Dr. Carnes will begin to probe those feelings, get Jody to pull them up, talk about them, wrestle with them and then try to dismiss them. It is the hardest work you'll ever do."

Jody asked, "Are you still angry?"

"Yes, Jody, I am. You'll never get rid of all of it."

"So how do you handle it?"

"I'm in a much better place, now. For the most part, I don't blame myself anymore. I'm still angry it happened. I've given up trying to find an explanation for why it happened, because there's no answer this side of Heaven. With Dr. Carnes' help, I'm able to live with what little anger I have left. Nothing will change the horror of what happened to us. All we can hope for is to move past it."

"That's a good way to put it, Mom. Moving past it. I haven't put it behind me yet. When we first got together in April, you said I needed to forgive you, not for you, but for me. I didn't understand it then, but I do now. You were right. I don't think I could deal with the rest of it until I forgave you."

Our server had made several trips to the table to take our order, but had the sensitivity not to interrupt what was a personal and emotional conversation. When our conversation turned to the mundane, I signaled to our server, she took our orders and the meal progressed. Helen wanted all the details about my new contract with R&R. After we finished with dessert, Helen shifted the gears of our conversation toward Jody and me.

Helen asked, "So what is going on between the two of you?" There was a little mischief in her eyes, and her smile turned her face into a symphony of wrinkles.

I waited for Jody to answer. She looked at me with a puzzled look.

I said, "I'm in love with your daughter."

"I know. You'd have to be blind not to see it. I want to know what you're doing about it."

I looked at Jody, then at Helen and raised an eyebrow.

"I'm not talking about that. I want to know where your relationship is going."

Jody responded. "I'm confused, Mom."

With effort, Helen leaned forward in her chair, pulling up her elbows onto the table. "When I first met you, Jack, all those years ago, you were head over heels in love. You beamed. The two of you were a perfect match, a blend of compatible personalities. In all my years, I've never seen such chemistry. You two were meant to be together. And because of what happened, what would otherwise have been a life-long relationship was cut short. Now you both have been given a second chance. You think you have all the time in the world. You don't. My message to you is don't waste one second. Don't let what you have slip through your fingers again."

Jody looked at me. Without a word, I knew she took everything her mother had just said to heart. When someone dispenses the truth in such simple terms, it resonates inside you. Helen put her finger on a place in my heart and released any remaining doubt in my mind about Jody. Helen was right. I was no longer satisfied with a status quo relationship. I wanted more and I knew Jody did as well.

When I left the Keys in April, it concerned me that my rapid attachment to Jody might be a rebound reaction to losing Emily. Emily's departure created a vacuum, I reasoned, and Jody filled it. Helen's succinct appraisal of Jody and me, made me realize that assumption was wrong. My feelings for Jody were no different than they were when we were kids. She was not just filling a void. We had never stopped loving each other. That's why our reattachment was so easy.

# 8

Jody and I slow walked Helen back to her rental apartment two blocks from Jody's house. Jody hugged her mother for the second time that day, which is miraculous given that three months earlier, Jody couldn't stand to be in the same room with her.

Then we strolled by the light of street lamps to Jody's. She sat down on the step to her porch and I dropped down beside her. The light from the street lamp beamed down through the tree, which had grown up around it. It left her porch in dappled shadows that moved with the evening breeze. The air was still warm and damp and smelled of the sea.

I picked imaginary lint off the knee of my pants and asked Jody, "So what did you think of your mother's admonition to do something with our relationship?"

"I wanted to reach out and hold her. She said what we both know to be true." She reached over and took my hand in hers.

"I know this isn't the most romantic way to do this, but I think we should get married."

"I feel like we are already. I've felt that way for a long time, Jack. And this," she looked around her small porch, "is romantic — just the way I'd pictured you asking me. Comfortable, intimate, just like our relationship. Now, would you please get your clothes from Billie's and stay with me?"

"Do you think I should stay at Billie's tonight? I wouldn't want to hurt her feelings," I teased.

"There's no way you're going to propose marriage to me and leave me standing on my porch. It isn't happening."

"I at least need to go get my clothes."

"Where we're going you won't need them."

"What about my toothbrush?"

"I bought one for you, remember? Would you just shut up and kiss me?"

I pulled Jody up from the step, and we embraced and kissed each other.

"You make me so happy, Jack." Jody pulled away from me, fumbled for her house keys in her handbag, unlocked the door and pulled me into one of the happiest moments of my life.

It was 3 a.m. when Billie called me on my cellphone.

"Jack, the fire department just called me. There's been a fire at the restaurant, and they think Joe is responsible. He suffered some burns, so they took him to the hospital. And the police think he did it. I'm going to the restaurant now to find out how bad it is. Could you meet Cynthia Pike at the hospital? I know he didn't do it.

"You worry about the restaurant. I'll go to the hospital."

I drove to the island's small medical center. The only entrance open was to the emergency room. The triage nurse pointed me to station number six, which was nothing more than a bed surrounded by curtains. A uniformed police officer stood guard at the nurse's station. I parted the curtain. They had wrapped Joe's left arm in heavy bandages. Joe looked pleased to see me.

"Jack, I'm glad you're here. You have to talk some sense into these people. They think I had something to do with the fire at Billie's."

As I was about to speak, the curtains rustled behind me and in popped Cynthia Pike. Her hair was disheveled and she wore a University of Miami T-shirt and jogging shorts.

Pike asked, "Alright, what's going on?" She yawned.

"I was just getting ready to tell Jack. I don't know what woke me up, but there was smoke coming from The Mangrove. It looked like it was coming from the back of the building in the kitchen area. I didn't have a key, so I kicked in the back door and the kitchen was in flames. I spotted a fire extinguisher on the opposite wall and made a dash for it. That's when the flames flashed up. I assume that's how I got this." He held up his bandaged arm. "I used the extinguisher, but there wasn't enough propellant to put the fire out. I raced back out the rear door, and a cop, the one out there," Joe nodded toward the nurse's station, "grabbed me, cuffed me, and called the fire department. When I broke through the back door I must have set off a burglar alarm."

Pike asked, "Did you explain this to the cop?"

"I did. But, he wasn't buying it. To him, I had no business being behind Billie's restaurant. He looked at my clothes, the fact that I'd kicked the door in and concluded that I either set the fire, or caused it to happen during the break in. The fact that I refused to surrender identification, and I won't tell the officer my real name, isn't helping."

"What're you waiting on?"

"His senior officer or a detective, I think. They want to question me. I know that much."

"So," Pike asked, "have they charged you with anything yet?"

"No, but I'm not free to go either." Joe turned to me and asked, "How bad is the damage to Billie's restaurant? The fire department had just arrived, when the officer took me to the hospital."

I said, "I don't know. Billie called me. She wanted me to check on you. She sent Cynthia and I to provide any help you might need."

"Does she think I did this?"

"She knows you're a suspect. But, no, she doesn't believe you had a part in it."

"Cynthia, will you represent me?"

"Joe, I'm not a criminal attorney. But I'll do the best I can. If I think it is beyond my expertise, I know of a good criminal attorney we can call. It sounds to me like a good fire investigator will vouch for your version provided what you're telling us is the truth. Where did you leave the fire extinguisher when you fled the building?"

"I just dropped it in the middle of the floor of the kitchen and got out of there."

"And if you in fact emptied the extinguisher, there should be chemical evidence where you attempted to put the fire out."

"That's not what worries me, Ms. Pike."

"Then what's your worry?"

"I need to talk with you under attorney-client privilege. Jack, if you're part of that discussion, a prosecutor could call you to testify to what I'm going to tell Ms. Pike. And this is the last place to have a confidential discussion. Needless to say, I don't want them to fingerprint me nor take blood samples or any other attempt to establish my identity."

"Joe, even with circumstantial evidence, if the police suspect you committed a crime, they can demand and they are within the law to demand identification. They could charge you with misdemeanor loitering and compel you to identify yourself. Then as a matter of routine . . ."

"Yes, I know, they'll run me for outstanding wants and warrants. Ms. Pike, I had permission to be on the property. Billie can put that to bed with a simple phone call."

"Alright. Let me go find out from the cop what the next step is. I'll be right back."

As Pike left, I asked Joe, "How's your arm?"

"Fine now. It's when the lidocaine and the morphine wear off. Then it could be a problem."

"What possessed you to run into a burning building, Joe?"

"I never thought about it. I just reacted like it had been my building."

Pike returned, "They're holding you for questioning. The officer is to escort you to the police department when the doctors release you. They'll call a detective named Dan McKenzie when you arrive at the department. Once there, tell them you want your attorney present during questioning. They'll call me. Before they question you, we need some time alone. I need to understand why you're so adamant about anonymity." Pike hugged herself. "This place is a freezer. I'm going to go home and try to sleep until they call me. Any questions?"

"Thanks for being here, Ms. Pike," Joe said.

"Cynthia. Call me Cynthia."

With a flourish of the curtains behind me, Cynthia Pike disappeared into the emergency room.

"Thanks for coming, Jack. You should be with Billie. I'm good. If you could come by the PD later and fill me in on the damage to the restaurant, I'd appreciate it."

I asked him if there was anything I could get for him. He asked me to tell the nurse he'd like a cup of coffee. I did and headed for Billie's."

The fire department packed their gear, rolled up hoses, and a firefighter blocked the entrances to the building with crime scene tape. Billie held a flashlight, the beam illuminating the smoke emanating from the structure. I caught her as she attempted to assess the extent of the damage.

She shined the light at my face, blinding me. "I'm sorry Jack. My thinking isn't clear right now."

"How bad is it?"

She walked to the back door and shined the flashlight into the smoky remains of the interior. The fire department soaked the entire structure. You could hear water dripping everywhere. Light from the fire truck still illuminated the clapboard siding of the building. "The kitchen is a total loss. I can't see the second floor over the kitchen, but as bad as the kitchen looks I'm sure the structure above it is gone, too. The fire didn't touch the bar or the courtyard. Thank God, my Banyan trees weren't affected. With the fire confined to the interior of the building, everything else remained unharmed."

"You don't seem upset."

"I was when I first got here, I was hysterical. Then the rational me, took over. We've been debating about whether to tear down this old building and start from scratch. We'd have had to gut the building to accommodate the kitchen expansion anyway, but decided to renovate due to the cost. It was a hard choice. Now there's no decision to make. During construction, we'd planned to rent two trucks to operate as our kitchen while construction was underway. We'd rent one truck equipped like a kitchen and the other as a refrigerator. And we'd planned to begin the project soon so that we could complete work before our high season begins after Christmas. It just means we speed up our schedule. And the bonus is we have good insurance on the building. Before, tearing down the old building and constructing something new would have come completely out of my pocket. Now, it looks as though insurance may cover much of it. So no, I'm not upset. Did you talk to, Joe?"

"He is okay. He has a nasty burn on his arm, but nothing serious. They're holding him for questioning. They think he may have set the fire.

You didn't tell him about any of your construction plans did you?"

"No. He knew nothing about them. No one in the restaurant except for Molly, the chef, had a clue. If any of them thought the restaurant might be closing, they'd bolt to find work elsewhere. I suppose I'll have to get everyone together and fill them in."

"So you're okay with this?"

"Yes. There will be inconvenience and loss of business, but I have insurance for all that. I'm just sorry Joe was caught up in it. Did Cynthia show up?"

"Yep, she has it under control. She's going into the police station as soon as they move him from the hospital."

"I think Joe's running days may be over. I feel bad that I may be responsible."

"Maybe we will get to the bottom of it and be able to help him."

"I hope so. There's a decent man under all the mystery, Jack. I think he risked his life to try to put the fire out. It takes a lot of character to do that."

"Is someone coming to determine the cause of the fire?"

"Yes, the fire chief told me before he left that an arson investigator will be here in the morning. He said their investigation should be complete in a few hours. Then I'll be free to contact my insurance company with a case number and begin the claim process."

"You worried about that?"

"No. The chief said he thought the source of the fire was the circuit breaker panel on the back wall in the kitchen. He said it looked like someone had tried to put the fire out with an extinguisher. He said he left the scene undisturbed for his team to look at in the morning. He said he saw nothing that would support arson."

"Well that would seem to corroborate Joe's story. He said he broke into the building to put the fire out and emptied the extinguisher, but it didn't help. Do you have an alarm system?"

"Yep, for both fire and police."

"When Joe kicked in the back door, he tripped the alarm and the police responded. His forced entry into the building, his vagrancy and unwillingness to identify himself, all contributed to his suspect status."

Billie turned off the flashlight to preserve the battery. "The arson investigators will clear him, won't they?"

"Yes. But his unwillingness to identify himself may take on a life of its own, Billie. And if he does provide identification, it may mean that whatever he's hiding from may come to light."

"It has to be pretty serious for him to go to all this trouble to disappear."

We agreed we could do nothing more until daylight. I told her I was going to run to her house, shower, change and then head to the police station. I said Joe wanted a damage assessment on her building. As we walked to her home, I informed her I was going to gather my belongings later in the day and bunk with Jody. I didn't say anything about our marriage plans, because I wanted it to be something Jody and I announced together. It surprised her it had taken this long and seemed happy, not offended, that I was making the move.

At the police station, the desk sergeant told me Joe was meeting with his attorney. Then he would meet with Detective McKenzie.

Since it appeared they'd tie Joe up for a while, I left a note for him that all was well at

Billie's and that he needn't worry. I wanted to do something to assist him, but his issues were all legal and only Pike was in a position to help him. Joe intrigued me. My mind raced with the potential reasons for his need to disappear. But the clues to his identity were too few to draw any concrete conclusions. If I were as determined to remain anonymous as he was, if I got out of the police department, I'd be into the wind.

I called Billie, gave her a quick update on Joe, and asked her to call me if there was any news about him or from the arson investigators. Billie was right. Joe was a captivating character.

# 9

    I called Jody and asked her to meet me for breakfast at the Hilton Resort. When I arrived, crews were removing Hilton signs and replacing them with "Westin." I couldn't imagine Hilton wanting to unload this property. It was the nicest resort on the island. Once inside, there had been other changes since we were here in April. They'd changed the name of the casual restaurant to Bistro 245 and had given it a face-lift. What I liked about this restaurant was their outside dining area by the water and marina, which is what I requested when I approached the host station. I left word that Jody would be joining me and gave her a description of "a beautiful blonde."

    Outside, wedged between the marina and the main building, was an outside dining area. It overlooked the bay between Sunset Key and Key West. The air was warm, humid and filled with sea birds of every description. A crow perched on a nearby piling squawked. Out in the distance, a cruise ship inched its way toward Fury Dock and soon the island would be bustling with tourists.

There was something genetic about me living by the water. I've always lived by the water. I couldn't imagine living in a place like landlocked Iowa. I'd feel claustrophobic. Mount Dora was about as far inland as I was comfortable. Then I had enchanting Lake Dora out my front door. My studio there had a panoramic view of the water. As I anticipated meeting with the Realtor this morning, I thought about how much of a factor living on the water would be in my search for a home. I looked out at the recent development on Sunset Key and saw million-dollar homes under construction. To get to it, you had to ride a launch from the Westin marina over to the island. That could be a significant inconvenience. But on the plus side, it was remote. That would take care of my need for privacy and seclusion. But at what cost?

I felt a hand on my shoulder. "What're you so deep in thought about?"

I stood up from the table, kissed Jody and gestured for her to take the seat next to me. "Just trying to think through what I want in a house."

Our server came, took our drink orders — we both ordered coffee — and disappeared back inside the restaurant.

Jody said, "So what're you looking for."

"I told you. I want Hemingway's house, on the water."

"Exactly like Hemingway's house?"

"No, like it. I like the separate studio."

"On the water? That's going to cost. Are you rich, Jack?"

"That's a question you should have asked before you agreed to marry me."

"You could be flat-broke and it wouldn't matter to me. You make me happy, that's all that matters. Anything on the water is going to be seven figures."

"My house in Mount Dora is worth about a half a million and it's paid for. My father left me a large amount that I need to invest in something. Bob Decker . . ."

". . . Your best friend who ran off with your ex-wife."

"Yes, that Decker. He was my financial expert and handled all my investments. And I've done well with him. I think the financial markets are on fire right now, and that makes me nervous. As soon as I have the opportunity, I want to pull a part of my investment out of stocks and invest in something else."

"Why? If stocks are doing so well, why not stay in the market?"

"When it gets like this, I worry a bubble will burst. The faster the markets rise, the faster they can come crashing down. I want to get out before that happens."

"And you think real estate is a better bet?"

"For now at least. Especially here in Key West. So Jody, what do you want in a house?"

"You, silly."

I smiled. "No, tell me."

"I don't have a place for my kids to stay when they come to visit. I don't like parking my car on the street and schlepping my groceries into the house. I don't like having to park my old van on the street for storage. And I have no place for a small garden. And you didn't answer my question, are you rich?"

"I guess by any reasonable standard, I am. I've done well with my writing and Decker has done well in investing my savings. If I never sold another book, we'd be able to retire."

"We. I like the sound of that."

We finished our breakfast and walked to the real estate agent's office on Duval Street. We met with Florence Keen, explained what we were looking for and left her to research available properties. We agreed to meet after lunch to look through what she'd found and then she'd set up appointments to see the homes we selected from the list. We agreed tomorrow after church would work best to tour the homes available.

We walked to The Mangrove, which was only two blocks from the Realtor's office. I saw a fire department SUV leaving the street next to the courtyard. A "closed" sign hung from the host station at the front gate. Someone had removed the crime scene tape from the entrance to the main building and we found Billie there sifting through the still smoldering heap.

Billie came out of the ashes, gave Jody a hug and said, "That was the arson guy. He confirmed the fire started in the electrical panel and corroborated Joe's story that he tried to put the fire out. He also said he was sending the fire marshal out to condemn the building. He thinks the structural damage was significant enough that we can't repair it."

"Is that good news? I asked.

"Yes, it means it just about rules out an insurance adjuster claiming we could salvage the building which I don't want to do. As soon as the fire marshal condemns the building, I'll call my insurance agent, file a claim and see if they can get an adjuster out here late this afternoon or first thing on Monday."

"How long before you can reopen?"

"Within a week. Maybe sooner. I don't know. They can deliver my food trucks on Wednesday. With Cynthia working on the permits for them, and accounting for food deliveries to stock them they could be operational by next Friday, just in time for the weekend. I'm hoping I can get the adjuster to declare the building a total loss. If so, I can have it taken down before I reopen."

"Have you heard anything about Joe's situation?"

"I had a visit from Detective McKenzie. He wanted to verify that I'd given Joe permission to be on my property. When I said I had, he said he didn't have a problem with Joe living on my property. He thought, though, that building code enforcement folks might have a problem with it if someone complained. McKenzie said it was a violation of city code for someone to camp out on commercial property. He said they were still going to hold Joe, pending the arson investigator's report. Then just before you showed up, Cynthia called me and said they were getting ready to release Joe."

"Did he have to identify himself?"

"She didn't say."

"Is Alex in town?"

"She's on her way from the airport now."

Just as we were getting ready to leave, Pike and Joe came through the front gate and ambled through the courtyard.

We greeted one another and Cynthia Pike said, "Well that was an interesting morning."

I asked Joe, "Did you have to identify yourself?"

"No. They wanted to charge me with loitering, but Ms. Pike insisted they contact Billie to confirm I had permission to me there. Once they did, they backed off."

Pike added, "And without any criminal involvement, they had no statutory grounds to demand that Joe identify himself. When the fire department verified there was no arson involved and in fact Joe tried to put the fire out and sustained injuries trying, they had no choice but to let him go."

Billie asked, "So what's this all about, Joe? Why all the secrecy?"

The smell of smoke wafted from the charred building. We all moved further into the courtyard to get away from it.

"I'm coming to that. Ms. Pike and I discussed my circumstances this morning and now I want to share my story with you." Joe looked around, "Could we all sit and I'll try to explain."

# 10

We all sat around a teak table and Billie went to the bar, unscathed by the fire, and came back with an assortment of cold drinks and snack food. Once she took a seat, Joe dove in.

"My name is Stephen Fitzgerald, but for the time being I want to continue to go by the name Joe. When I'm finished, you'll understand why.

"I'm an attorney. My home is Atlanta, Roswell to be specific. My father was a prominent attorney and served on the state legislature. He'd taken a little country law practice and had built it into a law firm of one-hundred attorneys. No one was his equal in his influence in Georgia politics. His clients included most of the major corporations in Georgia who curried favor with him to advance their own business objectives. He also represented some of the most influential men in the state.

"In the mid-1980s, the courts settled several civil cases regarding a lawyer's ability to advertise. No longer did the Bar forbid attorneys from running television or radio ads. One law firm in Atlanta began a heavy ad campaign soliciting personal injury cases. Using this new freedom to advertise, in just two years, John Baker, had built a law firm equal to my father's in size. But, even as successful as Baker was, he still had the reputation of an ambulance chaser; one who fed on the misfortune of others. His efforts to break into the respectable ranks of more established main line firms were unsuccessful.

"When I got out of law school in 1984, I went to work for my father's firm. In 1988, I made partner. While my father owned a majority of the firm, he gave me thirty percent stake. "Shortly thereafter, John Baker launched a two pronged conspiracy to take over control of my father's firm.

"In 1990, Baker hired private investigators to dig into my father's life to find out if he had any weaknesses he could exploit. My father enjoyed the company of high priced call girls. I'd no clue it was going on until it was too late. Baker, through surrogates, began blackmailing him. The amounts in the beginning were small, but they increased into hefty sums, which ended up in the coffers of John Baker. If dad had gone to the police when the extortion began, prosecutors would have excoriated him. But he could have avoided the more serious consequences that befell him.

"About the same time that Baker turned his investigatory dogs loose on my father, I met Melissa Baker or I should say Melissa Baker found me at a bar association function. She was a trial lawyer, gorgeous, desirable and aggressive in every respect and way out of my league. Within six months of our meeting, we were standing in front of a justice of the peace proclaiming our undying love for each other. The Fitzgeralds and Bakers were now family. Baker used that connection to begin discussions with my father about merging their two organizations together.

"Then Baker began to tighten the screws. By late 1991, the extortion amounts began to take huge hunks out of my father's fortune. These funds, once transferred into Baker's hands, became a war chest Baker would use to buy my father's share of the law firm. By the middle of 1993, with my father's fortune depleted, he began serious discussions with Baker on a merger.

"Baker had all the cards. My father had no clue Baker was behind the blackmail. Baker had my father where he wanted him and presented him and I with one of the most onerous merger agreements I'd ever seen. One of the heavier handed parts of the agreement was a morals clause. It stated that within twelve months of the merger date, if any immoral or illegal activities concerning the partners of the Fitzgerald Law Firm were made public, my father and I would forfeit any unpaid amounts of purchase price. Baker was offering a leveraged deal equal to seventy-percent of the book value of the company. He proposed terms of thirty-percent that he'd pay at closing and the balance he'd pay in three installments within twelve months.

"I begged my father not to take the deal. I didn't know then his fortune was gone and that he'd no choice. I was so angry with him. I refused to sign, so Baker wrote me out of the deal. But I didn't own enough shares to prevent the sale of the firm to Baker. My father sold his share for fifty-percent of its book value. He only received thirty-percent of that amount at closing.

"My refusal to sell my shares to Baker didn't sit well with Melissa. She was furious I'd insulted her father.

"Within thirty days of the sale of the law firm, Baker presented my father with a dossier of his sexual escapades. He told him he was behind the blackmail. He demanded my father sign a quitclaim for the rest of the funds owed to him by Baker or he'd expose my father's activities to the press. Like a fool, my father signed it.

"On the same day, Melissa filed for divorce, demanding fifty percent of all our joint assets which included half of my shares of the law firm. She also demanded $250,000 in alimony. Later that day, two security guards accompanied by John Baker, came to my office and fired me and escorted me out of the building.

"After my father signed the quit claim, and they served me with divorce papers, Baker leaked the scandalous pictures of my father in compromising situations with prostitutes to influential clients of my father's firm, and he made a special point of sending copies of the files to the judge who'd preside over my divorce from Melissa.

"The day after Baker exposed my father, he told me about the blackmail and that Baker was behind it. He said my marriage to Melissa was part of a grand conspiracy to take over my father's firm. Later that day, news of the scandal hit the press, and that evening my father shot himself in the study of his home.

"A month later, after hiring one of the best divorce attorneys in Atlanta, Melissa received half our assets. The judge, who was in Baker's pocket, awarded Melissa alimony of $250,000 a year. I stood behind the client table in the courtroom and couldn't believe what had happened. That was over three years ago. I was so angry I walked out of the court and swore I'd never pay another nickel to those thieves. And since my father took his life, I've no way to prove the extortion or that Baker was behind it. Ninety days later, after I missed the first three alimony payments, the Bakers convinced a judge to find me in contempt and issued a bench warrant. The choice is either pay the alimony or go to prison. Or, I could make it all go away by signing over the remaining shares of the law firm. That will never happen."

Pike raised a hand, "You should fight this, Joe."

"With what? I have no proof. I have no money."

We all sat in silence, each contemplating Joe's circumstances. I thought about the homeless people you see on the street and you have no idea of their circumstances or the horrors that have been visited upon them. Joe's story was heartbreaking and the extent of the ruthlessness of Baker and his daughter unimaginable. I had no suggestions to make and no encouragement to offer. I thought about telling him to swap his remaining ownership for his freedom, but if they'd done something like that to my father, I'd be as recalcitrant as Joe was.

I said, "Well, I understand why you don't want them to find you. But isn't running and hiding adding to the punishment they've already inflicted on you?"

Billie said, "You know, Joe. If this guy Baker is as evil as you portray, he has skeletons in his own closet. Perhaps you could do to him, what he did to your father."

"I'd never suggest extortion," Pike said, "but if Billie is right, and we had some compromising information on Baker, it might strengthen your hand in dealing with him."

"At the risk of repeating myself, if you haven't noticed, I don't have the resources to undertake something like that."

Pike said, "Let me make some phone calls and find the right investigator in Atlanta. Let's get an estimate of the costs before we decide to bag the idea."

Billie said, "I'll help with the cost."

Jody said, "Count me in."

"I'm in," I said.

Joe shook his head. "Whoa. Whoa. I don't want you to do this. I'm not asking you to do this."

"Before we get ahead of ourselves, let's get some more information," Pike said

Joe said, "I appreciate what you folks are trying to do, but you've no idea who you're messing with. Baker is . . ."

". . . Do you want to spend the rest of your life sleeping next to a dumpster, Joe?" Jody's question cut to the quick.

Joe looked around the table and down at his folded hands. "No."

Jody reached over, put her hand on Joe's, and said, "Let us help. When you get your life back you can repay us."

Pike said. "In the meantime, I want you to meet with the attorney general. If you decide to take on Baker, you'll need all the friends you can get."

"He can't know my identity. I can't risk that right now."

"He doesn't need to know."

# 11

I have an addiction to coffee. It would embarrass me to estimate how many cups I drink in a day. I share this addiction in common with my agent Lisa Catera. Until this past Christmas, my favorite coffee came from Dunkin Donuts. I know, my tastes are humble, but you know, good coffee is good coffee. That's until Lisa sent me a gift basket containing Barnie's, Santa's White Christmas flavored coffee. It had just come on the market and she'd been pestering me to try it. I blew through what she'd sent me in two weeks. While I'm writing, I'll have a pot going all day long. When I called her to find out where I could get more, she informed me they'd only made it for the holidays. I informed her that if she wished to remain my agent, she had to find more. She found a case on Long

Island and had it shipped it to me. Like I said, I'm addicted.

When I walked into The Marlin restaurant, the smell of coffee brewing made my return visit like a homecoming. The same server who had waited on Stephen and me on my first visit, caught my eye, poured me a cup, and followed me to the table Joe had already occupied.

Stephen started to stand.

I gestured for him to sit, extended my hand and sat opposite from him. He shook my hand and plopped back into his chair. While he'd combed his hair and beard, the wrinkles under his eyes, exceeded the wrinkles in his T-shirt. It occurred to me the police had placed his "camp" behind the restaurant off limits to him.

"Where did you sleep last night?"

"Jacob's Ladder."

"How did that go?"

"About as well as you might expect. I slept in a dorm with thirty snoring men. One of the guys was a Vietnam vet, suffering from PTSD. He awoke a couple of times last night screaming from battlefield nightmares. All night there was the parade of drunks traipsing to the bathroom two to three times a night opening and closing the bathroom door and flushing the toilet. I won't mention the smell."

While Stephen was clean, smells of the homeless shelter permeated his clothing and the area around him. It occurred to me how sheltered my life was. I was oblivious to an entire sub-culture of people whose life planning was limited to finding their next meal.

"Do you feel safe there?"

"Of course not, but I don't want to talk about that."

"Alright. What then?"

"Well, your offer to help. I can't accept it."

"Why not? It's obvious you need it."

"I don't need your charity, Jack." During my previous encounters with Stephen, he had presented a face of confidence and looked me straight in the eye. This morning, he peered out the window, down at his hands, at the server scurrying around the small restaurant, but he wouldn't look me in the eye.

"What's going on, Stephen?"

"Nothing. I just don't want to take charity from anyone."

"It seems to me you're doing just that. Where did you sleep last night?"

"I just want everyone to leave me alone. I don't need your help. I can work this out on my own."

"And how are you going to do that?"

"I'll figure something out."

"How long have you been on the street?"

"Two years."

"Closer to four. And what will you do to change your circumstances?"

"I don't know. These are people you don't want to mess with, Jack!"

"You're speaking of the Bakers?"

"Yes."

"You aren't afraid are you?"

"No," he said. His face reddened and his eyes bored into mine. He turned his head away, and wrung his hands. "It's a hornet's nest I don't want to disturb."

I tried to put myself in Stephen's shoes. Here was a young successful lawyer whose father was an icon in the profession who took his own life. The Bakers tricked him into marrying Melissa as part of a grand conspiracy to defraud him and his father of their law firm. He seethed when he described how the Bakers had extorted his father. But when he talked about how Melissa Baker had used him, the anger was laced with deep hurt.

"You loved her, didn't you?"

"What're you talking about?" he said, eyes narrowing, cutting glances at me and looking out the window.

"You're not afraid, you're wounded."

He said nothing, and dismissed me with a flip of his hand.

"I've been asking myself what could have happened that would drive you to live in this self-imposed nightmare. It's obvious your love for her was deep and to lose your father on top of it."

"Jack, I don't want to talk about this!"

"You're hurt, aren't you, Stephen? A deep hurt."

His eyes blazed. "Shut up. You've no idea what you're talking about."

"This hurt is so deep it's crushing you; you're powerless against it."

Stephen looked at me like a trapped animal. He pushed himself up from the table, threw his napkin at me and stormed out of the building. I reached into my pocket, flipped a twenty-dollar bill on the table and followed him. I jogged up the street toward Duval, until I caught up with him.

He turned and looked at me and yelled. "Stay out of this. You've no right to pry into my personal life."

I had to walk/run to keep pace with him. "I've been where you are, Joe. It's a dark place and unless you face it, it will destroy you."

He stopped dead in his tracks and turned to me. "What could you know about it? Look at you, wealthy, famous and in love. You've no clue."

Trying to catch my breath, I said, "Less than a year ago, I sat on the side of the road in my car and reached into the glove box for a gun to take my life. Depressed and without hope, I felt my life was over. I do understand."

"What stopped you?"

"Someone intervened, like I'm intervening now."

His shoulders sagged, he looked up at the sky and he struggled to maintain his composure. Right there, in the middle of the sidewalk he said. "Yes, I was in love. Her betrayal was devastating. My father had just ended his life. My life was in shreds. Then Melissa turned on me." Tears leaked down his cheeks. "It destroyed me. The brutality of the divorce and the pure evil that emanated from her during the entire process was the final straw. I ran and hid. She should have just killed me. It would have been better."

"You still love her don't you?"

He looked straight at me. His blue eyes were on fire. He looked away without answering my question. He looked down at his shoes, took a deep breath and gathered up his emotions.

I said, "You're at a crucial point, Stephen. Do you want to live or die?"

"I'm not going to kill myself, if that's what you're worried about."

"You might as well be dead. The path you're on isn't living."

He tried to erase an imaginary mark on the sidewalk with the toe of his shoe.

"Stephen. There are many ways I can help you, but I can't help you if you don't have want to."

111

"Want-to?"

"The desire to live, the motivation to fight. Do you want to climb out of the emotional coffin you're in and put your life back together? Or do you want to curl up into an emotional ball and sleep next to a dumpster? You can't give someone want-to. Either you have it or you don't. If you don't, this is a giant waste of time for me, for you, for everyone. So, I'll ask you. Do you want to climb out of that hole or not?"

"I don't know."

"What the Bakers did to you was criminal. What they did to your father was unconscionable. You need to right this wrong, Stephen. Don't you want to do the right thing for your father?"

"Of course."

"Then you need to stand up and fight, if not for you, for him."

He locked his eyes on mine.

"What Melissa did to you pales in comparison to what you're doing to yourself. Don't you see that?"

I remember from my own recent bout of depression that I'd finally had enough. I had reached a point that I was over it.

"Yes. But where do I begin?"

"You need to take on the Bakers. Earlier you said you didn't want charity or help. We can't take the Bakers on for you. You must take them on. This is your fight. If you want to set this right, we can assist. Do you want to take them on or not?"

"There isn't any other way is there?"

"That or let them railroad you into a jail sentence or forfeiting your stock."

Silence fell between us as we considered next steps.

He said, "I don't know whether I have the strength to do it?"

"It's there, Stephen. You may have to dig down for it, but it's there."

He looked at me and his vacant stare of a moment ago had changed. His eyes narrowed and the muscles in his jaw stiffened. "Would you help me? I'm not talking about the money. Would you stand with me? I'm not sure I can do this alone."

"Yes, of course."

He was quiet and thoughtful for a moment. "I've been thinking about Pike's advice to meet the attorney general. She's right, if I take on the Bakers, I'll need all the allies I can get."

"Agreed," I said.

"And the issue of homelessness seems like a pathway to make some good connections."

"Agreed."

We moved aside to make room for two kids on skateboards weaving their way toward Duval Street.

"I want you in on my meeting with Pike."

"Done. What're you going to do?"

"Pike said the AG talked about this homeless job being a paid gig. Maybe there will be enough for room and board somewhere."

"It's a beginning, Stephen."

"Yes, a beginning."

I encouraged Stephen to return to the restaurant. We ate our breakfast and revisited the circumstances that led up to the police taking him in for questioning. We analyzed the ramifications of Billie losing her main building in the fire. While I listened to Stephen wax about his concerns that Billie's insurance company would treat her with fairness, I knew I'd seen a sea change in Stephen's thinking. As he rambled on about how Billie needed to consult an attorney on her insurance claim, there was a spark in him I hadn't seen before. And, perhaps, his professed desire to take on the Bakers was his turning point, a reaching-out for a life preserver. But as I watched him talk with confidence about helping Billie get everything she had coming to her as a result of the fire, I had no doubt that I wanted to help Stephen in any way I could.

# 12

Later in the morning, Florence Keen called. She'd just gotten home from church and had several properties she thought would interest us. We agreed to meet at The Mangrove.

I had left Stephen and walked to Billie's restaurant. A sign on the front gate to the courtyard read, "Closed." Underneath, another handmade sign read, "Reopening Friday." The deserted courtyard, collapsed umbrellas and chairs turned up on the tabletops, seemed odd given it was a busy weekend. Next to where the main building had been, a lone umbrella remained open, and sitting under it, Billie labored away with paperwork.

Where the main building had once stood, a smaller excavator stood next to a pile of rubble it had created. Even after two days, smoke from the embers of the collapsed structure spiraled into the sun filled, morning sky.

When Billie heard me approach, she looked up, stood, smiled and hugged me.

I explained to Billie that I'd invited Florence Keen to meet here at the restaurant.

"All I have are drinks and snacks. I'm not set up to serve any meals," she said.

I assured her we would be fine.

"Where's Jody?"

"I was just getting ready to call her. You look awesome this morning."

"It's like being on vacation. Do you know how long it has been since I had a weekend off? To have a Saturday night off and to be able to sleep in on Sunday morning? You've no idea the time it takes to run this place. It's twenty-four seven, Jack. It never stops."

"And here you are, working," I said.

"This?" She looked down at a stack of paper. "This is nothing. This is a piece of cake."

"This is a big week for you isn't it?"

"Do you mean my visit to the fertility doc, or my food trucks coming, or getting the building construction underway?"

"Let's start with the fertility doc."

"Alex and I meet with Pike on Tuesday to go over all the legal papers related to adopting the embryos. After that, I have an appointment to run the final tests before they implant the embryos. After the tests, they start me on medications to increase the chances of fertilization. If all goes well, I'm hoping they can do the implantation procedure in a week or two."

Her eyes and gestures were expressive.

"You're excited."

"I've never wanted anything as much, Jack. I'm excited, but a little worried, I must admit. I ain't no spring chicken." She exaggerated her normal southern drawl. "And the thought of the possibility of multiple births concerns me. But I want a child and if this is the only way they can do it, I'm ready to risk it."

"And Alex is still on board?"

"Yes. Now that we made the decision, I think she's as excited as I am. The only down side is, if I do get pregnant, I'll have to carry the child during our busiest time of the year for the restaurant." She ran her fingers through her short rust colored hair. "My chef is going to have to do more to help me in the final trimester. Have you met Molly Flynn yet?"

"No, I haven't."

"She's ecstatic about the building burning down." She chuckled. "She said when I called her to tell her about the fire, that if it hadn't burned, she'd thought about doing it herself. Have I told you how much she hated that tiny kitchen?"

"Yes." Billie hadn't introduced me to Molly Flynn, but I liked her already.

"I forgot when you said the food trucks would arrive. They're like a freestanding kitchen aren't they?"

"Yep, a complete curbside kitchen in one and a refrigerator freezer in the other. Molly thinks the kitchen truck will have more space than her old kitchen had. They're coming on Wednesday. The electricians are coming tomorrow to set up temporary power service for the trucks."

"How's that going to work?" I looked around to the pile of burned lumber that used to be her main building. "Is there enough room for two trucks and construction of your new building?"

"I think so. It will be tight. I'm going to build a privacy fence right along here," she pointed to the area between the courtyard and the debris pile, "to hide the trucks and construction activity. The trucks will be all the way to the rear of the

119

property. It will be a pain schlepping food all that distance, but we've no choice. It's either do that or shut down."

"Construction?"

"The architect is working to change our building plans. When we had the old building, we were exempt from many of the new hurricane building codes. Now that we're starting from scratch, we have to meet all the new codes, which will increase the cost of the building. He's hoping to get plans approved and construction quotes this week. I'm not as optimistic. Everything moves pretty slow in the Conch Republic, Jack."

"Island time?" I asked.

"Exactly."

"A lot going on in your life, Billie."

"I gotta tell you, Jackie, when I think about it all, I get a little overwhelmed. It was just a few months ago we almost lost the restaurant. Thank God for your father's generosity in his will. I don't know where I'd be if he hadn't left me enough to buy the property. No sooner do we settle down from that, and wham, this fire."

Billie's landlord put her building up for sale and tried to prevent her from buying it because of her sexual orientation. She sued and forced him to sell the building to her.

"One day at a time, right?"

She took in a big breath and let it out. "One day at a time. That's more than enough to worry over, isn't it?"

I called Jody and asked her to meet me and the Realtor at Billie's. She arrived about ten minutes before our scheduled time and we both helped Billie make sandwiches and set up one of the courtyard tables up for our discussion. Once the table was set Billie, Jody and I took our seats.

Jody said, "I wonder what she's come up with? That was a pretty tall order you dropped on her, Jack."

Billie said, "There's an old house on Whitehead down the street from me. I don't know what they want for it, but it is gorgeous. The sign went up on it a few days ago. I've always admired that place. Someone told me it used to be part of the navy base; now they call it the Truman Annex."

"The Truman Little White House is there, isn't it?"

"Yes. The Navy carved the base up and sold some of the property off. The house used to be housing for officers stationed at the base."

"Is it on the water?"

Billie said, "No, but it's close to me. That's much better." Her full lips stretched into a broad smile.

Jody said, "There's the real estate agent at the gate." She pointed to a woman trying to get our attention from the front of the courtyard.

Billie got up, scurried to the front, let Florence Keen in and escorted her to our table. We all stood to greet her.

Florence Keen was a woman in her late sixties. She was lean, dressed to the nines and all business. Once we were all seated, she removed a manila file folder from her satchel, laid it on the table and turned to look at me.

"Jack, I want to start with some basics about Key West real estate. I don't know what you have in Central Florida, but in Key West, a fifty by one-hundred lot is a large lot. The amount of land around Hemingway's house is unusual, especially the closer you get to the docks and Mallory Square. Truman Annex, the docks, the navy base and Garrison Bight Marina take up a lot of the waterfront on Key West Island and there aren't many waterfront homes.

"As I mentioned to you yesterday, Sunset Key, is a new development five-hundred yards out into the bay near the Westin Marina. They've just started to construct homes out there and there are still many waterfront lots available. But they're expensive, and as I may have mentioned, the only way to access the island is by a small launch that operates from the marina. There's a lot on the island I want to show you, but you'd have to hire a contractor and build a home on it.

"On Key West island, I have two homes. One that I think meets your requirements, is close in, has a detached guesthouse but it is pricey because of its location. The other is out by the Casa Marina Hotel. It doesn't have the detached building you wanted. The house is a good size, though, and the lot is big enough to build your studio. It is a lot less than the other two options."

Florence Keen opened the file and gave us a flier on the Sunset Key lot. It was a copy of a plat, a map of the island showing all the lots. It was color coded to show which lots they'd sold and which were still available.

"Sunset Key is twenty-seven acres large. The people who own the Westin own the island. They're developing a portion of the island for guest cottages that will be part of their resort complex. They're developing the rest of the island for approximately sixty residential lots. I want to warn you, Jack. These lots are going fast. The one I want you to look at sits out on a point. It's a small lot, but I think it's the nicest one on the entire island. I don't know why it hasn't sold yet."

I looked at the plat. Situated next to the parcel she'd circled, was a much larger tract. The lot had no markings on it showing its status. I said, "What about this one?"

"It belongs to the owner of the Westin. I'm sure he'll build something spectacular there. That will add value to the lot I want to show you.

"Sunset Key used to belong to the Navy. They built it in the mid-1960s for a fuel storage dump, but never activated it. Ten years ago, the Navy sold it to a developer. In 1994, Westin purchased the island and began its development."

"How much is the lot?" I asked.

"Four-hundred-fifty thousand. Because contractors have to bring their material in by water, the cost to construct is double what it would be on Key West Island. But, the beach front lot is stunning and it's ultra-private."

Keen pulled out more fliers from the file and passed them out. She said, "This house is on Amelia Street. It was built in the late 1800s, is two-story and completely renovated. You told me, Jack, you liked the double wrap around porches on Hemingway's house. This house has porches around the front and one side, sits on a corner one-hundred by one-hundred lot. It is thirty-four hundred square feet and there's plenty of room for a separate studio. This house is four-hundred-ninety-nine thousand. By the time you build a new studio, you'll have close to seven in the property."

Jody said, "Doesn't look private to me. It looks like it sits right on the sidewalk."

Billie said, "Same as mine. My porch is only fifteen feet from the sidewalk. You can't sit on the porch without people gawking at you."

Keen said, "Yes but look at where your house is. It's not two blocks off Mallory Square."

"True," Billie said. "But Jack needs seclusion." She looked at me and winked.

Keen removed the remaining flier from the folder. "The last place I want to show you is just down the street from Billie."

"That's it, Jack! The one I was telling you about!" Billie said.

The flier showed a two story wood structure with double wrap-around porches. A waist-high stucco, concrete block wall separated the yard from the sidewalk and ran down the property line between the two adjoining homes. On top of the wall was a black-painted wrought iron fence. In the center of the front wall was a gate that opened to a used brick, paved walkway to the front porch. The house stood back some thirty feet from the gate. Behind the wall and fence was an eight-foot-high ligustrum hedge that had grown together to form an arch over the entrance gate. The photographer had taken the shot of the house through the gate with the hedge framing the picture.

While the southern colonial architecture was different from Hemingway's Spanish styled home, the double porches ran back along both sides of the house and resembled something you'd find in Charleston. There were some smaller pictures on the flier that gave a peek-a-boo look at the guesthouse.

"Any more pictures?"

"No, but if it is something you're interested in, I have appointments set up to look at both the Amelia home, this one and I've made arrangements for the Realtor handling the lot on Sunset Key, to show us the island."

"How much is the Whitehead Street home?" I asked, perusing the flier.

"One-point-two-million. If you're interested in Sunset Key, you'll spend one-point-five-million to build the kind of home you're looking for with a detached studio including the lot."

I said, "And there's Amelia Street."

Jody said, "Jack, I just don't think you'll be happy with that house."

"I agree." I turned to Keen. "Let's look at the Island and the one near Billie. There isn't anything else?"

"Sure, there are lots of homes available. I have homes on the water, on Key West Island, that are four to five million. But, I thought they'd be out of your price range. What's left doesn't come close to meeting your needs. If you don't like either of these two options," she held up the fliers, "we will just have to wait for others to come on the market or look for homes off of Key West Island."

# 13

Billie declined our invitation to tour Sunset Key in favor of enjoying her time off. A golf cart picked us up at the dock on Sunset Key and a young man gave us his spiel about the upside to spending a king's ransom on a small square of dirt. He repeated the statement, "Now is the time to buy," so often I began to count them. He handed us a new updated plat with several handwritten X's over lots, which were sold since they'd printed the latest flier.

The lot we liked was on the opposite end of the island from Key West. They'd just paved the road and yellow and blue ribbons streamed from stakes marking off the lots. The cart stopped in front of the one marked, "6." On our way from the dock to the lot, it impressed me how many lots had sold signs on them. We got out of the cart and trudged through the sand while the young agent droned on. The lot rivaled any beachfront setting I'd ever seen. I watched Jody, her blond hair streaming in the on-shore breeze. She strolled the lot trying to imagine herself living on this little square of paradise. Building a house from scratch gave me pause as I stood by the water's edge, admiring the aquamarine water and a sailboat tacking into the wind working its way back to the Westin marina.

First, was the time it would take to construct a new home. Finding a builder, settling on a design, getting approvals for a building permit, waiting for contractors to build, would take a year or more to accomplish. Jody's place was just too small, and I didn't want to impose on Billie, which meant renting something for a year. The other, was my experience of owning a home with Emily on the ocean at New Smyrna Beach. With our home right on the ocean, the corrosive effects of the salt air were destructive. It would be no different here. And the last consideration was the inconvenience of shuttling back and forth to the island by boat. Despite these reservations, I loved the lot. I loved the ocean. And the prospect of trying to make something work here was attractive to me.

I pulled the flier for Sunset Key out of my pocket, and I could see why Florence Keen had been so "keen" on this lot. It was on a point, it was on the quiet end of the island and secluded. And the major advantage is that I could design the house I wanted.

Florence Keen led the island salesperson away from Jody and me so we could visit in private.

"What do you think?"

"It's amazing, Jack. And private."

"The lot's pretty small, Jody. Once they build homes on either side, it won't feel private."

"Yeah, but look out at the ocean. It's pretty special. And I've the feeling the people who'll build homes here won't be full-time residents. They'll be snowbirds, or the rich buying vacation homes. I'll bet we'll have the island to ourselves most of the year."

I considered her observation. "You wouldn't mind schlepping groceries to the island?"

"Yes, that could be a nuisance, but when you look at this setting, don't you think it would be worth it?"

We completed our tour of the island. Keen tore us away from our Sunset Key salesman, who felt it is duty to remind us for the tenth time, "Now is the time to buy." We left Sunset Key with those words ringing in our ears.

The house on Whitehead Street was everything I was looking for and more. Large square columns across the wrap around porches on the first and second floor gave the house a formal appearance. While the house fronted Whitehead Street, we approached the house from the rear by car through gated access in Truman Annex. The owner stood by an open door to a detached three-car garage that faced a cul-de-sac behind the house. He led us through the garage into the courtyard behind the home, gave instructions in low tones to Keen and he departed. As we faced the back of the structure, a cottage hugged the property line to our left. On the right was a small shed/workshop. A giant Banyan tree covered the entire back yard. A six-foot block wall surrounded the yard and created the feel of a compound.

We toured the cottage first. To my delight, it was a near duplicate of my studio in Mount Dora sans the plate glass window views of the water. It was a one-room efficiency, with a single wall kitchenette, a single full bath, a Murphy bed, and a small sitting area. While it didn't have a plate glass window, three skylights washed the room in light. Two whirling ceiling fans ventilated the room. The set-up was perfect. I wouldn't have to do a thing to the cottage except install a desk and file cabinets. I looked at Jody who was nosing into nooks and crannies. She caught my eye and nodded her approval.

In the house, a master suite, study, living room, dining room and an enormous gourmet kitchen filled the first floor.

On the second floor, there were four bedrooms, two of which had their own bathroom and two shared a common, Jack and Jill type bath.

Every room had at least one ten-foot French door that opened onto a porch and the master bedroom had four. The owner had spent a fortune decorating a living-room sized screen porch on the back of the home. For a home constructed in the early 1900s, the interior looked like a brand new home. I'd watched Jody's reaction as Keen led us through each room. She'd get my attention, raise an eyebrow or smile.

We walked around the outside of the house. The concrete walls surrounding the house gave the property seclusion, even though the house sat in one of the busiest sections of town. Mature trees on the sides and back shielded us from the brutal July sun. Despite the heat, the back yard under the Banyan tree felt comfortable. After the tour, we stood where we began. I noticed that the guesthouse was only a few steps off the rear porch. Convenient, I thought.

While this house fit my needs to a tee, what it didn't have was waterfront. I didn't discount how much I enjoyed the lakeside views from my house in Mount Dora. Everything there was open and bright. Although quite appealing, I felt confined by a restricted view of the yard. That compared to the lot on Sunset Key which offered ocean views. It would be a hard decision. I was anxious to get Jody's reaction.

The only exit from the back yard to the street behind was through the detached garage.

Keen found the owner; we thanked him for his hospitality and made our way to the car.

"Are you sure you don't want to see the Amelia Street house?" Keen asked.

"Yes. I agree with Jody. It is too exposed to the street."

We all piled into the car.

Keen said, "Tell me what you think."

I looked to the back seat where Jody was sitting. "I can see why you picked these two properties to show us. They're so different, but both are excellent choices. Jody and I need to talk it over and we will get back to you."

"By the way, I tested the water on pricing. This house," she pointed toward the garage we'd walked through, "I think it's a little overpriced. His Realtor told me there's some room to negotiate and that we should make an offer. The price of the lot on Sunset Key is firm, and I think they're getting ready to raise their lot prices again. So if you've an interest . . ."

"Yes, I know. 'Now is the time to buy.'

# 14

Florence dropped us off at The Mangrove and we committed to get back to her that day. We found Billie where we'd left her. Only now, she sat with a man we didn't know.

We walked through the courtyard to her table. "Hi, Billie. Are we interrupting?"

"Jack, Jody, this is Tom Saleen, my architect. We were just finishing up with a review of the plans for the new building."

While Tom stood and extended his hand to Jody and me, Billie said, "This is my brother, Jack McNamara and our friend Jody."

"Nice to meet you both." To Billie he said as he rolled the plans up and placed them into a cardboard tube. "I'll make the changes we talked about, run them by you in the morning and, if there are no changes, we'll put the plans out for bid to the contractors we discussed. I've changed our permit from a renovation to new construction and got tentative approval from the city on the building plans pending any final changes we might make."

Tom Saleen placed the rest of his papers in a leather lawyer's brief case, gave Billie a hug and departed.

"I'm starting to get excited. The new building will be such an improvement. Molly is going to be so pleased." Billie scanned our faces. "All smiles. That's good. How did your house hunting go?" Billie sat back down at the table and we sat with her.

To Jody I said, "Well, tell Billie what you think?"

Jody looked at me, then Billie. "We go to see this stunning home on Whitehead Street and the first thing your brother wants to see is the little cottage on the back of the property."

Billie's eyes widened and she looked at me. "That house by my place has a separate cottage? That's what you were looking for, right?"

I said, "Yes, and it is a near duplicate of my studio in Mount Dora."

Jody gave Billie an enthusiastic room-by-room description of the Whitehead Street house. She pointed first to one and then the other Banyan trees that covered the courtyard around us. "It has an enormous Banyan in the back yard just like these. And, jutting off the back of the house is this covered, screened veranda. The way the owner decorated it, it could have graced the pages of *Architectural Digest*. It was like an outdoor living room, with couches, chairs, tables and lamps, television and wet bar for entertaining."

Jody's excitement about the outdoor living spaces shouldn't have surprised me. The main feature of her small conch-house was the small deck in the back yard. She had created this miniature tropical paradise with shade provided by mature trees and shrubs. Even in the hot summer months, Jody opened the French doors to bring in the outside. She opened them first thing in the morning and left them open until she went to work, or the heat of the day forced her to close them and turn on the air-conditioning.

"Didn't you go out to Sunset Key? What was it like?" Billie put her elbows up onto the table and leaned closer to me.

I started to answer, but Jody answered for me, "Breathtaking. Billie, this one lot we're looking at is on a point with a wide stretch of beach. The breezes coming off the water were spectacular."

Billie said, "Ever since they started developing the island, I've wanted to go out and look at the lots. With the restaurant, and everything going on here, I just haven't had the chance. I'll bet it is beautiful out there.

"It will be a tough choice to make." I said. "We'd have to build something new and I don't think the lot is large enough to accommodate a detached studio. But, like Jody said, the setting will get your attention. It would be nice to have a space to write and have that view out the window."

"Which way are you leaning?" Billie asked.

I waited for Jody to say something, but she looked at me and said, "Well?"

"The Whitehead Street place is perfect, in every respect. I wouldn't change a thing about it. If it sat on that lot on Sunset Key, I'd write a check right now. Even though it isn't on the water, there's a certain romantic charm that it's in the old section of town. Being close in is a negative, too. Traffic and the crowds coming off the cruise ships create noise. Even though the walls surround the property and give it seclusion, the property's still situated in one of the busiest sections of the city.

"Sunset Key is just the opposite. Where they located the lot, on the opposite end of the island from town, it's secluded and quiet, with an impressive view of the water. We could build a house of our own design. Keen picked the perfect spot on that island. Although the rest of the lots are nice, that one lot has a lot of appeal to me. The down side is access to the island is inconvenient. Having to park a car in a lot by the marina is a bit of a turnoff. Which way am I leaning? I don't know. What about you, Jody?"

"Once you buy the lot on Sunset Key and build a house, both houses would cost about the same. Yeah, building a house will take a few months, but it will take a little time to sell your house in Mount Dora. You can stay with me, and if you don't have enough privacy to write, you can always rent office space for a few months. I think it all boils down to which location do you like the best?"

I asked Jody if she'd a preference.

"Either one, Jack. I'm serious. Keen mentioned that the Whitehead Street homeowners were flexible on price. If you could buy the house for under a million, would it be any more attractive to you?"

"It might. But I'm having a hard time giving up the view of the water from my studio. Yet I like the fact that the house is close to you, Billie, the restaurant and close to your gallery, Jody. We can walk to everything."

Billie said, "Why don't you make a low offer on Whitehead, and see how much the sellers are willing to move off their asking price."

When I thought of the two pieces of property, I liked the old Whitehead Street house. While it was different from Hemingway's, it was similar, too. The separate studio, French doors in every room opening onto verandas and walls surrounding the property all impressed me. At the same time, I spent eight to ten hours a day behind a keyboard. I had to admit to myself, I would miss the view I had of Lake Dora. As I thought through scenes and dialog, I would look out at the water for inspiration. It was a tough choice.

"Billie, I think that's good advice. What kind of an initial offer would you make?"

"Eight-fifty . . . Nine. Somewhere in there. I'd like to see what they come back with."

"Alright. I'll call Keen and we'll make an offer."

Jody said, "Billie, since you don't have a restaurant to run for the next few days, would you and Alex have dinner with Jack and me tomorrow night? Alex will be in town, right?"

"Yes. Where?"

"Rooftop Café, at 7 p.m. I'm going to invite my mother and Stephen to join us, if no one has an objection."

Billie said, "That's wonderful. How are you and your mom doing?"

"Good. I'm feeling better – we are doing better."

Billie reached over and patted the top of Jody's hand. "I can't tell you how happy that makes me, Jody." To me she said, "Cynthia Pike called while you were looking for property. The attorney general will be in her office at ten in the morning and she wanted to know if Joe, I mean, Stephen, was going to be there. Stephen came by just before you got back and agreed to the meeting. He wants to meet with you at The Marlin in the morning before meeting with Pike. You okay with that?"

I told her I was. Billie and Jody resumed discussion about Jody's mother. They discussed how counseling was going. Jody expressed optimism about Dr. Carnes' help in rooting out her deep-seated anger.

As they talked, my mind drifted toward Stephen and the uphill battle that awaited him. It occurred to me that sometimes our feet are on a path we're powerless to change. Like a car without brakes, careening toward an uncertain danger,

140

circumstances beyond our control, can propel us. These events, and how we respond to them, define us. I read a book once where the author posited that you've no idea how troops will perform until you put them under the pressure of combat. I know from my own experience, you have no idea the depth of your character until you face a significant trial. It isn't success that builds character. It is when life has humbled us, crushed our egos and frayed our hope, only then do we dig down deep into ourselves and discover whether there's anything of value there. It was clear to me Stephen was skidding along his emotion bottom, searching for a seed of hope from which to grow his sidetracked life. While I was impressed by Stephen's many talents, they meant nothing until he found the inner strength to put them back to work.

In my own case, I'd reached out to God. In that moment of turning, God became my strength. To others, they find strength within themselves or through others who support them. I fill my novels with ordinary people placed in extraordinary circumstances. My joy in writing comes from watching my characters grow as they labor against overwhelming odds. As I contemplated meeting with Stephen in the morning, I was hopeful he'd find the strength to rise up.

Jody and I left The Mangrove and met Florence Keen at her office on Duval Street. From comparable sales on the island, Keen felt the Whitehead Street house was about two hundred thousand over market value. The exceptional quality of the home's reconstruction added back some value. She suggested offering nine-hundred-thousand and giving them twenty-four hours to respond to the offer.

"I've some bad news to share," she said, her face scrunched into a wrinkled show of sadness. "I just got a call from our salesman on Sunset Key. Lot number six sold ten minutes ago. I'm sorry."

"Now is the time to buy," I said aloud, to no one in particular.

# 15

Stephen already had a booth at The Marlin before I arrived. And while his hair was wet from a shower, he had the unkempt appearance that went with his current station in life.

"Good morning." I said.

"I hope it will be," he said, raking his damp hair with long, thin fingers.

"You worried about your meeting with the AG this morning?"

"Pike thinks this is a good connection to make. I'm not so sure."

"You're worried about the open warrant aren't you?"

"Among other things."

"What else then?"

"Baker is well connected," he said emphasizing the word is. "How do I know that Florida's AG isn't a friend of the Bakers?"

"Stephen, I think the AG has a lot bigger fish to fry than to pay any attention to a civil bench warrant. Besides, you don't have to give him your name. I agree with Pike. He's the top law enforcement officer in the state, and has connections in Georgia that could be useful to you."

"I wish it were that simple. You assume there are trustworthy people in the legal profession. My experience is it is a cut-throat profession; every man for himself."

"Based on what you've been through, I can understand why you feel that way. But not every attorney is like that."

Stephan gave me a wary look.

"Look Stephen, if you want to take on the Bakers, you need all the allies you can get. All you're going to do is meet with the man. Listen to what he has to say."

"What do I have to lose? Right?"

"Exactly. If Baker is as corrupt as you say, you're not the only person he's taken over the hurdles. You never know what an investigator can find. Maybe Baker has made some mistakes.

Perhaps he was careless and left some crumbs behind."

"Pike has the name of an investigator in Atlanta. When we finish the meeting with the AG, she wants us to call him."

"You're sure you want me in on this meeting?" Natural curiosity is a crucial element if you aspire to write. The selfish me wanted in on this meeting. But another part of me felt voyeuristic. This was personal and private.

"Yes. I want you there. And I want your active engagement. Every cell in my body wants to run from this—but I know I need to face it."

Stephen and I climbed the stairs to Pike's second story office on Duval Street. Her receptionist escorted us to Pike's office. Pike and an older man stood as we came into the room. Pike's eyes narrowed when she saw me. It was obvious Stephen hadn't told her I was coming.

"Joe, this is Albert Hall, attorney general for the State of Florida." Stephen and Hall shook hands. Pike introduced me and we all sat around Pike's desk. Hall was a rotund man, in his fifties, with a boyish face, dyed thick dark brown hair and dressed in an orange golf shirt and expensive, light gray slacks. Once she seated us all, Hall's hazel eyes scanned every inch of Stephen's person.

It was unusual for Pike to dress in casual clothes. It left me with the impression they planned to head to the golf course following our meeting.

To Hall Pike said, "I've already explained to Joe about your desire to meet with him. Perhaps you could go into more detail."

Hall looked at me and said, "Jack, I'm curious about why you're here?"

Before I could answer, Stephen said, "He is my friend. I asked him to be here because I value his opinion."

"Are you an attorney?"

"No, a writer. It is as Joe said."

"Newspaper writer?"

"Novelist. I'm Joe's friend. It's that simple."

"Alright." Hall shifted in his chair to face Stephen. He removed a set of granny glasses off the end of his nose and set them on the desk. "On Thursday, the governor, Ransome Downes, will announce the recommendations of the governor's taskforce on the homeless he formed to deal with the horrendous homeless problem the state faces.

He'll also reveal an outline of legislation he'll introduce to fix it. There will be a question and answer session following his announcement, and I'd like you to offer your reaction to what he suggests."

"You want me to offer my reaction? You don't know me from Adam's house cat. Why would you want my reaction?"

"Because I've read the taskforce recommendations and if our governor implements even half of them, many on the street will suffer. And he'll cut funding for the agencies that deal with the homeless."

Stephen said, "So I take it you're opposed to the governor's approach?"

Hall said, "Yes. Do you know anything about our esteemed governor, Joe?"

"No."

"Before the people elected him to office, by one of the slimmest of majorities, he was a new car dealer in Fort Lauderdale."

"Do you watch TV, Joe?"

"Not in a long time."

"Then you're not familiar with the nauseating television ads he ran for his dealership.

Our governor used to mount a white horse, wear skintight western shirts and pants, a white hat, black boots and a black mask. He called himself, the 'Lone Arranger.' At the end of each commercial, he'd raise the horse up on his hind legs and wave his white hat in the air. Then he'd say, 'Let me help you into your next new car.'

"When he ran for governor, he leveraged the white hat into his campaign. 'Ransome Downes, the good guy.' He ran as a 'clean the house' candidate, an outsider. He'd grab headlines with his buffoonery and insulted his opponents. In his attack ads, his ad agency would Photoshop pictures of his rivals in black hats. It became Downes' trademark."

I said, "You don't sound like a fan."

"He's a blow-hard incompetent. He uses the phrase, 'for the people,' but he wants to dismantle every program designed to help the less fortunate in the state. He's taken to calling them 'black hat' programs."

Stephen said, "And you're in his cabinet?"

"Yes, but not in his party."

"So you want me to do a hatchet job on the governor."

"No. Not at all."

"What do you want from me?"

"Cynthia, I mean, Ms. Pike, told me you'd be a good representative of the homeless. She said you're articulate, believable and homeless. That if there were anyone who could speak for the homeless, you were the right guy."

"Experts abound. Why do you need me?"

"This is a political fight. There are agencies and experts lined up on both sides of this issue. What's dumbfounding to me is there isn't one shred of input from people who're homeless anywhere in that taskforce document. The taskforce skewed the whole report in favor of cutting funding. They pushed the problem off on faith-based organizations. The loan arranger says these organizations 'are better able to deal with the problem.' What I want you to do is be the voice of people who'll be most affected by these changes. I want you to be the voice not tied to any special interest. What you say isn't impugned because you're not affiliated with this group or that."

"You're expecting me to oppose the governor's proposals."

"I don't see how you couldn't be."

I asked, "Have you seen the governor's proposed legislation?"

Hall said, "No, he's keeping his cards close to the chest. But if it follows any of the taskforce recommendations, it will be a disaster for the homeless who depend on state aid, or state agencies for survival. It proposes huge cuts to funding."

Stephen asked, "Ms. Pike mentioned something about compensation?"

"I was thinking about room and board, for five days, plus four hundred dollars for your time."

I asked, "If Joe accepts compensation from you, won't he then represent a special interest? Yours? Doesn't that conflict concern you?"

"Not at all. Joe has the freedom to respond to the governor's proposal in any way he wishes. I'm just convinced that once he hears Downes' proposal that there will be no question of the damage it will create."

Pike, who'd been quiet since she made the introductions, said, "Joe, I've known Albert a long time. We went to law school together. I think what he wants is to make sure the people who'll be most affected by this legislation have their voice heard. Yes, he and I aren't fans of our current governor. We just feel the governor wants to fast-track this legislation and none of the people who'll be most affected by it will have had any input."

"I'll need to think about this," Stephen said.

"Joe, I need to know now. The governor's speech is in two days. I've another person lined up in case you decide against it. But I need to know now."

"And how will this go again?"

"The governor will hold a press conference at the Westin Resort this Thursday. He'll give a speech and open it up to questions and answers. I'll stand and suggest that we hear from you. I'll ask you to stand and answer a series of questions related to the proposals the governor makes. Since I don't know what they are, I can't prepare you for them."

"Will the governor know in advance you plan to call on me for a reaction?"

"I hadn't planned on it. No."

"I've a problem with that. It sounds like an ambush to me."

"If I make the governor aware, will you agree to do it then?"

Stephen looked at me, then at Cynthia Pike. "Yes."

"Good." Hall reached down beside his guest chair, pulled a brief case up to his lap and opened it.

He pulled out an envelope and handed it to Stephen. "This is a voucher for your stay at the Pier House. It covers a room and meals." He withdrew a second envelope, withdrew some cash and handed it to Stephen. He handed the envelope to Pike. "Here is two-hundred dollars. I've authorized Ms. Pike to release the other half to you after the press conference."

"No strings attached?"

"None other than you doing what you agreed to do. The presser is at two p.m. I'd like you to be there an hour before." To Pike he said as he stood. "I'll see you in an hour?"

"Yes. I want to meet with Joe for a few minutes and I'll be on my way."

"Joe," Hall extended his hand and Stephen shook it. He repeated the farewell with me.

As I watched Albert Hall walk out of Pike's office, it surprised me there was nothing untoward about Hall's motives. I waited until we all sat down again and asked Pike, "Is there anything going on between Hall and the governor we aren't aware of."

"Yes, he was active in Jake Reardon's campaign. He ran against Downes for governor."

"Hmmm."

"I know what you're thinking, but Albert isn't that way."

"I'm just worried he might use Stephen in some sort of political feud."

Stephen said, "Jack, it's fine. He didn't attach any strings to this, and I don't feel obligated to take a position." To Pike he said, "Hall referred to a taskforce report. Is there any way to get a copy of it?"

"Albert and I were talking about that before you came. He's worried if you studied the document and were familiar with it, you might reference it in the press conference. It might appear to others that Albert was using you to go after the governor."

"But isn't that what he's doing?"

Pike leaned back in her chair. "Yes, I'm sure that's in the back of his mind. I also know he's angry that no one has spent time gathering input from the people who it will affect the most; the homeless. He thought if someone could be at the presser, who could speak for those affected, it would put a human face on the problem."

"Why, me?"

"When Albert told me the governor had selected Key West to announce his legislation, and that he wanted to find a spokesman for the homeless, I thought his idea was crazy. When he asked me to help him find a spokesperson, the idea seemed impossible. Then you showed up at Billie's restaurant. In spite of your legal issues, you fit the bill."

"With the press there, and given the role Hall wants me to play, I might as well take out a full-page ad and tell the Bakers where to find me."

I said, "It all boils down to a simple question, Joe. Do you want to go after the Bakers or not? If you do, it doesn't make any difference. So, what do you want to do?"

"I'm ready to face it." He looked over at me. He was sitting forward in his chair. The inflection in his voice was firm, definite. "I'd still like a copy of the taskforce report."

"I'll try to get it for you."

# 16

Cynthia Pike hooked her blond hair behind her ears. "I asked Albert Hall if he knew any investigators in Atlanta who could handle a fraud case like yours. We need someone who's a specialist in forensic accounting. He called a friend in the Georgia attorney general's office and they suggested Trimble Davis Investigations. They handle high profile cases and Albert assures me they're the best. I called their offices, spoke with Davis, gave him a thumb nail and asked if we could call him this morning."

"Have you used my name in any of these discussions?"

"No, Joe . . . I mean Stephen. I'd never do anything like that without discussing it with you. But if we call Davis, you have to give him details."

"I understand."

"We good?"

Stephen nodded.

Pike dialed a number and she placed her phone on speaker. She introduced us and asked the receptionist to put us through to Davis who was expecting our call.

"Davis." The voice boomed over the speaker.

Pike introduced everyone including Stephen.

"Stephen Fitzgerald?"

Stephen said, "Yes."

"The third, right?"

"Yes."

"When Ms. Pike called me and gave me an outline, I wondered if it was about your father's firm."

"You're familiar with what happened?"

"I know a little. I've done work for your father. I knew him well. It shocked me when I learned of his sui . . . death. I'm so sorry. Ms. Pike gave me the bare bones. Could you give me a summary of what happened? If you decide to hire us, I'll want to interview you in detail."

"Are you still retained by the Fitzgerald Law Firm?"

"No. No conflict of interest. Baker tossed all your father's consultants out in favor of his own. I haven't done any work for the firm since your father's death."

Stephen ran through the story he had told all of us at Billie's restaurant. His account was succinct and delivered without emotion.

"And what's your goal in hiring us, Stephen?"

"I'd like Baker to go to jail for what he did to my father. At a minimum, I'd like to get out from under the outstanding warrant and the alimony I'm required to pay. Baker defrauded my father and me of the equity in my father's law firm. I want that returned to me."

"To bring criminal charges against Baker involves working through law enforcement. Extortion is difficult to prove. Blackmailers seldom keep receipts. From what you've told me, all the meetings that took place between Baker and your father were private; without witnesses."

Stephen said, "You don't sound optimistic."

"No, I don't. Working through the legal system, especially with a case like this, will take time. If you came to Atlanta, and went to the police, they'd arrest you for the open warrant and they'd chalk up your complaints against Baker as sour grapes. To get the police to launch a serious investigation will mean you presenting them with a fleshed out case. You'll need to provide convincing evidence that supports your claims of extortion and fraud. That will be time-consuming and expensive. But there's another way to approach this.

"We dig into John and Melissa Baker. I get my folks to take his life and finances apart. We go on a skeleton hunt. Just as Baker did to your father, we find out how clean Baker is. I'm betting, based on what he did to your father, his lack of character will show up in other places. Maybe we will get lucky and find a smoking gun proving Baker blackmailed your father. Maybe not. But it is my hope that we don't have to dig real deep to find leverage."

"And if you do?"

"We use it to get you out from under your legal issues."

"Aren't we blackmailing him?"

"No, not at all. We would try to influence his decision-making. Your father was a master at this. He found weaknesses in his opponents and used it in negotiations. It was one of the reasons your father was so influential."

Stephen said, "Looks like Baker turned the table on him."

"That may be, but it doesn't alter my strategy. My goal is to get enough advantage to make your legal issues go away. If we find enough, we may be able to get the settlement you want. If we stumble onto more, maybe we take a run at criminal charges. It depends on how far you want to go and what we find. If you agree, I want to fly down to Key West and dig down into the details with you."

Pike said, "The financial arrangements we discussed, Mr. Davis, remain. You'll bill my office for your services." To Stephen she said, "Do you want Mr. Davis to proceed?"

Stephen said, "Yes, I definitely do." To Davis he said, "And I agree with your approach, Mr. Davis."

"Call me Trim."

"Trim it is."

Davis said he'd meet with Stephen. They set a date and time later in the week and we ended the call. Pike reached into a desk drawer, pulled out a small box containing a new cellphone and slid it across the desk to Stephen.

"Here. If I need you, I want to be able to get a hold of you." To me she said, "I wrote the phone number on the box in case you wanted it, Jack."

Stephen started to object.

"I'm giving you this as a convenience to me, not you. I don't want to run all over the island looking for you." She stood, neatened some papers scattered on her desk. "Gents, I need to run. The Florida Democratic Party is sponsoring a golf tournament at the Key West Golf Club. It seems our coffers are empty following our unsuccessful campaign to take back the governor's office. Albert Hall is the guest of honor."

"You a golfer?" I asked.

"No way! I suffer this humiliation once a year. The heat and humidity are dreadful. But the various civic organizations love it because it draws business to the island at a time of the year when we need it." She reached back to her credenza for a purse and car keys.

Pike showed us out of her office, walked with us down the stairs to the street, and bade us goodbye. I put the number for Stephen's cellphone in my cellphone contacts.

"Where are you headed?" I asked Stephen.

"I'm going to gather all my worldly possessions and head over to the Pier House. I have to tell you it blew me away when he told me the voucher was for the Pier House. That's the nicest place on the island."

"I was, too. The Democratic Party, no doubt, has a block of rooms there for the golf tournament and their bigwig guests. Don't look a gift-horse . . ."

"Believe me, I'm not. I'm not sure how the Pier House will react to a guest of my social standing." He grinned. He said, "We should get together before the governor's press conference."

I agreed.

As I watched him saunter down Duval Street toward the Pier House, I hoped he would have a respite before war with the Bakers erupted.

I walked to Jody's gallery. As I passed the front of her shop, I noticed her rearranging her window display. I stopped and watched her switch out several pieces of sculpture. She replaced them with three burled cypress bowls an artist had turned on a lathe, stained and brought to a high gloss. I stood there for several moments wondering how long it would take her to notice me. This morning she wore her hair down and as she moved about, she kept flipping her hair out of her face. When she noticed me standing by the window, it gave her a start. When she recognized who it was, she shook a fist at me and smiled.

I walked through the door and she backed away from the display.

"You scared the you-know-what out of me."

"I stood there for ten minutes before you noticed me."

"Ah, huh. I thought you were a dirty old man ogling me."

"What if I was?"

"I'd have put on a little show." She fluttered her eyelashes.

"Ah, huh."

"So, tell me how your meeting went?

"Stephen hired an investigator and agreed to work with the attorney general." I gave her a quick summary. "The AG put Stephen up at the Pier House, of all places."

"Hear from the Realtor?"

Just as I was about to answer her, my cellphone rang in my pocket. I pulled it out, looked at the caller I.D., it was Emily. She was the last person from whom I'd expected a call. I debated whether to answer or let it go to voice mail. Jody was uncomfortable with Emily. I said, "What the hell" to myself and answered it.

"Emily." I looked at Jody and she raised an eyebrow.

"Hi, Jack." The volume on the phone was up to max and Jody could hear every word.

"What's going on?"

"I got a call from Nathan Barksdale." Barksdale was the CEO of R&R, my publisher. "He wants an update on the progress of your next novel."

The truth was I hadn't written very much. I had some ideas, a rough outline or two, but nothing had marinated long enough to resemble a plot. I'd just completed negotiations with R&R in April for a new contract. I was on the hook to write two novels by April of next year. In March, I had finished two novels in ninety days and that drained me. The creative well was dry. Then there was the divorce. When I returned to Mount Dora, after deciding to move to Key West, I spent the last couple of months packing and sorting through a lifetime accumulation of junk. After fifteen or twenty trips to the thrift store, I had whittled my possessions down to the bare necessities and declared myself ready to move. As I prepared to come to Key West, I questioned the wisdom of leaving my studio there. I was nostalgic about the number of novels I'd written in that space. What got me past it was the recognition that it was also the self-made prison of my multiyear bout with depression. To sum it all, I just hadn't felt like writing. I was in a good place. While my prospects excited me, I hadn't written a thing.

"I haven't started on anything yet. I'm trying to get settled here. I haven't found a place."

"You should give Nathan a call. He's sensitive about you living up to your commitment."

While I was in my depressed state, I couldn't write for a two-year stretch. Barksdale had already paid me to write the novels and R&R was suffering from the loss of revenue from my books. Under the threat of a lawsuit, and some help from Jody and Billie, I got my writing back on track and fulfilled my obligation. I understood Barksdale's concern about my performance.

"I'll call him."

"You should call Lisa, too."

"Alright."

"Jack. When do you think you'll put your house up for sale?"

"As soon as I find one here. Why?"

"I think I may have a buyer."

"Who?"

"Me. I mean Bob and me."

"Emily, that's just too weird."

"I know. I know, but Bob has always liked your house."

"That's not the only thing Bob liked that was mine. Emily, I have to go."

"If you're going to sell it, what do you care who the buyer is. Think about it, will you?"

"Emily. I'll talk to you later." I hung up.

Jody asked, "'That's not the only thing that was mine?' What was that all about?"

"Decker. I'm done with both of them."

"What does that mean, Jack?"

"I don't want to have anything to do with either one of them."

"What about her editing and managerial skills? Don't you need her?"

"I'll get someone else. I don't have a book in progress. I'm moving. It's the perfect time."

I don't know why her expressed desire to buy my house triggered the avalanche. Perhaps it was my unquenched anger at Bob Decker. While I may have forgiven them both for their betrayal, I hadn't forgotten. I'd already called Decker to inform him I had hired another financial advisor and removed his authorization to trade stocks in my portfolio. He said he understood and hoped in time we could remain friends. It was a short conversation. Their desire to buy my house was too close to home and it fanned the fading embers of my anger.

On impulse, I called Emily back. She answered on the first ring.

"Jack?"

"Emily we need to talk."

Jody wore a puzzled look as we both stood in the middle of her shop.

"Is this about the house?"

"Emily, I want to make some changes. I'd hoped we could work together, but I don't think it will work."

"This is about the house isn't it?"

Jody moved closer to hear Emily's part of the conversation.

"There are many issues. The house just put it all into focus."

"Are you firing me, Jack?"

"That's a crude way of putting it, but, yes, I guess I am?"

"I must confess I was wondering how long it would take. I'd hoped we could work through it."

There was a long silence and I waited her out.

"I'm sorry it didn't work out. My offer on the house still stands, though. I have some of your belongings. What do you want me to do with them?"

"Do you still have a key to my studio?"

"Yes."

"Just leave them there with the keys."

"This is a shame, Jack. We're such a good team."

"Were, Emily. We were a good team."

I flipped my phone closed.

"Wow!" Jody, reached out and squeezed my arm. "You okay?"

"I should have done that in April when she first told me about her and Decker."

"You were dealing with a lot, Jack. And she was knee deep in your negotiations with Barksdale. Then wasn't a good time; now it is."

"Do you need to call your agent? What's her name again?"

"Lisa Catera. No, she and Emily are close. Emily will call her if she isn't on the phone with her already."

My phone rang again. I expected it to be Lisa.

"Mr. McNamara. I got an answer to your offer on the Whitehead Street property. Can you and Ms. Holland come by my office for a minute?"

I held my hand over the transmitter, "Can you close shop for a few minutes. It's the Realtor."

Jody nodded.

"We'll be there in a minute."

"Did they accept our offer?" She clapped her hands together. "This is so exciting."

"I don't know. She didn't say. But we will know soon enough."

Jody already had her keys out, ready to lock the door.

# 17

The realty office was quiet for late morning. The receptionist dialed Keen's office and announced our arrival on the intercom.

Florence Keen brushed a spray of dyed, light brown hair from her forehead and ushered us back to her small cubicle. She borrowed a chair from another office and we sat across from her in the cramped space.

"Well, they gave us a counter offer." She gave us copies of the modified real estate contract. "They came off fifty-thousand, to one-point-one-five-million."

"Is that a final offer?" I asked.

"They didn't say. I tried to feel out their Realtor, but he wasn't a big help. It sounds to me like they're expecting a counter-offer from us. I did some more checking. It is hard to find comparable values on a house like that since it is so unique, but I still think it is a little high."

Jody asked, "What do you think it's worth?"

"My opinion hasn't changed. I think a fair price is right around a million."

I said, "Let's counter at a million."

"May I ask how you're planning to make the purchase? If it's an all-cash deal, and they don't have to wait for loan approvals from a bank, that may motivate the seller."

"Yes, we'll be paying cash."

"Alright, let me write it up and send it back to them. Twenty-four hours to answer?"

"Yes, let's get this done." I said.

Jody said, "You know Jack. I was thinking about furnishings. I don't know what the seller's circumstances are, but I love that house just the way it sits. I don't know what kind of furniture you have, but I've nothing that would be appropriate for that house. If they aren't willing to come off the price, perhaps they'd sell it furnished. The way they decorated the back porch is stunning. It would cost a fortune to duplicate it."

"Florence, let's counter at one-point-one-million furnished, as it sits."

"I think that would make an interesting offer. Before we start shuffling papers back and forth, let me call their Realtor and run this past him. Let's see how the seller's react."

Keen wiggled out of her cubicle, told us she'd be back and she disappeared into the maze of cubicles behind us. I looked at Jody.

She raised her eyebrows and grabbed my hand. "Keep your fingers crossed."

"You like the house?"

"Jack, it's perfect. I loved the lot on Sunset Key, but when I walked into the big ole house it felt like home."

"Yeah, me too."

Keen returned all smiles. "I spoke with the Realtor. When they first listed the house, he says the sellers had intended to offer it furnished, but he had talked them out it. He felt it would be harder to sell. I told him the price of our counter-offer and that it was an all-cash deal. He said he felt sure the sellers would accept it. He wanted me to write it up and get it to him right away."

"That's marvelous," Jody said.

"I'll get this typed up, get it over to them and let you know as soon as I hear something."

Jody and I ducked into the Hard Rock Café. We sat inside rather than swelter in the heat on their patio. We ordered burgers. Ceiling fans labored overhead. Our table sat under an air-conditioning vent that blew refreshing air on us. They'd decorated the walls with memorabilia from five decades of rock and roll. People queued up outside to buy Hard Rock Café T-shirts from their sidewalk store.

Jody said, "So, how many people will be at the dinner tonight? I need to call the Rooftop and give them a number."

I said, "There's Billie, Alex and your mother. Did you call Cynthia Pike?"

"Yep, she'll be there. Then there's Stephen Fitzgerald."

"Counting you and me that makes seven. If we get asked when we're going to get married, what do you want to tell them?"

"Yesterday," she said with a mouth full of her burger.

"What do you think about having the ceremony in our new house, after we move?"

"We haven't even got a contract yet and you've already moved."

"Yeah, I'm jumping the gun a bit. Assuming we can get together, what do you think?"

Jody wiped her mouth with a napkin. "I love it. That would be perfect." She set her plate aside. "I can just see the ceremony on that incredible back porch. We could have the reception in the backyard under that beautiful Banyan tree."

"Good. That's what we'll do."

I walked with Jody back to the gallery. Tourists window shopped her store. When she unlocked the door, they drifted in after her. I told her I had errands to run and patrons swallowed her attention.

I spent most of the afternoon in local jewelry stores shopping for an engagement ring. What I knew about diamond rings was microscopic. Salespeople educated me about the four C's in picking a stone: cut, color, clarity, carat weight. After two hours, my eyes crossed and, in the end, I picked one I thought was stunning. It could have been zirconia for all I knew, but I liked it and I thought Jody would, too. By four o'clock, I had

Jody's ring. I knew she didn't expect a ring, so I was hoping for a complete surprise.

Shortly before five, I went by Billie's restaurant. I found her at the bar with Alex. They were drinking margaritas and huddled together. Billie was still dressed in the sweatshirt and shorts she'd been wearing earlier. Alex had her black hair piled on top of her head and wore black shorts and a sleeveless black top.

"Alex, it's good to see you."

She pulled herself away from Billie, stood and gave me a warm hug. "I haven't seen you in a while." She smelled of perfume mixed with full day's perspiration.

I said, "It's good to see you. You look wonderful."

Billie said, "I've filled her in on all the recent events. Did you notice they hauled off all the debris?"

I looked to the rear of the courtyard. The excavator and debris pile from the torn down building were gone. "That was quick." To the rear, where the building had stood, electricians had installed two stub poles that looked like sawed off power-poles. Attached to them were gray boxes to provide temporary power. "The electricians have been here too, I see."

"They just left."

Closer to us, there stood a stack of cypress fence panels and a stack of four by four posts.

Anticipating my question, Billie said, "The fence people come in the morning. As soon as the trucks arrive on Wednesday, the real work begins. We need to stock them and Molly needs to organize the kitchen truck to suit her. But for now, this," she looked around at the empty tables in the courtyard, "is marvelous. I feel like I'm sitting in the eye of a hurricane. Dead calm, but you know it won't last long."

Alex said to me, "I don't know how she does it."

"What're you going to do during your pregnancy, Billie?" I asked.

"Alex and I were just talking about that. Assuming the procedure is successful, we've several options. The first two trimesters shouldn't be a problem unless there are complications. That gives me six months to train Molly to assume more of the day-to-day operational duties. We've been talking about adding a second chef during the high season and I want to scale back the physical work I do anyway. The business has grown enough to support more staff. What worries me is getting this building done before my final trimester."

"And before Christmas," Alex added.

"Yes, when the snowbirds invade the Conch Republic. By then, I hope we have our act together."

Alex said, "I have some vacation time I haven't taken, and if Billie begins to have trouble, I can take a leave of absence."

I asked, "What're the chances of problems, Billie?" This all seemed so risky to me.

"IVF is pretty safe, Jack."

"I've read that IVF success rates decline after a woman reaches forty," I said.

"The issue is with the quality of the egg. As women age, the viability of their eggs can decline. As women approach menopause, the success rate for women using IVF with her own eggs declines. It isn't that way for donated eggs. The fertility success rate for women using donated eggs is about the same for younger and older women."

Alex volunteered. "I'm concerned about that, too, Jack. The doctors said, nationwide, women over fifty have better than a fifty-percent chance they'll go to term. At the clinic Billie is going to in Miami, they claim to have a seventy-five percent success rate. The risks are the same for any woman going through pregnancy: gestational diabetes, high blood pressure and pre-eclampsia the most serious. For women over fifty there's a higher risk of miscarriage, pre-mature delivery and low birth weight. But the docs say if Billie takes care of herself, takes medications as prescribed and stays on track with follow-up visits, they believe there's a low risk of complications. As a last resort, if there are issues, they can always end the pregnancy. And here is something interesting. Fertility clinics have IVF restrictions for women over a certain age. Not because of health concerns so much, but out of concern a mother might be too old to provide adequate care for a child."

Billie and I'd already discussed most this at some length, but it was good to see that Alex had worked through it and offered this upbeat assessment.

"Alex and I meet with Pike in the morning to go over paperwork. Once she files the papers with the court, the docs can proceed. We were just discussing how many embryos we wanted to implant."

"Why is there a decision?"

"The more eggs they implant the higher the percentage I'll get pregnant. The more eggs implanted the higher the risk of twins or triplets, which creates its own set of issues. Our docs won't implant more than three. They're suggesting two. Since implanting two might result in twins, we've been talking about whether we should go with only one embryo."

Alex said, "These procedures are so expensive, Jack. We've been weighing the possibility of the cost of multiple attempts versus the risk of having twins. Billie would be in her late sixties when our child would be in their teenage years. I'd be in my early sixties. That would be challenging enough with one child much less two."

I tried to think of some fragment of wisdom I might offer. Since I've had no children of my own, I couldn't imagine what it would be like to have a child that late in life. "What've you two decided?"

"We're still talking about it. I'm leaning toward two. Alex is still chewing on it." She looked at Alex. It was clear they weren't having a disagreement about the number, but they both wanted to make a wise choice."

Alex asked me. "Do you have any thoughts on this?"

"If you decide on two embryos, I think you should assume you'll have twins. I would plan on it. So I'll ask the question, 'Do you want twins?'"

They both looked at one another for several moments without speaking.

Alex finally said, "We haven't decided yet. We've been talking about it. And we're running out of time to decide."

# 18

I enjoyed the second-story, open-air bar at the Rooftop Café. Once the sun set, even on the hottest of days, there was always a cool breeze to wash the cares of its patrons away. Soft lights and limbs from surrounding oaks gave it a tree-house feel. While you could order food in the bar, the restaurant was next to it, but indoors.

Stephen stood waiting on the sidewalk on Front Street at the base of the stairs leading to the entrance. He had on new clothes: khaki shorts, white golf shirt, beige ball cap with 'Key West' embroidered on it and flip-flops. It would be hard to distinguish him from the garden-variety conchs who inhabited the island. He'd trimmed his long hair and full beard.

"Hey, Stephen," I said. "What've you been up to?"

He spread his arms out to show off his new threads. "Did a little shopping and had a couple of margaritas watching the sunset at the Pier House sunset deck."

Jody said, "I never get tired of that. It's so beautiful. I think it's one of the finest traditions of the island."

We ascended the stairs to the bar and discovered Cynthia Pike had already pulled six barstools around a single counter-top height cocktail table. Still decked out in her golf clothes, Pike dropped down off the stool, came around the table and greeted everyone with a hug. Her face was red with sunburn and her eyes a little red from the heat.

"How did golf go?"

We all found seats around the table.

Pike said, "Humiliating. I hate golf. I finally gave up, quit playing, and rode in the cart with Albert Hall. That was after I teed the ball up and took three swings at it without ever hitting it. I was so embarrassed. Thank God for those little carts with beer on them."

I said, "It has been a while since I've played, but I know what you mean. Golf requires a lot of skill, something I have in short supply. The only thing I'm good at is losing golf balls."

Pike lifted a frosty mug of beer in the air in a mock toast. "I'll drink to that."

The server came, took orders from Stephen, Jody and I and shuffled off to another table. Stephen ordered a margarita and Jody and I ordered house wine.

Jody had her hair down and wore a long one-piece, white, sleeveless dress and sandals. She had on only a touch of makeup, a string of pearls and dangling earrings to match. As the four of us engaged in light conversation, waiting for Alex and Billie to arrive, I couldn't keep my eyes off her. Her light brown eyes were brilliant. She'd laugh at Pike's self-deprecating recount of her golf outing and send the warmth of her personality to each of us. She looked as happy as I can remember. And while there may have been laugh lines at the corners of her eyes and some softness in the skin at her jawline, she hadn't changed since we were kids on the beach in Hollywood, our skin tanned and hair bleached from the sun. She turned away from Pike and caught me looking at her and I could have sworn she blushed.

I'd never seen Billie wear a dress, but tonight she wore a floor length, high-waist, coral print dress. Alex had on white shorts and an orange

T-shirt. After greetings, our server brought drinks for Stephen, Jody and I. Then she took margarita orders from Billie and Alex. After our server returned with drinks for Billie and Alex, my cellphone rang. I excused myself and stepped away from the table. It was Florence Keen.

When I returned, I suggested, since we all had so many events today, that each person give an update. I asked Stephen to go first.

He provided a brief synopsis of his meetings with Albert Hall and Trimble Davis and that he'd moved in at the Pier House. He said, "Today, I took two positive steps to return to the land of the living. I can't tell you all how grateful I am for all your support and help." He raised his margarita in the air. "I'd like to propose a toast to Billie. If she hadn't injected herself into my life, today would have never happened." With his glass still raised, he said, "God bless you, Billie."

We all raised our glasses. I pointed to Billie. "Billie, you're next."

"Just before Alex and I left to come here the food trucks arrived. I wasn't expecting them until Wednesday. Stephen you and Jody haven't seen it, but they hauled off the debris from the building and they ran electricity for the food trucks. Our architect called and said he had a set of plans ready for Alex, Molly and I to review."

I said, "And you're going to reopen Friday."

"Yep. Cynthia pulled all the permits. The city will inspect everything on Friday morning and if there aren't any problems, we open Friday for dinner."

"Alex?"

"The merger with Southeast Airlines is complete. My seniority is high enough I can command the schedule I want, and this weekend I took my check ride for certification to fly 747s. Now I can fly international, something I've wanted to do since I started flying." Alex raised her glass, nodding her head and we all offered congratulations.

"Jody?"

"Jack will tell you about some news we have to share. But I wanted to give you all an update on my mom. I asked her to come tonight, but she was not feeling up to it. She and I've gone through several months of counseling, as you know. In the past week or two, we've had several breakthroughs. She's been through a lot and I've come to understand and appreciate that. I've forgiven her. Stephen, Jack will fill you in on the story at some point, but you all know, given the circumstances how difficult it was for me to do this. I've come to understand we both have been victims of something horrible. Once I understood that, I began to see what a courageous and strong woman she is to have endured such hardship.

"Most women who go through what she did, end up taking their own lives. Instead, she turned these unspeakable circumstances into an opportunity to help women all over the world who suffer from this sickening disorder. When I see what she's done with her life, it is an inspiration. I share this because I'm optimistic she and I are on the mend. I want to have a relationship with my mom. And that's the news I want to share."

There were no toasts or congratulatory statements. Alex, who was closest to Jody, put her arm around her shoulder and hugged her. Jody took my hand. It was a tender moment for her, but she held her emotions in check.

Jody said, "Jack, why don't you share your news."

"Alright. I just got off the phone with Florence Keen. Jody and I are now the proud owners of the house on Whitehead Street. Because this is an all-cash deal, we will be able to close in a week or two."

Jody's mouth fell open. "Jack, you're serious."

"That was the call I just took. They agreed to the offer and are selling the house furnished, just as it sits."

Billie started to lift her glass.

I held up a finger. "And there's something else." I looked around the table trying to build some suspense. I reached into my pocket, pulled out the box and took the ring from it, reached for Jody's hand and slid the engagement ring on her finger. Her eyes were the size of silver dollars. She held her hand up in the air as someone might shade his or her eyes from the sun.

"Oh, my God!" She threw herself at me, her arms around my neck. She pulled away, held her hand out at a distance and surveyed the ring. "Jack, it is gorgeous. Oh, my God." With her mouth open, she held out her hand for everyone at the table to see. She hugged me again.

"I'd already asked Jody to marry me. We wanted to wait and share it with everyone. As you can see the ring was a little surprise."

"Now, can I make a toast?" Billie said.

I nodded to her.

"If there were two people in this whole world meant to be together, it is the two of you. Congratulations."

Billie raised her glass. We all followed suit.

This time Jody couldn't contain her emotions. She hugged me again and told me she loved me. "You make me so happy, Jack."


The six of us moved into the restaurant and feasted on baked yellow-fin tuna and filet mignon. When they cleared the plates away, we refreshed our drinks several times and Stephen regaled us with stories from his youth that kept us all in stitches. In my forty-eight years, I can't recall a happier evening. Hope filled us all and the stars in all our lives seemed to be in perfect alignment.

# 19

The next morning, after a late evening at the Rooftop Café, Jody and I slept until well after eight. When Jody awoke, she got me up and said she wanted to look in on her mother before she went to the gallery. She'd tried to call her, but she wasn't getting an answer. After showers, we walked the two blocks to her mother's apartment.

We let ourselves in with a key her mother had given her. We found her in bed.

"Mom. Mom?" Jody said, in a raised voice.

She walked around the bed and put the palm of her hand on her mother's forehead. "She's burning up." She lifted her mother by the shoulders. "Jack, wet a dish cloth and bring me a glass of water. Mom, can you hear me?"

I went into the kitchen, wet a small towel, poured some water and I returned. Jody had propped some pillows up behind Helen. She was lethargic and disoriented. Jody lifted Helen to a sitting position, took the glass from me and held it to her mother's mouth and she drank in small sips. Once Helen finished half the glass, she laid her mother back against the pillows and she washed her face with the cloth. She folded the material into a small rectangle and laid it across her forehead.

Helen looked around the room and then at us. "Yes, I can hear." She tried to sit up but gave up and fell into the pillows. She looked like all the blood had drained from her face, almost an ashen color.

"Mom, I think we need to get you to a hospital." Jody looked at me, panic written in the lines of her face.

"No! You mustn't do that."

Jody pulled the covers back. Helen looked emaciated, her bedclothes damp and smelling of perspiration. She felt her forehead again. "Mom, this is serious. I'm going to call an ambulance." Jody pushed herself up from the bed.

Helen summoned the strength to reach out and restrained her by the wrist. "We need to talk, sweetheart. There are some things I haven't told you."

Jody sat back down on the bed. "What things?"

"I have terminal cancer." Helen looked at me then Jody. "It began as undetected ovarian cancer. They did a hysterectomy and tried to remove all the disease they could see, but it had already spread. They did some radiation therapy to slow the progression down, but it only bought me some time."

"Why didn't you tell me?"

"When I first came to Key West to see you, I didn't want you to agree to counseling out of pity for me. It would have never worked. I talked with Dr. Carnes and she agreed we should withhold my cancer. When you were well along in counseling, we were going to tell you. But our relationship was going so well, I didn't want to spoil it. I figured you'd know soon enough."

The first time I had seen Helen at the Westin, I should've seen the signs. Her frailty, the dark circles around her eyes and her stooped over posture. In my defense, I hadn't seen her in thirty-five years. I'd remembered her as diminutive and birdlike. I had chalked up her appearance to advancing age. Now it was altogether clear, Helen's motivation to reconnect with her daughter was a dying wish. I chose to think about it in positive terms, that they'd reconciled. And I understood her reasons for secrecy. Jody needed to heal and knowledge of her mother's true condition could have interfered. I hoped Jody was drawing the same conclusion.

"How bad is it, Mom?"

"Stage V. It's in my liver, sweetheart. And time is short."

"How short?"

"I'm guessing, based on how I'm feeling, perhaps a few weeks. And that may be optimistic."

"Can't they do something?"

"Everything they could do has been done. If I go to the hospital, I'll just be miserable. The IVs, the noise, the constant vital sign checking, it would be awful. I'd rather be here, with you." She pushed herself up into a sitting position. "There, I'm starting to feel a bit better." It was when Jody tried to straighten her covers around her that Helen noticed the engagement ring. She reached for Jody's left hand and held it up for inspection. She looked straight at me. "You've made this old woman happy, young man. It is such an exquisite ring."

"We announced our engagement last night. I'm sorry you weren't there, Mom."

"Honey, I wish I'd been there, too. But this old body was just not in the mood to cooperate."

Jody put her hand to her mother's forehead. "We have to get this fever down."

"There's some aspirin on the kitchen counter. Jack, would you bring them to me?"

I walked to the kitchen and returned with the bottle. She placed two tablets in her mouth and emptied the glass of water. She still had no color in her face. She said to me, "Would you please hand me my robe?"

I stepped over to the chair next to her bed, retrieved her robe and handed it to her.

"Are you sure about this, Mom?"

"I need to get out of this bed for a while. We will all be more comfortable in the living room."

I stepped out of the room while Helen dressed. With great effort and leaning on Jody, Helen emerged from the bedroom and shuffled to a lone club chair in the sparsely furnished room. Jody and I both picked up chairs from a dinette set and pulled them close to her mother. We all sat in awkward silence.

"Are you in any pain? I asked her.

"No, I'm just weak. The weakness comes and goes. I'm fine. I'm feeling much better."

I had to admit, her face started to show some color.

"Look, you can both stop worrying. I've already been to an oncologist in town. I explained to him my desire to avoid a hospital stay and he's agreed to make house calls when we reach the point I can no longer make it to his office."

Helen pointed to a coffee table in front of a couch. "On the top of that stack of papers is the name of a registered nurse the doctor recommended. She'll stay with me as needed, again, when the time comes."

"Mom, wouldn't you be more comfortable in your own home? I'd be happy to take you there and stay with you."

"Nonsense. You have a life to lead right here. And where you are, is home to me. Are you okay with that?"

"I'm not going to let you stay another night in this place." Jody looked around inspecting the space as though for the first time. "You're going to come and stay with me."

"I couldn't let you do that," she gave a weak protest.

"Mom, I'm going to grab a few of your belongings, Jack is going to get my car, and we're going to take you to my place right now." Jody looked up at me for confirmation and I nodded. "Once we get you settled, Jack will come back for the rest of your clothes and let your landlord know you're leaving."

"It's only a month to month lease, Jackie. And I don't have that much here."

You could see the joy in Helen's face at the prospect of being with her daughter.

By the time I walked to Jody's, got her car and returned, Jody had some of her mother's possessions packed and ready for the return trip. I double-parked on the street in front of Jody's, helped Jody transport her mother up the steps and into her house. I returned to Helen's apartment. I rounded up clothing I found in the closet and dresser drawers, and packed them into a large suitcase.

In the living room, I found a laptop, a cellphone, several hardbound books, psychology trade publications, a large, canvas handbag loaded with junk and a minimal amount of foodstuffs in the pantry and refrigerator. It took me less than fifteen minutes to corral her possessions. Helen had given me her landlord's phone number. I called her and gave notice she was leaving.

When I returned to Jody's, I found them sitting at the dinette, Helen drinking water and Jody blowing the steam off a fresh brewed cup of coffee. Jody found room for Helen's clothes. That was a challenge since Helen's apartment was larger than Jody's home was. It was obvious I'd have to return to Billie's. It would be at least two weeks before we could close on the Whitehead Street home. We'd all move into the house as soon as we could. Until then, there wasn't enough room for the three of us here.

I waited until later in the morning, when Jody helped her mother with her shower, to gather my clothes and toiletries and put them in her car for transport to Billie's. If Helen saw me packing up, it would have made her feel bad that she was forcing me to move. Since she didn't know I'd moved in with Jody, she'd be none-the-wiser.

When I was putting the last of my belongings in Jody's car, Florence Keen called me on my cellphone and said a final contract reflecting the agreed upon terms and selling price was ready to sign. While Jody settled her mother, I walked to Keen's office and signed the contract. The only change I made was to set the closing date in two weeks. That would mean the seller would have to make immediate preparations to move. Since they had no furnishings to worry with, it would lighten their burden.

By the time I had returned to Jody's, Helen was in Jody's bed and sleeping. We exited to the deck in the back yard. The heat was sweltering, but the shade and slight breeze made it tolerable.

"Is she doing alright?"

"The aspirin helped to reduce her fever. I called her doctor's office, gave an update and the doctor sent word that he wanted to see her this afternoon. He said he'd come by after rounds at the hospital."

"She looks so frail. If she weighs eighty pounds it would surprise me."

Jody pulled her hair up into a ponytail and tied it in a knot. "You didn't have to move out. We could have worked out something."

"I know. But you don't know how much time you have with her. You can focus on her without worrying about me."

"I suppose. This is so upsetting. I should have seen the signs. Now it seems so obvious."

"She's right, though. If you'd known from the beginning, the wrong reasons would have motivated you. Even though you'd have had empathy for her, you'd have felt pushed into dealing with your feelings."

Jody reached across the table for my hand. "I'm not angry about her keeping her cancer a secret. Not at all. You're right. She and I wouldn't be where we are now had she told me. If anything, it elevates my respect for her. She could have played that card and she didn't. It proves what I've come to know about her, she acted out of complete selflessness and love. When she told me she was dying, I knew in an instant how much I loved her. It was her dying wish that I would no longer be burdened with what happened to us. It was such an unselfish act."

I was proud Jody had come so far with her mother. She'd cast aside her feelings of anger and even hatred toward her mother and replaced them with love, which was impressive. It had begun with forgiveness. She found it somewhere deep within her. Her expressions of love for her mother, given everything that had happened, were a testament to her deep character and inner strength.

We spent the next hour talking about adjustments we needed to make to care for Helen. Jody called one of her friends who helped at the gallery on occasion. She'd open the store up and clerk in Jody's absence. I called Billie and told her I'd be staying with her until we closed on the house. I explained what was going on with Jody's mother, and she at once volunteered to provide meals until we could get Helen settled in the Whitehead Street house.

Jody and I agreed to take turns sitting with her mother, so someone would be with her at all times.

I looked at Jody and wondered how she'd handle the loss of her mother, especially given the emotions involved in their reconciliation.

I tried to clear my head of the sadness and Lisa Catera came to mind. I needed to call her, shore up our relationship. With Emily out of the picture, I needed her now more than ever.

# 20

My relationship with Lisa went well beyond a professional association and I'd neglected her. During our talks with R&R, I had yanked the early stages of contract negotiations out of her hands, which tested the limits of our friendship. In the end, while she finished putting an excellent contract together, her calls after that were infrequent. In the last couple of months, I've talked with her once. I just wished my motive for calling her now hadn't been about my lack of performance on this new contract.

I wanted to call Barksdale and assure him I had everything under control, but I'd bruised Lisa with the contract and I dared not go around her on something so important.

I walked to The Mangrove, past the "Closed" sign and found a place in the courtyard to make the call.

"Lisa."

"Hi, Jack. I was just getting ready to call you."

"About Barksdale?"

"Well, that, too."

"Emily called you."

"Yep. I wish you'd given me a heads-up."

"That's why I'm calling, Lisa," I lied.

"Why did you fire her? I thought you guys had worked things out."

I explained the exchange about the house, the awkwardness of having to deal with my ex-best-friend Bob Decker and that I wanted my manager and editor close at hand.

I filled her in on buying the house, my engagement to Jody, Jody's challenges with her mother and all of Billie's news. As I ticked off each of these events, I felt more embarrassed. In the past, I was on the phone with Lisa daily, even in the midst of my two-year case of writer's-block. Now I was sharing with her the news of life changing events as I would to a stranger. I knew my lack of communication about all this would hurt her.

"Am I next?" Her wounded words were like a dagger through the phone lines.

"Lisa. Of course not."

"Are you sure? Because it appears to me, you don't trust me anymore. That doesn't even touch on our personal relationship. Ever since Emily filed for a divorce, you've walled me off and treated me like a leper. What's going on, Jack?"

I responded without thinking. "You and Emily are so close; best friends." My answer surprised me.

"Is that what this is about?"

I hadn't thought about pushing Lisa away. But when she coupled my recalcitrance with Emily's divorce I saw it, and the reason why. I was angry at her siding with Emily. "I thought you were on Emily's side."

"And how did you come up with that?"

I could hear Lisa's breathing deepen.

"When I called you and told you I wanted to fire Emily and find another editor, you fought me on it. When it came time to negotiate with R&R, I find out Emily has been involved in the R&R discussions."

"Whoa. Whoa, Mr. McNamara. We need to put the brakes on this right now. First, I've been friends with Emily because Emily was your wife, manager and editor. I treated her as if she was a part of you, because she was. But you make no mistake, my loyalty has been to you and only you. When you were so sick, Emily enlisted me to get you the help you needed. I was her friend, because that's what you needed, the people in your life confronting you on your depression.

"When she started pulling away from you, it broke my heart. I was not concerned for Emily. You were my concern. I loved Emily as long as she loved you. When her affections changed, I tried to protect you from the carnage. But there was only so much I could do.

"On your contract, you told Emily, to go out to look for another publisher. You'll recall we had a conversation about your prospects of finding another outlet given your history of depression. You got angry with me, and gave the job of finding another publisher to her. What you don't know, and what Emily hasn't told you, is that I'd been in discussions with R&R from the moment they fired you. I was the one who brought them back to the table not Emily. Yes, she was successful in finding other publishers interested in your work despite your history. She proved to both of us I was wrong and that we had a stronger bargaining hand than I thought. Because you'd given her the job of finding your next publisher, when R&R came to Key West to try to work something out with you, she told me you wanted her to deal with R&R. So, that was you're doing, or Emily's, not mine.

"She wanted to salvage her job with you so she threw her weight around. She didn't care whether I was fired or not. In the end, it was my relationship with Nathan Barksdale that saved the deal. It was our attorneys who figured out how to structure the deal so both you and Nathan got what you wanted. It was not Emily. Was Emily my best friend? No."

"Did you know she was cheating on me?"

"Now we're down to it aren't we? You think she confided in me and I didn't tell you about it."

"Did you know?"

"No. She talked to me about how unhappy she was. That she couldn't handle your depression any longer. But, no. She never talked to me about an affair. She gave no hint of it."

"Well, it appears I owe you an apology. I'm sorry."

"Jack, I may be your agent, but I've always been your friend first. I'd never do anything to hurt you."

"I'm sorry, Lisa. Forgive me."

"Now tell me why you called."

"Barksdale. Emily told me he's getting panicky. She said I needed to call him."

"And you called me first. That's a good sign."

"And, I wanted to talk to you about a replacement for Emily."

"Well, you know R&R will provide an editor at their cost. You have me to manage your affairs. Do you really need to replace her?"

"I still want my own editor. It would embarrass me to send one of my unedited, rough draft manuscripts to Barksdale."

"We have people here in the agency who could handle that for you."

"Lisa . . .?"

"I figured you wouldn't budge. So after Emily called me and told me you'd parted company, I started making some calls. As it turns out, one of R&R's own editors retired and moved to Big Pine Key, right up the road from you. I called her. She said she'd welcome the part-time work. She'd worked on some of your previous novels and she would be happy to meet with you. Her name is Betty Worth."

Lisa gave me her phone number.

"I remember her. She was excellent. I enjoyed working with her."

She said, "I have a couple of more names if she doesn't work out, but Nathan tells me she was one of his best.

"I'll call her."

"Now let's talk about your novels."

I explained to her what my ideas were for the two action adventure novels Barksdale expected. I also told her I was thinking about basing a novel on Jody's reconnection with her mother. That it would be "fiction" based on a true story. She liked the concept. I also gave her a thumbnail on Stephen's experiences and told her I was thinking about approaching him for permission to tell his story depending on how it all worked out.

I gave her an idea on when the wedding would be and asked her to put it on her calendar. I warned her that things were subject to change depending on how everything went with Jody's mother.

"I talked to Barksdale after I visited with Emily on the phone. Since I had nothing to report to him, I told him I'd call you, get a status report and get back to him. But, he wants to talk to you in person. He said it was personal. You should call him."

I told her about the conversation I had with Barksdale at the Pier House in April about his daughter's attempted suicide and his own regret he hadn't stayed in touch with me during my bout of depression. "I think he just wants to make sure I'm okay. If it's anything more, I'll let you know."

"Jack, are we okay?"

"Yes, I'm glad we talked."

While our conversation ended on a good note, I acknowledged there was still some distance. I'd bruised her. I felt bad about it. I knew our phone conversation hadn't fixed it. I committed to spend time with Lisa when she came for the wedding.

At The Mangrove, workers had constructed a part of the fence between the courtyard and the back lot and busied themselves with its completion. I waved at Billie who directed a food service delivery driver on where to unload supplies. I could see her chef, Molly, scurrying about the stainless-steel food truck, preparing for the opening on Friday. Billie waved back at me and then turned her attention to stocking the refrigerator truck.

I called Nathan Barksdale's personal cellphone number. He answered on the first ring.

"Jack. Good to hear from you."

"You too, Nathan. How is your daughter doing?"

"That's why I wanted to talk to you. She's doing marvelous. We found an excellent psychiatrist who put her on the right medications. She joined a support group and it's made a huge difference. She's motivated. She says she isn't ever going back to being depressed. It is a real turnaround, Jack."

"That has to be a relief."

"You never stop being a parent and you never stop worrying about your children. Relief? Her progress is a godsend. How are you doing?"

"As far as the depression goes? I couldn't be better." He didn't ask about the progress of my novels but I briefed him on my ideas and he seemed pleased in particular with a novel based on Jody's Story. "Nathan. I'll meet my deadlines."

"I've some news to share. *The Tainted Lady* just broke into the New York Times top ten. I'm working with Lisa and a studio on the movie rights."

*The Tainted Lady* wouldn't be my first book made into a movie. While there was good money in writing novels, selling movie rights was the real payday. A movie boosted sales of all my other books.

"So Lisa knows about this?"

"I asked her not to tell you, Jack. I wanted to share the news with you in person. I was just about to call you when you called me. I was going to wait until we had a firm deal, but I just couldn't keep it from you."

To say my relationship with Nathan Barksdale was different was a complete understatement. Six months ago, he fired me. While greed brought him back, I think his daughter's emotional challenges gave him insight into the hell I'd been walking through. I had let him down. I think he was able to get beyond it because of his experience with his daughter. Even in the best of the times my relationship with Nathan was distant. We seldom talked. All our communications came through Lisa. Since his daughter's bout with what I could only assume was Bi-Polar Disorder, we made a personal connection and I saw a side of Nathan I'd never seen before, compassion and caring.

We chatted for another twenty minutes. I filled him in on our wedding plans. He asked me when the wedding was and I got the impression he wanted to come. I told him he was welcome to be there and that I would send details when we finalized them. I told him I'd purchased a home in Key West, and put my house in Mount Dora up for sale. He told me he wanted to retire to Florida in the next few years and expressed an interest in the details of my home, although I thought he'd be happier in Palm Beach or Naples. I imagined Nathan living in more splendor than my home there afforded. Finally, we got to the subject of Emily's departure.

"I have to tell you, Jack. Negotiations almost fell apart in Key West because of Emily. If it hadn't been for my long standing relationship with Lisa, and my overriding desire to salvage our relationship, I'd have walked away. I know you respected her skills, but she was not helping your cause. She trampled all over Lisa. I'm surprised Lisa didn't quit on the spot."

"Thanks, for telling me, Nathan."

We hung up, and I just sat there ruminating about his comments. Mentally, I was defending Emily. In the light of all that had happened with her, I knew my feelings were irrational. As I considered Lisa, though, guilt swept over me. It redoubled my determination to repair our relationship. It also affirmed my decision to sever ties with Emily. I'd screwed up. And it was Lisa who pulled me out of the fire.

# 21

After I briefed Billie on Jody's mother and as I departed her restaurant, I received a call from Stephen.

"Albert Hall wants to get together."

"Where?"

"At the Chart Room here at the Pier House. I guess he wants to make sure I'm going to show up. Can you make it?"

"What time?"

"Three."

"Alright, I'll be there."

Jody and I made sandwiches and sat on the back deck so as not to disturb Helen. The breeze from earlier this morning had retreated. The sun was a white, blaring smudge overhead and the humidity intense.

"She's still weak. In fact, she seems worse. After her shower, I couldn't keep her awake. The doc called and he'll be here soon. He finished his rounds and asked if he could come early." She sat facing the house and peered over my shoulder through the sliding glass door.

No sooner had we finished our lunch we heard knocking at the front door.

I followed Jody through the house and stood behind her as she opened the door and greeted the middle-aged man.

"Sean O'Brien," He extended his hand. "I'm Dr. Holland's doctor."

Jody shook his hand introduced herself, then me. She showed him to her bed, which was only a few steps away.

"I appreciate you coming, Doctor. When we went to her apartment this morning, we had a difficult time waking her, and she was weak and running a high fever. Even with help, it took every bit of her strength to walk even a short distance. We moved her here, to my house. I'd have brought her to your office, but she didn't have the strength. She was adamant about not going to the hospital. She said she'd discussed that with you."

O'Brien was tall, thin, balding and his face, from his eyes down, had a dark tan, but his head was white as a snowbird, an angler's tan. He removed his sunglasses, set his bag at the foot of Jody's bed.

O'Brien said to Jody, "You're Dr. Holland's daughter, correct?"

She nodded.

"Your mother is in the advanced stage of ovarian cancer. Unfortunately, she caught it late, and her cancer has spread to her liver."

Jody interrupted. "Yes. She told me this morning. Is it too late for treatment?"

"When she came to Key West, her condition had already advanced beyond curative treatment. More chemotherapy might have slowed the spread of the cancer some, but she'd have suffered more than necessary. The treatment might have extended her life, but not more than a few weeks. She rejected that option immediately. She said she'd been through enough of that. All I tried to do at that stage was to make her comfortable and buck her up with vitamin shots."

"How far has the cancer advanced?"

"Let me look at her, and we can talk some more."

Doctor O'Brien sat on the bed next to Helen, and awakened her from sleep. She was groggy and disoriented as she'd been this morning. She looked at the doctor, a little startled, until she recognized him.

"Dr. Holland? How are we doing today?" He felt her head and face.

"Not so good, young man."

He reached for his bag, pulled out a stethoscope, digital thermometer and blood pressure cuff. He slipped a penlight from his shirt pocket and shined it into her pupils. I could see the whites of her eyes had a golden tinge. He took her vitals, pulled down the covers and palpated the right side of her stomach. She grimaced.

"Does that hurt?"

"Ah, huh."

He held out his hands, asked her to grab them and pull herself up. She complied, but it took every ounce of her strength to do so. Once she was in a sitting position, he listened to her heart and lungs.

"Your fever is coming from an infection in your lungs."

"Pneumonia?" Jody asked. She'd sat at the head of the bed, next to her mother and opposite the doctor.

O'Brien nodded at Jody, then addressed Helen. "Your distended stomach, painful liver and the jaundiced appearance in your eyes tells me your liver is failing. Have you been eating? I don't have a scale, but you look like you've lost more weight since I saw you last week."

"I have no appetite. I know I should be eating."

"No surprises there, Dr. Holland. Your symptoms are consistent with advanced liver cancer. Do you still have the prescription for morphine I gave you last week?"

"I have it, but didn't fill it. It hurts, but it isn't unbearable."

"You should fill the prescription and begin to take it is as prescribed; one to two tabs every four hours. From this point forward, you'll no doubt need them. I'm also going to give you a script for penicillin to combat the infection in your chest. That should reduce your fever and make you feel better." He gathered his equipment and placed it in his bag. He reached for Helen's hand. "You have any questions?"

"Time?" Helen asked.

"Your liver is failing, Helen."

"Days?"

"Perhaps, it is hard to say. Everyone is different."

O'Brien stood, and addressed us all. "You have my cellphone number. If the pain becomes problematic, give her medication every three hours. If that doesn't help, call me. Call me if her condition changes. I only live a few blocks from here. You should have Dr. Holland's nurse come twice a day. I'll call her and give her instructions."

"Dr. Holland . . . Helen, at this stage, rest and sleep are your best friends. Take advantage of them."

The doctor gathered his equipment, shook our hands and left.

"Mom, what're your thoughts?"

"I'd say, if I remember my medical training, I don't have much time."

Jody said, "What can I do, Mom?"

Helen began to cry, "You've already done it, Jody. Your expressions of love and your being here with me now are answers to a million prayers. I'm beyond happy. You've filled my heart. I can't think of anything more precious to take from this life."

Jody fluffed up Helen's pillows, straightened her covers and fussed over her until Helen assured her she was comfortable. I offered to run to the pharmacy and get the prescriptions. Jody found the script for the morphine and the other prescription the doctor had just given us. She gave them to me and thanked me for getting them filled. Jody pulled one of the dinette chairs up to Helen's bed, and as I turned the knob to open the door I heard Helen say, "I just hope God has forgiven me for what I've done."

I paused to hear Jody's response.

"Mom, you were sick. You didn't know what you were doing. Of course he'll forgive you."

I opened the door and left.

When I returned from the pharmacy, Helen was asleep again. Jody was sitting at the dinette. She looked up at me, but it was clear her mind was somewhere else. I sat at the table, next to her and waited for her to share her thoughts.

"I had hoped she'd stay up so we could give her the antibiotics, but as soon as you left it was a real struggle for her to keep her eyes open. I tried to talk with her, but she kept drifting off. I finally gave up and let her sleep."

"How are you doing?"

"You mean with my mom and her dying?"

I nodded.

"While you were gone I was thinking about that. I lost my mother in 1961. She was dead to me. In the years following the loss of my family, I grieved for all of them, including my mother. So I've already gone through the process of losing her. Everything that's happened since we've reconnected is a gain not a loss.

"Yes, I'll be sad that we didn't have more time, but when I look at it through her eyes, she gets to leave this world with a weight taken off her shoulders. And with her help, I'm now able to free myself of the awful burden of it all. So I'm happy, grateful and pleased for her. She set about to make this right between us and she did. I want to grasp on to that and celebrate it. So far, while her health has declined from the cancer, she hasn't dealt with a lot of discomfort and as far as I can tell, she hasn't suffered. I'm sure as the cancer progresses, the pain will, in time, become an issue. I don't want that for her. The circumstances of her life have caused enough hurt."

We discussed the doctor's pessimistic view of Helen's longevity. Jody decided she wanted to call Dr. Carnes and talk with her. I explained Stephen's desire for me to meet the AG with him. She encouraged me to go, and said she'd use the time to speak with Dr. Carnes.

These conversations were all too familiar. I had just buried my Aunt Ruby a couple of months earlier. I'd spent hours dealing with the legal issues involving her death. As I reflected on the experience and the final wishes of the dying, I remembered a commitment I'd made to Ruby, to find her adopted sister Millicent. In the melee following her passing, I had forgotten it. This was a commitment I needed to keep.

My thoughts about Helen were bittersweet. It was her intervention in the early stages of my writing that launched my career. But her temporary flight from sanity and the destruction it caused was an enormous stumbling stone in my life, not to mention Jody's. Had it not been for the murders committed by her, Jody and I would have likely married and could have spent our entire lives together. I regretted what happened. At the same time, I was grateful Jody and I, in the end, were together and we could still love one another all these years later. I was grateful, too, for the opportunity Jody had to repair some of the emotional damage from that event and the pivotal role Helen played. Given all that happened, I couldn't think of a better outcome.

It was my hope, as I walked from Jody's to the Pier House, that the assurances Jody had given me that she was in a good place, were more than just words.

# 22

The Chart Room Bar at the Pier House was empty. I'd gotten there early and the server greeted me and told me to sit wherever I wanted. I chose a table in the corner, one I thought would be the most private.

The room was rich in wood tones, and nautical artifacts. It was small and cozy. I asked if she could make coffee. She said she'd just made some for herself. Soon, she appeared with a cup, cream and a square ceramic container holding a variety of sweeteners. Just as I was about to explain to her that others would be joining me, Stephen appeared in the doorway, followed by Albert Hall. Stephen wore jeans and a work shirt. Hall had dressed in golf attire. I wondered if he'd just come from the golf course. His shirt was moist and smelled of perspiration. We shook hands and took our places around the table. The server hovered nearby to take drink orders.

Hall told her to charge the drinks to his room, and he gave her his room number. He ordered a rumrunner and Stephen ordered a beer. I sat between Stephen and Hall as I dressed up my coffee.

"Jack, I didn't expect you to be here?" Hall's tone was sharp.

Before I could answer Stephen said, "I asked him to come."

I offered to leave, but Stephen waved me off. And he didn't try to explain my presence to Hall.

"I was hoping we could talk in private."

"Whatever you have to say to me, you can say to Jack."

The grimace Hall wore on his face was overt. He narrowed his eyes, flexed the muscles in his jaw and stared me down. Instead of finding the confrontation intimidating, it elevated my interest. What could he want to discuss with Stephen that would warrant such a need for privacy? I was not about to leave. I returned his glare with a smile. I said nothing and waited for Hall to kick off his meeting with Stephen.

When it was obvious to him I was not moving on, he said to Stephen, "Did you read the taskforce's report I sent you?"

"Yes."

"Well? What did you think?"

"Whoever wrote it filled it with stereotypical assumptions about the homeless that aren't true. I think it oversimplified the problem, casts blame in all the wrong places, cuts funding for the wrong programs and recommends more funding for a broken system that's failed to deal with the real issues."

"Can you give me illustrations on what's wrong with it?"

"To begin with, the report is reactive. It focuses on how to handle problems the homeless create. It doesn't address what's causing the homeless problem to begin with. It cuts funding for meaningful programs, and aims to sweep the problem off the street and to fund organizations who can maintain the status quo."

Albert Hall's face beamed. "Are you prepared to repeat this tomorrow?"

"It depends on how you want me to do it."

Hall rubbed his hands together as one might prepare to dig into a scrumptious meal. "It is my understanding Governor Downes will hit the highlights of the taskforce study, and announce the main points of his own legislative proposal. Once he's done so, he'll open the meeting up to questions and answers. At the appropriate time, I'll stand and say that there was no one at the presser who was homeless who could represent the people the legislation would affect. That I had asked you to come to offer a reaction."

"Have you told the governor you're going to do this?"

"No, not yet."

"I only agreed to do this with your promise that you'd give the governor advanced warning."

"I'm going to tell him in the morning."

"Just before the event?"

"Yes. I'm afraid that's the best I can do."

"So, it was your purpose to catch him off guard. To embarrass him."

"Joe, Ransome Downes is a political neophyte. He rode a wave of anti-government sentiment into the governor's mansion as an outsider. He's a lightweight and, with regard to the taskforce, special interests are playing him. If I can't find a way to slow him down, he could do some serious damage to the state while he's in office."

"It doesn't alter the fact that you're attempting to use me to do a hatchet job on the governor."

"I'm not asking you to say anything more than what you just told me. I'm not asking you to sandbag him, just offer your opinion."

"How will I know you'll follow through and tell him what you have planned?"

"I'll introduce you to him. I'll explain why I asked you to come."

The right side of Albert's mouth turned up into a smirk. It was as though he were imagining the look on the governor's face when he introduced Stephen and the effect it might have.

Albert said, "I'll live up to my end of our agreement. And I expect you to live up to yours."

"And now that I know it is your intent to harm the governor, what if I decide I don't want to do this?"

Hall turned and looked straight at me as though weighing his next words. I had the feeling we were coming to the reason Hall didn't want me here.

"Because, Mr. Fitzgerald, there are a couple of legal issues you may need my help with."

Now Stephen cut his eyes to me, then back to Hall. "How did you find out about that?"

"That's not your concern. What your concern should be is that I can be either your friend or enemy. It wouldn't be wise for you to renege on our agreement."

I immediately thought of Cynthia Pike. Could she have confided in Hall? Stephen's jaw muscles tightened into knots. I considered Trimble Davis' strategy of digging into someone's life looking for issues one could use as leverage to influence their decisions. It was obvious the tactic had no geographic boundaries. I wanted to accuse Hall of extortion but thought better of it. I didn't want to say anything to hurt Stephen.

After a long silence, Stephen said. "Mr. Hall, I don't know how you found out about me, but it doesn't matter. You should do whatever you feel is right. But understand this, you won't push me to do anything I don't feel comfortable with, and I won't stand up in that press conference and say anything untrue. You're correct. I did agree to do this. You introduce me to the governor, explain my purpose for being there and I'll do my part."

"Excellent." Hall said exhaling in relief. He rubbed his hands together again and pulled his elbows up on the table. "I knew your father. Or I should say I knew of him. After the press conference, we should talk and you can tell me about your situation. I'd like to help if I can."

Hall was a master of carrot and stick diplomacy. He maneuvered Stephen into a position where there would be a downside if Stephen didn't help Hall advance his agenda. Stephen sat in silence and bit his lip.

"The press conference starts at two. You need to be there at one." Hall stood up, drained the remains of his rumrunner in one swallow. "Jack." He extended his hand to me, which I accepted. "It's Stephen, isn't it?" Hall extended his hand to Stephen, and said, "I'll see you tomorrow at one."

When Hall had left, Stephen and I sat down.

"I thought you handled him with skill, Stephen."

"My negotiation skills are a little rusty, but I'm okay with where it ended. How do you think he found out about me?"

"If I had to guess, I'd say Pike, when she was selling you to Albert, gave him your name. She, no doubt, was trying to enlist his support on your behalf and confided in him."

"I'm not sure I care for the way she handled that."

"At least you know he has no plans to pursue you for the warrant."

"Yeah, there's that. I guess it doesn't matter. Soon it will all be out in the open anyway. Might as well be now.

I explained the crisis with Jody's mother and that I needed to get back to help if I could. He asked me if I'd come with him to the press conference, but he said he'd understand if I couldn't.

# 23

News photographers and videographers muscled with each other for space to set up their equipment along the back wall of the conference room. Workers had placed a stage at the front of the room, on top of which they placed a podium flanked by two green-skirted tables. The lectern carried the seal of the State of Florida. Nameplates lined the dais.

Media technicians were installing mics and performing sound checks and, somewhere in the room, a boom box played Phil Collins', Another Day in Paradise. Hotel staff had filled the room with chairs arranged theater style.

I searched for signs of Albert Hall then I retreated to the foyer to wait for his or Stephen's arrival. I was surprised they were late. I people watched as conferees trickled in. My assumption was they were members of the press angling for front row seats.

Hall arrived bedecked in a light gray suit, white shirt and a solid red necktie that hung long over his protruding stomach. He toted a leather lawyer's bag in his left hand, and extended his right for me to shake.

"Where's Stephen?" he said, looking around the foyer.

"I don't know. I just got here myself."

He turned and looked toward the lobby then back at me. "The governor will be here any moment." He dropped his bulky bag on the floor.

"He will be here, Mr. Hall."

"Why are you so confident?"

"I think Stephen is a man of significant character."

"You mean the kind of character that causes a man to fail to pay alimony?"

"You shouldn't pass judgment until you understand the circumstances."

"That's fair. You're right, I don't know the circumstances. He's fortunate to have Cynthia Pike as his attorney. If anyone can help him navigate his issues, she can."

"He needs more help than that."

"What help will I need? Stephen said, standing behind us.

I said, "I was about to suggest to Mr. Hall, that you might need his help."

Hall said, "I'm glad you're here, Stephen. Cynthia is already lobbying me on your behalf. She hasn't told me what's going on, but when the time is appropriate, we will get to the bottom of it. The governor will be here shortly. I want to pull him aside for a moment, explain what I want to do and then I'll call you over and introduce you. I want to keep it short and simple."

"Alright," Stephen said.


There were a few awkward moments when neither of us had much to say. Then the governor came through the front entrance flanked by his security detail and entourage. Ransome Downes was taller than I'd imagined and younger. He wore gray slacks, a navy-blue sport coat and white dress shirt with an open collar. Albert Hall left us standing in the foyer and intercepted the governor. He spoke and Downes nodded as he did. Finally, they both turned and looked at Stephen and, for a moment, Hall signaled for Stephen to join them. I was not about to let Albert exclude me from the confab so I tagged along, much to the unabashed annoyance of Hall.

As we approached, Downes looked at me and a grin spread across his long thin face. He extended his hand. "Jack McNamara, right?"

I shook his hand. "Yes, that's right." I looked over at Hall with a smirk on my face.

"I'm your biggest fan. I knew you lived in Florida . . . Mount Dora, I believe . . . but I didn't expect you to be here. My wife and I love your books."

I said, "My connection with Joe is recent. But I've come to understand the plight of the homeless through him."

"And, Joe is it?" Downes extended a hand to Stephen.

"Street name. My real name is Stephen Fitzgerald. Mr. Hall felt like my experiences as a homeless man might be of value."

"Yes, Albert was telling me."

"And, Jack, I'm a little confused about your role here?"

I said, "I'm here to be a friend to Stephen, just to be of support."

To Stephen, Downes said, "I assume Albert has explained what the press conference is all about. How do you feel you can contribute?"

"Didn't Mr. Hall explain . . .?"

". . . I'd prefer to hear it from you, Stephen."

"The way Mr. Hall explained it to me, after you gave your speech, Albert would ask me to offer my reaction to your plan from my experience as a homeless man."

Downes scratched his chin, looked at Albert Hall then back at Stephen. "He did, did he?" He looked over my shoulder into the conference room and the chairs were filling up. "Alright." More chin scratching. "Stephen, your input will be welcome. Welcome, indeed. My goal is to provoke a debate and to succeed in doing more than just putting more whitewash on a serious problem. I'd love to get your reaction."

Downes excused himself and bounded off into the conference room.

"Well, that went well," Hall, said.

"How did you expect it to go?" I asked.

"Not like that. We need to get in there. I want Stephen and me down on the first row."

I took it to mean I wouldn't be sitting with them.

On the dais with the governor, were the mayor of Key West, the chief of police and the secretary of Children and Family Services. I found a seat in the back next to the television cameras and press photographers. The mayor came to the podium, welcomed the press contingent to his city and introduced the governor.

Downes stood, brought a black bound spiral notebook to the podium. He looked around the room. The graying temples of a full head of black hair gave him a presidential appearance. I had a hard time imagining him wearing the Loan Arranger costume astride a rearing white stallion.

He recognized the political dignitaries in the room, city officials and the heads of charities in Key West who provided services to the homeless.

"The homeless situation in the State of Florida has reached critical level. On any given day, more than fifty-seven-thousand people—about the population of Daytona Beach—are homeless in Florida. According to a report by the state Department of Children and Families, the population is growing by twelve percent a year.

Nowhere in the state is the problem more acute than here in Key West.

"As you're aware, one of my campaign promises was to improve the plight of the homeless. After taking office, I assembled a taskforce and charged them with finding solutions to the problem. And today, I'm prepared to lay out the broad outline of legislation I hope the state house and senate will take up later this year."

There was a noticeable pause in the governor's speech. He looked over and down to Albert Hall and Stephen sitting on the front row to his right, then back out to the audience. He closed his notebook.

"It has come to my attention this morning, in my search for input about the homeless, I've overlooked the people we're trying to help; the homeless themselves. Albert Hall, our fine attorney general, has suggested this would be an excellent forum for that input. And here with us this morning, I'll call him Joe, has agreed to share his experience with us.

"So, Joe, if you wouldn't mind coming up to the podium I think we'd all benefit from your perspective."

The governor backed away from the podium and gestured for Stephen to take center-stage.

In a stroke of pure genius, Downes had just turned the tables on Albert Hall. If Stephen got up and made a fool of himself or refused to get up to speak, Hall would look like a fool. And if Stephen made even the most perfunctory of comments, Downes would look magnanimous. If Stephen had any significant input, it would give Downes the opportunity to make changes to his speech on the fly. While it may have been a brilliant move for the governor, it put Stephen in a terrible spot.

From my vantage point, I couldn't see Stephen's face. I could only imagine the thoughts running through his head and the deep regret he must be feeling at having agreed to Hall's scheme. But in a moment, Stephen stood. His first two or three steps toward the stage were tentative. He looked at the audience and almost tripped over the first step leading to the dais and podium. The governor stepped out of his way, and returned to his seat. As he stood at the lectern, his nervousness was palpable.

"My name is Joe." His voice cracked. "I'm homeless by choice. Many of you may assume a large percentage of us are on the street because we want to be. You'd be wrong. Less than six percent of those who're homeless choose that lifestyle. Some of us have broken the law and hide on the streets. Others, like me, are running from something they don't want to face. Even though we choose to be on the street, only a small percentage of us want to be there.

"For the other ninety-plus percent of the homeless, circumstances have forced them to the street. Roughly thirty percent are mentally ill. Those addicted to alcohol or drugs make up another thirty percent and the disabled, many veterans, make up the remaining twenty percent. Of those, a third are women and children and twenty-five percent are veterans, many from the Vietnam War. A third of the homeless have jobs with insufficient income to lift them off the street.

"First, no manmade program will put an end to homelessness. Enormous progress can be made, but not with current programs, many of which enable homelessness instead of providing a pathway out of it. Let me share with you the experience of a local pastor from my home state, Georgia.

"He'd just replaced the pastor of the church who'd been running a homeless shelter and a soup kitchen for over twenty-five years. The church provided a weekly bus service to carry people to the employment office and day labor jobs. He noticed the same people showed up every day for food and shelter but not for the buses to find work.

He concluded that the church provided the basic living needs but no incentive for the homeless to find work and to rejoin society. He began to ask hard questions about what they were doing. He redesigned his ministries to provide 'temporary' help that moved people toward health. He turned those away unwilling to work. He focused on the addicted who wanted rehabilitation. He provided psychiatric treatment to the mentally ill willing to submit to a doctor's care. He enrolled the disabled and undereducated willing to go to school. Soon, his ministries began to show good results.

Hospital emergency rooms determine the type of illness before prescribing treatment. The goal is to treat the emergency and release the patient. The patient must submit to treatment or there can be no cure. This is a good model. If we ran a hospital the way we run the homeless system we'd fill the rooms with patients who would never leave.

"The homeless situation in Florida and Key West is complicated, with complicated solutions. There are two approaches. Build programs to treat the symptoms or design a scheme to attempt to cure it. In my opinion, the only way to reduce the cost of homelessness is to focus on curative treatments rather than addressing only the symptoms it creates.

"The first step is to resolve that homelessness will no longer be acceptable. Stephen stopped, scanned the room, and allowed his words to take effect. "I want us to think about this for a moment. Homelessness should not be tolerated. All the incentives for the homeless to remain in that condition should be removed." He paused again, and I could hear murmurs in the audience. "As my pastor friend discovered, the current system provides incentives to the homeless to remain in that current state. And the ranks of the homeless will continue to grow until these incentives are removed. The homeless need to be swept off our streets, but not under a rug.

"The second step is to create pathways for the homeless to receive the help they need. People will remain on the street until we have a system in place to handle their unique needs.

"An organization trained to diagnose the individual causes of homelessness is needed. People should be channeled into programs that provide the help they need. But, none of this will work unless and until the option for someone to be homeless is removed.

"The mentally ill are the most distressing problem on our streets today. In 1975, the Supreme Court, in the Connor v. Donaldson case, ruled we could not hold the mentally ill in institutions against their will. But there were caveats. First, they couldn't be a threat to themselves or others. And they had to be capable of taking care of themselves. Following this ruling, many of our mentally ill were dumped on the street. States, to cut costs, closed many mental health facilities. Towns that housed these shuttered hospitals had an instant homeless problem they were ill equipped to handle. Many homeless, mentally ill folks need to be in institutions. They're beyond treatment and they're incapable of taking care of themselves. They need help.

"Connor v. Donaldson created the unintended consequence of fear by local governments to deal with the homeless. Many in law enforcement misunderstand the law to mean the mentally ill have the right to live on the street without interference. And these rights—to live unmolested on the street—apply to anyone. Cities, afraid of violating someone's constitutional rights, don't enforce vagrancy laws.

"Part of their fear is if they arrest a mentally ill person for vagrancy, what would they do with them? If you put them in jail without dealing with the mental health issue, they'll be right back out on the street once released from jail.

"On the legal issue, once a person is incapable of taking care of themselves for whatever reason, they become a burden to society. They should be forced to submit to treatment until they can be restored to full participation. At the same time, society can't begin to enforce laws that limit freedoms of the homeless until they have the help they need. One without the other is a waste of time.

"What about the homeless addict who refuses treatment? Or what about the mentally ill who don't want to undergo treatment or take their medications? And what about the homeless who refuse to work? These cases reflect the conundrum that must be dealt with. These individuals have become burdens on society. They are incapable or unwilling to take care of themselves. There must be consequences for their non-compliance. There must be loss of freedom. Chronic addicts and the mentally ill who're beyond treatment should be institutionalized. Those who can work but refuse to do so and can't support themselves should be incarcerated. In the case of the latter group, they should remain in this state of lost freedom until they are willing to rejoin society and support themselves.

"To some, this might seem harsh. Without curative pathways, it would be."

"Most people on the street live desperate lives and many have lost hope. These people need and want help. But they need the right kind of help. They need help that can restore them to productive lives. Homelessness is a disease that can be cured. There's no question the problem is challenging and it will take men, money and material to fix it. All that is needed is the will to do it."

Stephen scanned the faces of the audience and smiled. "Thank you."

He stepped back from the podium. The press and audience applauded with enthusiasm.

Governor Downes stood, took a few steps to where Stephen stood, shook his hand and gestured for Stephen to return to his seat.

From the back of the room, I could see Stephen return to his seat in the first row, but I couldn't see Albert Hall's reaction to Stephen's speech. As the governor opened up a notebook, adjusted the microphone and prepared to start, I couldn't get over how impressed I was with Stephen's performance. He spoke without notes, completely off the cuff and gave one of the best explanations of the homeless situation I'd ever heard. He was articulate and polished. And except for his initial nervousness, his delivery and stage presence were flawless. His thoughts were bold, controversial and I was anxious to hear the governor's reaction.

# 24

Governor Ransome Downes looked out into the standing room only audience.

"Before I get started, I want to react to Joe's excellent analysis of the homeless dilemma and his thoughts on a solution. He's right on target, Our aim must be to cure the homeless problem. Anything short of that leaves in place a system that, at best, maintains the status quo and in the worst case enables the problem to grow worse. I also agree whatever we do, we must have the attitude that, as a society and a governing body, we will no longer accept homelessness as a condition."

The governor held up the taskforce report on homelessness. "As you all know, several months ago, I assembled a taskforce of some of the best minds in the state to make recommendations on dealing with the homeless." He set the report back down. "And while I feel there's much good information in this report, like Joe, I feel there's too much emphasis on reacting to the problem and not enough on eradicating its existence.

"One of the recommendations of the taskforce was that we declare war on homelessness. As my cabinet and I began to wrestle with the recommendations of the taskforce, this one recommendation stuck with me, declaring war. I'm convinced this is the wrong approach. These unfortunate folks aren't the enemy. We aren't at war. I like the term Joe just spoke about, that these are people living desperate lives, and only a small percentage of the homeless are on the streets by choice. Regardless of the reason for their homelessness, these people need help—our help.

"So the initial goal of our administration, in whatever steps we take, is to find solutions. And as we dug into what various government and private organizations have done, we found we spend a tremendous amount of money with mixed and sometimes disappointing results. We found that these efforts weren't well coordinated and at times operated at cross-purposes. Like Joe expressed with eloquence, many of the programs, without meaning to, created a culture of homelessness without offering individuals a realistic way out.

243

"Our administration learned the complexities of the issue and the difficulty coordinating all the private and public agencies that have a stake in the problem. We soon learned that anything we do, will cost more money than the state can provide. It will take both private and public funds together. And as Joe pointed out, unless we have a coordinated, well-defined structure to treat each individual, we're wasting our time.

"In thirty days, I'll appoint a cabinet level position to focus this administration's effort on fixing our state's homeless problem. This secretary will coordinate between the state legislature, existing state agencies and the governor's office. We will create a quasi-state organization funded by governmental and private agencies. This cabinet appointee will oversee, coordinate and manage our statewide effort. While the state would direct the efforts, we will staff it with people from the private sector. This group will design and develop a structure within which all governmental and private bodies could operate. The state will train, certify and supervise participating organizations. Private groups who don't wish to take part would no longer be eligible for state funding. This organization will identify, train and certify private physicians, treatment centers and other groups who'd participate in the treatment, rehabilitation and education of the homeless. This organization would evaluate state and municipal vagrancy laws to insure the legal structure exists to remove the homeless from our streets and to create legislation and statutory models that counties and municipalities can adopt. They'd identify potential locations within the state where we could provide temporary housing to the homeless while they undergo treatment, training and job placement. These centers would include shuttered military installations, vacant state buildings, or the creation of new treatment centers that are capable of handling, at the start, large numbers of people.

"In summary, the homeless issue will receive my full attention and that of my administration. It is a problem we have allowed to languish long enough. I intend to do everything within my power to correct it. Now if there are any questions, I'd be happy to try to answer them."

For the next half-hour, the governor answered questions.

One question stuck in my memory. "What happens to the people who refuse to cooperate? Aren't they free to do that?"

He answered, "In the Connor v. Donaldson case, the court ruled that we can't hold the mentally ill in institutions against their will, if they weren't a threat to themselves or others and they were capable of taking care of themselves or could be cared for by others. I think this is an excellent test. We should apply this standard to all who're homeless. If they're a threat to themselves or others or incapable or unwilling to provide for their own support, then they're a burden to society and we should help them. These individuals, by circumstances beyond their control or by free choice, rely on others or the state to care for them. These folks need help, and if they're unwilling or unable to accept help, we should institutionalize them until we can rehabilitate them and they're capable of supporting themselves."

That seemed harsh to me. But the more I thought about it what was the alternative? Which would be worse? To force a man into drug treatment and attempt to salvage his life, or to let him rot on the street, sleeping in urine stained doorways and stealing from people to maintain a drug habit. Or what of a man who just didn't want to work, who panhandles for money, takes up precious bed space in a homeless shelter and clogs up city parks interfering with the rights of other citizens to enjoy them?

The rest of the questions the governor tackled fell into two broad categories. From the liberals there were questions related to the potential violation of the "rights" of the homeless. Conservatives raised questions about how the governor planned to pay for this sweeping program.

But after the governor ended his presser, I was most curious if Stephen's performance ran counter to Albert Hall's goals. From where I sat, Stephen helped the governor not hurt him. As the people filed out of the room, I made my way to where Stephen and Hall stood. Governor Downes remained on the dais besieged by reporters and well-wishers. As I rounded the first row, there was an awkward silence between Stephen and Albert Hall. Hall was first to speak.

"I was wondering where you got off to. I was curious what you thought about the governor's talk, and what you thought the reception was by the crowd?"

I looked over at Stephen and his face masked his own feelings.

I said, "Well, Downes impressed me as a Republican sounding much like a Democrat. It seemed like he cared for the people on the street and was attempting to find a solution that would work."

Hall said, "Both the Downes' plan and your assessment of the situation, Stephen, shocked me. I assumed after reading the taskforce's report and recommendations, Downes would take the standard republican approach, which would have been to wipe the homeless off our streets without trying to deal with why they were there in the first place. And even though the governor and I are on opposite sides of the political fence, I agreed with most of what he proposed. So, it surprised me." And turning to Stephen, he said, "You gave an excellent account of yourself." He extended his hand to Stephen and Stephen shook it.

"I agree, Albert," a voice boomed from behind me. I turned to see the beaming face of the governor. "Joe . . . I thought you did a marvelous job up there." He turned and pointed to the podium. "You gave one of the best summaries I've heard on the issue. You showed the polish of an attorney."

Stephen said, "It's Stephen. Stephen Fitzgerald. And I'm an attorney or I was until recently."

Downes said, "This sounds like a long story, and I have to leave for another engagement." Turning to Hall he said, "I'm impressed with Stephen's grasp of the issues of the homeless. I'd like to explore ways to involve him in our efforts. The two of you should explore that option and find a way to make it happen."

"I'd be happy to," Hall said. He sounded sincere.

The governor shook everyone's hands. As he shook Stephen's hand he said, "Again, good job." And off he went immediately swallowed by his security detail, who whisked him from the room.

I excused myself.

# 25

When I arrived at Jody's, she'd just gotten off the phone with Dr. Carnes. She sat at the kitchen table across from her mother's bed.

"Still asleep, huh?"

"Yes, and she hasn't budged since you left."

"What did Dr. Carnes have to say?"

Jody said, "She said she's known about my mother's cancer from the onset. She didn't want my mother's illness to interfere with our reconciliation and Mom made her swear to keep her condition a secret. She told me Mom had already made her final arrangements. That she wanted to fly down this afternoon and visit with Mom while she still had the opportunity. She said she'd go over everything with us this afternoon when she arrived. How did Stephen do?"

"It couldn't have gone any better. The governor reversed the tables on Albert Hall and asked Stephen to speak to the group before he gave his speech. Stephen was so impressive. He was a little nervous to start, but he was articulate, well informed and offered creditable suggestions on how to fix the problem. The governor talked about his proposed legislation. It was like he and Stephen had met before the event and planned what they were going to say, their talks were so similar. While Albert was going to use the press conference as an opportunity to embarrass the governor, it turns out they both were in agreement and didn't know it. Typical politicians."

"So what do you think will happen with Stephen?"

"That's the incredible news out of this. Hall had already dug into Stephen's background and knew of his legal issues. When the three of us met at the Chart Room to go over what Stephen would say at the presser, Hall threatened Stephen. He told him if he didn't come to the press conference, the Georgia warrant might become a problem.

"Hall was expecting the governor to announce some right leaning program that would do nothing to fix the problem. He was going to use Stephen to embarrass him. After the press conference was over the governor said to Hall in front of Stephen, that he wanted to get Stephen involved. He asked Hall to work with Stephen to make it happen."

"The governor offered Stephen a job?"

"No, I wouldn't say he went that far, but it was clear this was the goal of Hall and Stephen working together."

"What about the warrant outstanding against Stephen?"

"Hall told Stephen before the press conference, when we were at the Chart Bar, that he'd try to help Stephen any way he could. He said he knew of Stephen's father."

"That's wonderful news!"

I walked over to the bed where Helen was sleeping. Jody had covered her in a light bedspread and you could see the covers rising and falling with each breath she took. "It is hard to believe how far you two have come since she sent you that letter expressing a desire to meet."

Jody got up from the table and stood beside me at the foot of the bed. She slipped her hand in mine. "Our reconnection was a godsend. I'd have gone to my own grave hating her. She was right; I needed to forgive her. Once I did, I could see what an amazing woman she was. Despite the horrible events, she endured—we both endured—she was able to make a life for herself, when so many other women couldn't. The selflessness of a dying woman coming here to save me from myself is an act of love I'll never forget."

"It is pretty amazing. And sad at the same time."

"I choose to look at it this way. We have righted a terrible wrong. Love prevailed. And we both can face the rest of our lives knowing our love was strong."

"You're right, Jody. I like your version better."


It was almost five in the afternoon when Dr. Carnes arrived at Jody's. Jody greeted her at the door with a warm hug. Dr. Carnes wore black slacks and matching long-sleeved blouse. She dropped her handbag into a chair, sought me out and wrapped her arms around my neck.

"Jack. It is so good to see you." She set me free and pushed back away from me. "I'm afraid I've neglected you over the past few months. I've been so involved with Helen and Jody."

"I understand, Doctor."

"Call me Janis."

Jody said, "I'd like that, Janis."

"How long has your mother been sleeping?"

"All day."

Dr. Carnes walked around to the side of the bed, sat next to Helen and picked up her frail hand. She turned her hand over, and rubbed her palm, calling out her name.

"Helen. Helen. It's Janis."

She patted her hand until Helen's eyes began to flutter, and she awoke out of a deep sleep. She opened her eyes not recognizing Dr. Carnes at first, but then her face broke out in a symphony of wrinkles.

"Hey, sweetie." Helen's voice was course. She put Dr. Carnes hand in both of hers. Helen scanned the room until her eyes connected with Jody and me. "All the people I love are here. That's marvelous."

"How are you feeling, Helen?"

"Weak. And thirsty."

"Let me get you some water, Mom." Jody moved off to the kitchen, retrieved a glass, filled it with cold water from the refrigerator and returned to the bed. She handed the glass to Dr. Carnes, who lifted Helen to a sitting position and helped her drink from the glass. She placed a second pillow on top of the first and laid Helen back down.

"Are you in any pain, Mom?"

"If I try to move it hurts a little. But if I'm still, I'm fine."

"Do you want some pain-meds?"

"I'm fine, Jody. I can't keep my eyes open now. If I take the morphine tabs, I'll be out of it."

We were all silent for a few moments.

"You all look like someone is dying." She chuckled at her own joke. "Well, I guess I am, aren't I?"

Following her lead, Dr. Carnes said, "Yes and you're doing it so well. Of course you do everything well, don't you?"

Helen said, "You didn't bring me a sympathy card? Why is that anyway? Cards aren't given out until after someone has passed away. Now that's out of whack, isn't it?"

Dr. Carnes said, "What do you want your card to say? I'll go get one made especially for you."

She thought about it a moment, even putting the tip of her finger to the side of her head "How about an "I will miss you" card. Then she lost control of her emotions. Her eyes turned red and watery.

Dr. Carnes looked at Jody, at me, then back at Helen. "The card will say we will all miss you. But you're still here. And we should enjoy this time and make the most of it."

Helen sniffed back her sorrow. "I wish we could all go down on Duval Street and have some ice cream, but I don't think I could make it ten feet."

I said, "Well, we may not be able to go to the ice cream shop, but it can come to us. What's your favorite ice cream, Helen?"

"Oh, that's easy. Butter pecan."

"You want it on a cone or in a cup?"

"How about one of those waffle cones?"

To Jody and Dr. Carnes, I said, "Can I get you anything?"

Jody said, "I'll have what Mom is having." Dr. Carnes nodded her agreement.

I asked, "Do you have a small ice chest?"

Jody went into the backyard and came in with a small Styrofoam cooler.

This late in the afternoon, with conchs making their way down Duval to the sunset decks for their evening ritual, there was a line at the order window at the ice cream shop. I queued up for what seemed like an hour. Finally, after a twenty-minute wait, the teen behind the counter, stood up four cones in the ice chest. She added ice and closed the cooler up for the journey.

When I got back to Jody's, Helen had fallen back asleep.

Jody said, "She tried to stay awake until you got back. But, bless her heart, she just couldn't do it."

"I'm sorry it took so long. But with the late afternoon heat, the ice cream shop was overrun."

I asked if anyone wanted ice cream, but none of us wanted it.

Dr. Carnes said, "I want to share with you what her last wishes are. I brought her living will, her will, and a Do-Not-Resuscitate order."

"Do Not Resuscitate?"

"DNR for short. It means she doesn't want anyone to extend her life by artificial means. She asked me to be her healthcare surrogate, someone who'd make decisions about her health care if she were unable to make them for herself. We completed those forms before she reconnected with you, Jody. So I may have the legal right to make those decisions, but I'll make them at your direction."

"I hope we don't get to that point," Jody said.

"Her will is straight-forward. She leaves her institute to a trust along with the majority of her financial estate. She wants her work to continue. She's also set aside part of her estate in trust for you. She wanted to make sure, if you needed any further counseling, those funds would be available. After five years if the funds aren't used, you'd return them to the institute trust. She's adamant she doesn't want a funeral or a service. She wants her ashes spread over the graves of her children and if you're willing, she wants you to do that. Your well-being and the financial health of the institute and its ability to continue to help women suffering from Postpartum Psychosis were her primary concerns. That's pretty much it."

"It won't be long will it?"

"No. Weakness, lack of appetite, the jaundiced appearance of her eyes and distended stomach are all signs we're near the end." To Jody, Dr. Carnes said, "I'd like to stay with her and you. She's my closest friend. I love her. Would you mind?"

"Of course not. You're more than welcome. You can have the couch, and I have a comfortable air-mattress for the floor."

"Are you sure?" Dr. Carnes said, looking at me.

"I'm staying with my sister. Don't worry about me."


While Helen slept, we ordered takeout pizza and Dr. Carnes recounted stories of Helen's life and work until late in the evening. At about eleven, I said goodnight and walked to Billie's, letting myself in the back door and following the stairway from the kitchen to my bedroom on the second floor. I was just starting to take my clothes off when my cellphone rang. It was Jody. She told me that shortly after I left, Helen's breathing became erratic and she died. She'd just called 911 and the funeral company and they were both on their way. She said it pleased her that she'd died in her sleep and appeared not to be in any distress.

I reversed course back to Jody's, and we three consoled each other. By one o'clock in the morning, the medics had pronounced Helen dead and the funeral company had removed her body. Jody's home was silent as each of us began to mourn our loss. It was five o'clock when we all collapsed on the floor and the couch.

# 26

After a couple of hours sleep, by eight a.m., I was ready to get up. Dr. Carnes and Jody were still sleeping. Rather than wake them, I decided to walk down to The Marlin for coffee. Sitting in one of the booths was Stephen. I joined him and gave him the news of Helen's passing.

"I'm sorry to hear that, Jack. How is Jody taking the news?"

"As well as you could expect. Estranged for many years, they just recently reconnected. It now seems it was her mother's dying wish."

"Billie told me the story. Remarkable. When did it happen?"

"Late last night. No one got to bed until five this morning. I could only sleep for an hour, so here I am."

"Anything I can do?"

261

"I appreciate your concern—but, no. Helen's best friend arrived last night. She's also the executrix of her estate. She understands exactly what Helen wants."

The server came bearing coffee and I declined ordering breakfast—wanting to wait to have breakfast with Jody and Dr. Carnes. I realized last night was the final day of Stephen's stay at the Pier House. I said, "Now that you've completed your deal with Albert Hall, where will you stay?"

"I guess my deal," he emphasized the word deal, "with Albert Hall isn't over. I was going to call you this morning to tell you about it. The governor wants to hire me."

"The governor offered you a job?"

"I guess, at least that's what Albert said, assuming I pass a background check. I don't think they know how they want to use me, but he wants me to take the Florida Bar exam and he wants the issue with my former wife to go away."

"Did you explain the situation to him in detail?"

"I did."

"Including how Baker defrauded your father?"

"Yes. That, too. Anyway, we left the conference center and went into the restaurant and he interviewed me for the job the governor has in mind. I told him I went to Georgia State law school and gave him a run-down on my experience working in my father's firm. But he was the most interested in where my knowledge of the homeless and their issues came from."

"Where did it come from?"

"The City of Atlanta hired my father to review their ordinances on the homeless and to offer policy suggestions that would help improve the problem. My father assigned the project to me. I was a legal consultant to the city's taskforce on the homeless—dealing with the same issues Florida is dealing with."

"What did they finally do?"

"The city ignored most of the legal counsel we gave them and chose to gloss over the problem, throwing more tax dollars into failed programs and kicking the can down the road for another administration to have to deal with."

"Well that experience had to help your cause with Albert Hall."

"He was pretty pumped after the interview. And it was good for me, too. A confidence boost."

"Well you did a jamb-up job at the press conference. I can't tell you how impressed I was. You didn't look like you needed a confidence boost to me."

"You've no idea the depths to which I've sunk over the past three years."

"Why, Stephen? It is obvious you have so much talent; so much going for you."

"When Melissa left me, it destroyed me completely. She was beautiful, sexy, intelligent, and funny. I was crazy in love. When I found out she'd used me in such a personal way, it devastated me. Even after a few years, the hurt has been paralyzing. It wasn't until I talked to you that I began to see that the way the Bakers had treated my father was unconscionable. And, now that hurt has turned to anger."

"As well it should be."

"My only fear about any of this, Jack, is that I have to face Melissa again. She humiliated me. I don't know whether I can do it."

"What John Baker did to you and your father was criminal. What Melissa did to you was beyond criminal. You shouldn't let her get away with it. They both should go to jail for what they did."

"Anyway, that defeat and humiliation kept me on the street. I didn't care what happened to me. I just wanted to be as far away from the Bakers as I could get. Thanks to you, I'm ready to take them on.

"I was going to call you. Trimble Davis is flying in later this morning from Atlanta. We're going to have lunch at the Pier House. Would you like to join us?"

"What useful purpose could I serve in being there?"

"Moral support. Another set of ears. I'd feel better if you were there."

"What time?"

"The Chart Room at twelve-thirty."

"Stephen, I'll try. But I want to be sensitive to Jody and what she's going through. I haven't talked to her this morning. And I've no idea what her plans are. But if I can make it, I will."

"This is going to be expensive, Jack. Are you sure you want to front me the money on this? And I've no idea what it will cost?"

"Listen, Stephen. I wouldn't have offered if it wasn't something I wanted to do. I'm not concerned about it. I have a good feeling about this.

It will be a small price to pay to get your life back. And it sounds like you're well on the road to recovery."

"Thank you, Jack. Thank you for all you've done. And one more thing. Albert said he talked with the county attorney and the police chief in Key West. He said he explained my situation to them and told them they should refer any attempt to serve a warrant on me to his office.

When I returned to Jody's she and Dr. Carnes were up and huddled over two cups of steaming coffee at the kitchen table. They were still dressed in pajamas.

"You were up and out early," Jody said.

"You both were sleeping when I got up. I couldn't sleep, so I went to get coffee. I found Stephen at The Marlin. The governor was so impressed with Stephen they're trying to create a job for him working on the governor's homeless initiative."

"Jack, that's wonderful. Where will he stay until he gets settled?"

"I asked him, but we got distracted and he never told me. I wish we'd a place to offer him?"

Jody looked around the cramped one-room house and said, "Me, too. If he can wait a week or two, after we move into the new house, he's welcome to stay here."

"He meets with that private investigator for lunch today at the Pier House. He asked me to be there. Since I didn't know what we're doing, I told him I would have to let him know."

"Janis and I were just talking about some kind of memorial service. The funeral home will cremate her over the weekend. We were thinking about a ceremony the second half of the week."

Dr. Carnes said, "I know Helen wouldn't have wanted us to make a fuss. But there are so many of her colleagues and friends in Tampa we will disappoint if they can't express their sympathy."

Jody said, "We're thinking about finding a hotel near the cemetery in Hollywood for the service. After the memorial is over, you, Janis, Billie, Alex and I will go to the cemetery and spread Mom's ashes as she asked. Are you okay with that?"

"Of course."

"With this being Friday, it will take Janis and me all afternoon to make arrangements and to contact people who worked with Mom and her friends."

"Can I help?"

"You should go be with Stephen. Afterward, you can help us call people and invite them to the memorial service."

"How are you doing? You look tired. So do you, Janis."

"I'm okay," Jody said, curling a spray of hair around her ear with her finger. "I'm sad she's gone and I wish we had had more time. But I'm so grateful for the time I spent with her."

Dr. Carnes said, "You were important to her, Jody. Your reconnection was an answer to lifelong prayers. I can't begin to express how happy you've made her."

Jody said, "I know. That's what I want to focus on. It has made me happy, too."

I showered and dressed. I marveled at the speed with which Jody had found a hotel in Hollywood, arranged catering and secured permission from the cemetery to spread her mother's ashes there. As I left to meet Stephen, both

Dr. Carnes and Jody were working through a list of invitees.

# 27

Trimble Davis was an enormous man in his fifties. I hadn't expected his shaved head, bulbous nose and obesity. He and Stephen had on casual clothes. I suspected the reason Stephen and Davis were sitting at a table in the middle of the bar was that Davis wouldn't have fit into a booth. As I approached the table, Stephen stood and made introductions. I shook Davis' fleshy hand and I sat next to Stephen across from Davis.

"I was just telling Mr. Davis about your books. Turns out he's a big fan."

To me Davis said, "Please call me Trim. I was on surveillance one night six or seven years ago, and one of my associates had just finished one of your books and gave it to me to read. Hooked me on the first page and I've been a fan ever since."

The irony of his nickname made me chuckle to myself. "I'm pleased you like my books."

"I asked Mr. Davis, I mean Trim, to hold off his questions until you got here."

Davis said, "Let me get my recorder. I want you to start at the beginning. I know you gave me the basics over the phone, but now I need details." His bushy eyebrows moved in dramatic fashion as he talked. His gray eyes were clear and focused.

For the next half-hour, Stephen recounted his experiences with the Bakers from the time he met Melissa Baker to the time he arrived on the streets in Key West. His recollections were a mirror image of what he'd shared with Billie, Jody and I a few nights ago.

"And you say your father handled all these payments to Baker in cash?"

"I didn't say that. I've no idea how he paid him. I know this. Over the course of twelve months, Baker's blackmail reduced my father's considerable fortune to zero."

"And what would you estimate his net worth to be?"

"More than fifteen million. Perhaps more."

"And what value would you place on the law firm you claimed they stole from your father?"

"Annual gross revenues were fifty million. After expenses, my father's share as a senior partner was five to seven million. I'd say it was worth about twenty-million, give or take."

"So between the loss of your father's estate, and the law firm, you claim you lost about forty million dollars?"

"I'm not claiming anything. You asked for my opinion. It would take an accountant to do a proper job of that."

"Just a figure of speech. For Baker to take in that kind of money in twelve months, moving around those large sums would be difficult to hide. Even if he worked with someone skilled in laundering money, a large bulge in income would stand out like a scarecrow. We will need to have access to all your father's financial records and track the liquidation of your father's assets. I'm surprised moving all that money didn't raise the ire of the feds."

Stephen asked, "Assuming you can document the withdrawals from my father's estate, how can you prove those funds went to Baker?"

"Stephen, I have some of the best forensic accountants in the U.S. If there's any trace of the funds moving between your father and Baker, we will be able to find it."

"But so what! What if you do find a trail? What does that prove?"

"It supports your claim that the Bakers blackmailed your father."

"And then what?"

"We can go two directions. The first option is to take this information to either the attorney general in Georgia or the FBI. From what you've told me about the Bakers connections with judges and law enforcement in Georgia, I'd want you to file a complaint with the FBI."

"Why the FBI? How would this be a federal crime?"

"Extortion on this scale, if it involved interstate commerce in any form, would be a federal matter. If Baker used a telephone, the U. S. mail, or moved funds around through the banking system there's a good chance he violated federal laws. Then you'd file a federal complaint. None of the information we get will be admissible in court, but it will convince the FBI that laws have been broken and they can get a judge to issue search warrants to collect the information legally."

"What's the second option?"

"When we first talked on the phone, I suggested you might be able to turn the tables on Baker. We dig into Baker's finances, prove the extortion and threaten to go to the FBI with our findings. As I said when we first talked, when someone like Baker and his daughter engage in such a well-thought-through conspiracy, I doubt you're their only victim. Someone that vicious wouldn't be able to contain their greed. I can assure you there are others he's extorted."

"Why do you say that?"

"I've been doing this for more than thirty years. When Baker went after your father, he used your father's proclivities against him. I'd be willing to wager a year's pay Baker is up to his ears in vices; vices that would make your father's issues look tame."

I asked Davis, "Why are you so sure of that?"

"Any man, who'd sacrifice his daughter on the altar of greed, is capable of anything. I don't think we will have to dig deep for the leverage we need."

"Why didn't my father think about that?"

"He was too busy trying to prevent the destruction of his own career."

"How long do you think this will take?"

"Depends on the direction we go. If we go the law enforcement route, it could take months to perhaps a year. If we go the private route, it will take a month or so, perhaps less."

I asked, "Why can't you do both?"

"We can. Let's say we find something on Baker we can use against him. We could threaten to take what we have learned to the authorities if he doesn't meet our demands. We exchange what you want from him for our silence. After you have what you want from Baker, you can always go to the FBI."

Stephen asked, "We use extortion—the same way Baker did against my father?"

"I wouldn't use those words. We strike a bargain." Davis winked at Stephen.

I asked, "Stephen is making connections with the Florida attorney general. Couldn't he use those connections to begin an investigation into Baker's activities regardless of any deal you might strike with him?"

"Perhaps. It depends on what Stephen's demands are." He turned and looked at Stephen. "What are your demands?"

Stephen paused a long time before answering. He looked at me with a vacant stare. He turned to Davis and said, "I want the money they stole from my father. I want the law firm back. I want to be out from under the alimony to Melissa. I want out from under the bench warrant. And I want John and Melissa Baker to go to jail."

"That's it?" Davis was incredulous. "You're not asking for much," he said with sarcasm.

Stephen sat up, squared his shoulders—his eyes clear. "No, I don't think it is a lot to ask. I can't get my father back, but I can try to undo the damage that's been done. I want you to dig into Baker and find the dirt we need. I want to break free of my current legal issues. When you meet with Baker, I want to be there with you. I want him to think that once he finishes with me, that he's safe. While all this is going on, I want you to dig into my father's case, and anyone else Baker might have blackmailed. I want to take what we find to law enforcement, whichever agency we've the best chance of getting action taken. I'm serious. I want him to pay for what he did to my father."

I didn't say anything but I liked Stephen's strategy. He needed to get out from under the legal cloud, take the Florida Bar exam and take advantage of the opportunity with the governor. This was an immediate issue. If Stephen waited for Baker's conviction, the opportunity he had might disappear.

Davis said, "I think it's doable. In anticipation of our meeting, I've already put Baker under surveillance. And I'll get my folks working on your father's case. It is my understanding I'm to bill Ms. Pike for my time and expenses?"

Stephen looked at me.

I nodded

Stephen said, "Yes, that will be fine."

Davis explained the investigation would be expensive. Stephen asked him how much it would cost?

"I'm guessing, two-hundred-fifty-thousand for starters. Could be a half-a-million depending on how long the investigation takes."

I nodded to Stephen. Stephen extended a hand across the table to Davis and Davis shook it.

Stephan said, "I want you to call me every day."

I explained that Jody needed me at home and I left them at the bar. What struck me about the meeting was Stephen's growing emotional strength. There was fight in him. As he gave instructions to Davis on what he wanted done, he delivered the instructions with force, confidence and a bit of anger. This is a different Stephen than I first met that night at Billie's. My respect for him had grown and I had confidence he'd prevail over Baker.

# 28

When I returned to Jody's, she and Dr. Carnes were on their phones calling people about the memorial service. Between calls, Jody handed me part of the list, gave me instructions on what to say and we spent the better part of the afternoon calling her friends and colleagues. When we completed the calls, Dr. Carnes packed her belongings, bid us goodbye and started her journey back to Miami.

Just as Dr. Carnes was leaving, Billie and Alex ascended the porch and hugged Jody.

Billie said, still in Jody's embrace, "We're so sorry about your mom, Jody."

Alex took her turn, wrapping her arms around her. "Are you okay?"

Jody said, "Yes, I'm good."

Alex released her and there was an awkward moment of silence.

Jody said, "Come inside. Let's get out of the heat."

Billie looked at Alex, then at Jody, "We can't stay. I've got my hands full trying to open the restaurant tonight."

Alex said, "We just wanted to come by and offer our help. If we can do anything . . ."

"I know. And if I can think of something, I won't hesitate. But Mom had everything in order. Not much to do." Jody filled them in on the memorial service in Hollywood. "That's right. Tonight is the night you reopen."

Billie said, "Yep, everything is ready. We have a limited menu. I hope it's enough. It looks a little funny having the trucks there instead of a building. I'm hopeful my customers will understand."

I said, "Don't worry. I'm sure they will, Billie. You serve wonderful food and have the best bar in town. Everything will be fine. Besides, I read an article recently that, out west, food trucks are the next big thing."

Billie combed through her rusty short hair. "I hope so, Jack."

I asked, "What do you hear from your contractors?"

"The architect's got all the permits. The contractor should be able to start next week." Billie rocked on her heels. "Well, we need to be getting back. I have folks waiting on me." She turned toward Jody. "Again, I'm so sorry."

Billie and Alex both hugged Jody again and left for the restaurant. Jody and I stood alone on the porch. Jody sat on the steps to the porch and I joined her, sitting close to her. It was the first time we'd been alone since Helen came to stay with Jody. She laid her head against my shoulder, I wrapped an arm around her shoulder and she began to cry. We sat there for a while and I waited for her to sort through her feelings.

After what seemed like half an hour, she said, "This has been such a whirlwind since that letter from her arrived telling me she wanted to meet with me."

"It has been a lot."

"It has, Jack. It has. It's been liberating."

"The power of forgiveness."

"Yes, there's that. But there's more." She pulled away from my embrace, wiped the tears from her eyes. "I may have needed to forgive her for my own mental health, but she needed forgiveness from me. We were both hurting. Both of us needed the other. We both had emotional holes only the other could fill. I'm very sad we won't have more time together. But I'm incredibly happy she and I were able to make each other whole again."

She leaned into me, and again I wrapped an arm around her. The trees provided shade, but the air was moisture laden and it approached ninety degrees. Despite the heat, we sat on the porch mostly in silence. My own thoughts rested on Jody and I marveled at how she'd handled the whole experience. The encounter could have gone so many different ways. I'm not so sure I would've been as forgiving as she was. But when I'd seen the difference it had made in her, the outpouring of love that resulted, there was no question her response was correct and that both Jody and her mother had benefitted greatly from their reconnection.

It was Friday and Billie's reopened at 5 p.m. with happy hour. Jody and I showered, changed clothes and headed to Billie's a little early thinking we might visit with her before the gate was opened. The line of folks, waiting to get in, extended halfway down the block. Patrons filled the courtyard. There was not an empty chair at the outdoor bar. The host recognized us, waved us through the host station, and pointed toward Billie, where she held court with a small knot of customers at the end of the bar. Billie was wearing an orange sleeveless long dress and when she saw us approach, she held an arm out and drew us into her small group.

After she made introductions, she led us away from her patrons and said, "I have a table toward the back reserved for ya'll. She pointed to a long table where Alex and Cynthia Pike had already seated themselves and they engaged each other in conversation. Also seated with them was Molly Flynn, Billie's chef. Billie remained with her group, and we wended our way to Alex.

When Alex, et al, tried to stand to greet us, I motioned for them to remain as they were. I sat next to Pike, while Jody sat between Molly and Alex. We all greeted one another. Pike offered condolences to Jody and Molly started to get up.

"Well, I'll leave you guys so you can enjoy the reopening."

I said, "Please don't leave yet. We hardly ever get a chance to visit with you. You're always so busy."

Molly sat back down. She was in her late-thirties, a freckled happy face, somewhat heavy set, with bright emerald eyes. "You're right."

I said, "So tell me about all the changes. How are you going to pull this off?"

"Well, you're not going to believe this, but there's as much room, perhaps more room, in the truck than I had in the old kitchen. And everything is newer."

"Then why the limited menu?"

"Well, it's about food storage space. In the old building, we had a large walk-in refrigerator. And the refrigerated truck has about half the space."

"Will that be a problem?"

"Not really. Our smaller menu includes all of our most popular dishes. Our menu had a few seldom ordered items we kept to please older customers. They weren't ordered often, but we still had to devote refrigerator space for them. So the reduced menu should make us more efficient. I'm hoping Billie will phase out some of those items, and give us an opportunity to try some new dishes when our building is finished."

Jody said, "This has got to be stressful for you, especially this week."

"Not at all. I'd have burned that old building down myself, in order to work in a decent kitchen. Everything has worked out perfectly. And look at the line," she said, pointing to the line down the block to get in. "It certainly doesn't look like it hurt business at all."

I said, "And Billie was so worried."

"Billie worries about everything." She pushed herself up from the table. "I really have to get to work, or we're going to have some angry customers." We said our goodbyes and wished her well with the food truck.

When she was out of earshot, Alex offered, "Billie is so fortunate to have found her. She's so talented in the kitchen and an excellent manager of the kitchen staff. I don't know where we'd be without her."

"It certainly seems that the conchs like her cooking," I looked around to the packed tables in the courtyard.

"You met with Stephen this morning, Jack?" Cynthia Pike said.

"I had breakfast with him. He's so pumped up."

"What did you think of the job he did at the press conference?"

"He was amazing; so confident and professional."

Pike said, "He blew Albert Hall away. He was in my office before he left for Tallahassee singing Stephen's praises. He said the governor was so impressed, he wants him on staff to help with the homeless initiative."

"That's what he told me. He said Hall wants to help him with his legal woes. Have you been stoking the flames on that one?"

"Yeah, I may have stepped on the line of attorney client privilege, but Albert could be an enormous help to Stephen. In fact, I think he's already made some inquiries with the AG in Georgia. He told me they were going to "unofficially," she made quotation marks in the air with her fingers, look into the matter. It seems John Baker has made some enemies in the AG's office there and they didn't need much of an excuse to "look into it." Again, she made finger quotation marks.

"Did Stephen tell you about his meeting with Trimble Davis?" I asked.

"Yes. The AG route will take time. It sounds like Davis is going to take a much more direct approach."

"You okay with doing that? The extortion, I mean?"

Pike curled some hair behind her ear and said, "One of my previous office managers wrote herself checks for ten-grand from our law firm escrow account. When I discovered the embezzlement, I threatened to go to the police if she didn't return the money. Blackmail? I don't think so. This was the same case with Stephen. The Bakers conspired to steal from his father and from him. If Davis finds anything to use against Baker, I wouldn't hesitate to use it."

"Did you get your money back?" Jody asked.

"Yep. She had a small child. She didn't want to go to jail. She had to go to her father to get the money. Here is the thing. Had I gone to the police, there's a good chance I would have never seen a dime of that money. If I'd pressed charges, she'd have no incentive to return my money to me. Sometimes the threat of the police is so much more effective than going to them."

Alex asked, "Are we talking about the homeless guy?"

I answered her. "Yes, Billie, Cynthia and I have been trying to help him get his feet on the ground."

To Alex I asked. "When will you start flying international?"

"Soon. I'm so excited about it. I'm in the top ten-percent in seniority now, so I'm able to bid on European flights and hold those lines."

Pike asked, "What's so good about that? Seems like they'd be long and tedious flights?"

"The fact that they're long is good. If I fly domestic flights, they're short flights and I have to fly more of them to get in my hours for the month. Flights overseas are longer. I have to fly fewer routes to get my hours in, in a shorter timeframe. Then I have more hours off, at home.

Pike said, "I've always wanted to travel in Europe."

"That's why I'm so excited. Other pilots, who fly to Europe, tell me they're so tired when they land there, the last thing they want to do is go anywhere. They stay at the hotel at the airport and never venture very far. I hope that isn't the case for me. I hope I have the time to see some of the sights. The old timers who have flown those routes for years say the romance of flying to Europe wears off quickly and that in the end, it's just a job."

Billie floated over to the table and sat down in a huff. "What's just a job?"

I said, "Alex's flying off to all these exotic locations." I looked at Alex and smiled.

Billie said, "People think owning a restaurant is romantic, too. Alex knows better, don't you, sweetie?"

Alex said, "I never see her. I'm the jealous girlfriend and Billie's girlfriend is her business. I could be gone for a week and she'd never know it."

Billie laughed. "She's right, I confess. I'm a lousy wife."

Pike said, "Here's too us, workaholics all." She raised her glass of wine and took a long drink. Since we hadn't gotten to order drinks yet, Jody and I raised imaginary glasses in the air.

Billie took the cue, and flagged down a server who took drink orders and departed. "While you're all here, I have some news to share. My In-Vitro is scheduled in a week."

We all took turns offering congratulations.

Billie said, "We've decided to implant two embryos."

"Why two?" Jody asked.

Alex answered, "If they implant more than two, there's a higher risk of multiple births which carries its own set of risks. If they only implant one, the risks of not having a viable pregnancy increase and there's the huge cost of a second try. Two embryos balance all those risks."

Jody asked, "Are you prepared for twins if both embryos survive?"

Billie and Alex answered "yes" at the same time. They both laughed.

Billie said, "That would be awesome."

"And the timing would be good. Billie hopes to get the new building built before she enters her seventh month of pregnancy," Alex said.

Pike asked, "And what about you, Jack? When will you be closing on your home?"

Jody answered, "Two weeks, and I can't wait."

I said, "I was going to call you and ask you to represent us at closing."

"Well, in Florida, you don't need an attorney to close the transaction. It is traditional that the company through whom you purchase title insurance will act as closing agent. I'd be happy to look over all the closing documents and the results of the title search on the property, but once that's done it takes about an hour to close the sale."

Billie said, "It will be so nice to have you a few doors down from Alex and I."

The wine arrived in two iced buckets. They delivered hors d'oeuvres on two platters. Our own celebration of Billie's reopening began. I looked around the table and saw an empty chair.

I asked Billie if she was expecting someone else.

"Stephen. He said he'd come."

I stepped away from the table and called Stephen on his cellphone.

"We're at Billie's ready to begin our party. You coming?" I asked Stephen.

"I'm on my way. I'm at the police station again. It appears the Bakers have found me. They saw my picture in the newspaper from the press coverage of the governor's press conference."

"Are they going to arrest you?"

"No. But I had to use Albert Hall's get-out-of-jail-free card. The chief told me the law required them to serve the warrant. But they called Albert, and he told them he'd handle it personally. I have the AG of Florida as my attorney."

"What's he going to do?"

"Stall. They want an extradition hearing and Albert will drag his feet. He wants to give Davis time to do his thing. And he's reached out to his counterpart in Georgia and made some inquiries. He's trying to get the warrant quashed in Georgia and asked for a hearing there instead. Again, he wants to stall until we can find out about the Bakers."

Stephen said he'd be there shortly and we hung up. When I returned to the table amid laughing and storytelling, I thought about Stephen's dilemma. Had it not been for Billie and her kindness, Stephen would still be sleeping on cardboard somewhere in Key West.

# 29

Jody had wanted to have the memorial service at the Diplomat Hotel on Hollywood Beach. It had shocked us to learn the storied hotel had fallen on hard times, closed and had been recently demolished. Once frequented by Arthur Godfrey, Jacky Gleason, Frank Sinatra, and Sammy Davis, Jr., the hotel, like so many Miami Beach resorts withered as the theme parks of Central Florida redirected the attention of the tourist trade. Now all that remained was an empty lot with speculation the new owners would construct a larger, more luxurious Diplomat.

Jody had considered the Little Flower Catholic Church, the place where her family's funerals had taken place back in 1961. She decided the connection was too close.

In the end, Jody found a hotel downtown that had a banquet room large enough to handle a hundred people. Invitations were sent to more than two-hundred-and-fifty friends and colleagues. Just over one-hundred people committed to come.

Flowers choked the meeting room. The hotel staff set up chairs theater style, with a center aisle. They'd placed a lectern at the head of the room. To the left, a large picture of Helen Holland stood on an easel.

Dr. Carnes placed a table outside of the meeting room with nametags for all the attendees. An assistant from Dr. Carnes' office sat at the table and made sure everyone had a nametag. When I first saw the name badges spread across the table, it finally dawned on me that Jody and Dr. Carnes had not invited any of Jody's relatives or Helen's brothers or sisters. I could only assume Helen's estrangement from her family or Jody's family had not been Helen's doing. Knowing Helen, she would have tried to make the effort.

Jody, Dr. Carnes and I stationed ourselves at the entrance to the room. We'd created an impromptu receiving line and greeted attendees as they entered the room. Dr. Carnes did most of the greeting, introducing Jody as Helen's daughter and me as Jody's fiancé. As we greeted each person, some offered anecdotes depicting how their lives intersected with Helen's or praised the work Helen had done with them or on their behalf.

Once everyone arrived, Dr. Carnes navigated around the room greeting everyone by name. Jody and I took seats on the first row, as Jody was one of the speakers.

Dr. Carnes moved to the head of the room, tapped the side of a drinking glass with a ball-point-pen and asked everyone to take their seats. The room was pungent with the smell of flowers and the blending of many different perfumes.

As the din from the crowd subsided, Dr. Carnes stood before the lectern and said, "My name is Janis Carnes. Helen Holland was a patient of mine, my colleague and my friend. Like you, I was a small patch she'd woven into the quilt of her life. We're all connected by her life. If you're like me, you're a better person, a richer person because of that connection.

"If you're not familiar with the life of Helen Holland, you will be as her daughter and friends come forward to share their stories with you. You'll come to understand what a remarkable woman Helen was. Despite the horrendous circumstances of her life, not only did she persevere, she thrived. PPP caused unspeakable consequences in Helen's life. But, we will celebrate the life of a woman who overcame those circumstances and dedicated her life to helping women with PPP avoid the ravages of that disease.

"Before I open it up for you to come forward and share, I want to introduce to you Helen's oldest daughter Jody." Dr. Carnes nodded to Jody, backed away from the lectern. Jody got up and took Dr. Carnes' place in front of the gathering.

Jody had on a tan pantsuit and a white blouse. She had her hair piled on top of her head, and wore silver pierced earrings.

"In 1961, Helen, my mother, suffering from PPP or postpartum psychosis, took the lives of my father and four of my brothers and sisters. She tried and failed to take my life. And while she may not have taken my physical life, what she did to our family took away my emotional life. I'd grown up hating her for what she'd done to our family. I'd built my life around that hate. You see, PPP not only destroys the life of the mother, it often destroys the lives of those around her. And if the mother survives and doesn't take her own life, society will brand her as a psychopath and family and friends will abandon her.

"But this isn't where my mother's story ends. It is where it begins. And it is a beautiful story. It is a story of redemption, love and forgiveness.

"In 1961, the courts ruled my mother incompetent to stand trial, and they incarcerated her in a mental hospital not far from here. She underwent treatment and while the PPP subsided and melted away, the emotional damage didn't. She languished in the hospital's care until the mid-sixties when Dr. Carnes took over my mother's case. My mother couldn't get past what she'd done until the courts sent another PPP patient to the hospital. She'd also committed infanticide. As my mother had gotten to know the other woman, it was plain to her that what the woman had done was not deliberate, that it was the result of the psychosis. From her, my mother learned three key truths that would drive her for the rest of her life. PPP women weren't alone, they weren't at fault and that PPP was a preventable, treatable, temporary disorder.

"Dr. Carnes nurtured my mother, and encouraged her in her efforts to help other women so afflicted. My mother became a doctor of psychiatry, built the institute in the Tampa Bay area and advanced the cause of PPP women around the world. She clawed her way back to mental health and brought many PPP women with her. She was successful by any measure you could use. Her life is inspiring and I'm so proud of her. But, in my mind, all these successes pale in comparison to one of her greatest achievements.

"You'll remember I had built my life around hating her for what she'd done. I hadn't seen or spoken to my mother since the events of 1961. Several months ago, she sent me a message that she wanted to meet with me. When I consented, she said I needed to forgive her for what she did to my family. I NEEDED TO FORGIVE HER, for what SHE DID. It was the most preposterous thing I'd ever heard. She said I needed to forgive, not for her benefit, for my own. She said if I didn't let go of my anger, it would haunt me and ruin my life. You won't believe this, but she told me I need counseling. ME! I can see you all chuckling." Jody smiled. "I can tell you've had one of these sessions with my mother, too.

"As much as it offended me for her to tell me I was the one who needed help, I knew she was right. I was living with the damage of that hatred every day. I'm getting married soon, to this wonderful man on the front row," she pointed to me, "and I didn't want this emotional baggage dragged into my relationship with him.

"My mother and I began counseling and it was soon obvious my mother was motivated by love and concern for me. It was genuine. Soon, I fell in love with my mother again. And I was able to forgive.

"What I didn't know at the time was she was dying of cancer and she had a small window of time to help me. She didn't tell me she needed my forgiveness as much I needed to forgive her. Her greatest success, above all the successes of her life, was to restore her relationship with me. She gave me the opportunity to forgive her and save my own life. In so doing, she received the forgiveness she needed to save her own.

"And now I'll make my point. Because of the horrendous events in her life, she needed to pour herself out into all our lives. And what we offered her in return is the redemptive power of love. With each one of us, she gave of herself and in return she received back the life that PPP had taken from her."

I couldn't contain my own emotions as Jody backed away from the podium and joined me on the first row. I hugged her and we sat down as Dr. Carnes opened the service up to others who wanted to share their remembrances.

For two hours, people filed to the front to share their stories of how Helen had contributed to their lives. Of all the stories told, none was more touching than the woman who came forward who'd driven her three children into a lake during a PPP episode. Rescuers saved her but not her children. While she pled temporary insanity in criminal court, that state didn't recognize PPP as a mental disorder. They convicted her of manslaughter and sent her to prison for fifteen years before they paroled her.

Within six months of her release from prison, she attempted suicide. Her family contacted Helen Holland's institute for help. She finally received the psychiatric intervention and counseling she needed. Once restored to health, she had remarried and started a new family. She held up a picture of her two healthy toddlers and praised Helen Holland for rescuing her from a dark place. I was fascinated with all the good that had come from the horrible events in Helen and Jody's lives.

Later in the day, at the Memorial Cemetery less than a mile or two from the Hotel, Billie and Alex, Jody, Dr. Carnes and I stood before the five graves of Jody's family. Her father Paul had a large headstone that read, Paul Holland, husband and father 1922 to 1961. Flanking his headstone, were four more flat granite plaques. Their markers gave the children's names and date of birth and death. While others decorated their graves with artificial flowers, there was nothing embellishing the graves of Jody's family. Grass had almost covered the children's markers and I felt for Jody that the cemetery hadn't been more diligent in caring for the sites.

"I've only been here once, Jack," Jody, said. She held the urn with her mother's ashes. "It was just too painful to be here."

"And now? What're you feeling?" Dr. Carnes asked her.

"Like it is over. Placing mom here has completed the circle. "

"What do you mean?" I asked.

"Mom would have been here with her family had I not intervened in her attempted suicide. Now she's with them in eternity. I hope if there's a heaven they're all there and that horrible wrong has been made right."

The profound impact of Helen Holland's life on her daughter was clear. But my thoughts were about how she'd affected my life. Because she liked my writing, she was responsible for giving my career as a fiction writer a kick-start. I owed her a lot.

The orange sun was low on the horizon, and the afternoon sea breeze sent the palm tree fronds into thrashing motions. Jody looked at me, opened the urn, bent over and started to sprinkle her mother's ashes around her sibling's markers in birth order, the same order Jody's mother had taken their lives from them. She emptied the container in front of her father's head stone.

Jody put the lid on the empty container and placed it on the ground. She embraced, Janis Carnes, Billie, Alex and me. There were no tears.

"You okay, sweetie?" Dr. Carnes asked.

"Yes. I'm good."

We all stood with Jody. I wondered what she was thinking about, but refrained from asking. I just wanted to stand with her as long as she wanted to stay.

We said our goodbyes to Dr. Carnes and started our journey back to Key West. Billie and Alex were going to spend the night and head back in the morning. Although we had a room reservation in Hollywood for the evening, Jody wanted to go home. We made it to Islamorada as the last of the light disappeared in the sky. Just before midnight, we were sitting on Jody's front porch.

Jody said, as we huddled together under the light of the streetlamp, "I wish my mom could have made it through the wedding."

I said, "I was thinking about that as we came over the Seven Mile Bridge."

She was silent for a time, leaning into me as we sat on the steps to her porch.

"What're you thinking about?" I asked.

"I wish we'd had more time. Everything seems like such a blur, it moved so fast. I feel she and I had a meal at a drive through restaurant, when I would have preferred a leisurely dinner; one she and I could have lingered over and enjoyed each other. We filled so much of the time with counseling and moving past issues, I didn't get a chance to enjoy her company. I'm grateful, mind you. We gave each other the gift of healing, but I just wish there had been more time."

"A sign of a good relationship is when you leave that person you wished you had more time with them. You look forward to the next encounter."

"When I was laying the ashes on the gravestones, I was thinking about the next encounter as you put it. I was thinking about whether Heaven is real, whether there's life after death, whether I'll see my mom and my family again."

"And what conclusion did you come to?"

"I'd prefer to believe it's true."

We fell exhausted into bed. I could tell from the pace of her breathing Jody had fallen asleep almost immediately. As I drifted off to sleep, her words "I'd prefer to believe it's true," played over in my mind. She described how I felt. There was hope in those words; comforting hope.

# 30

I got up at about seven in the morning and Jody was still sleeping. I thought about trying to write, but wasn't in the mood. Not wanting to wake her after the events of the previous day, I dressed and strolled down to The Marlin for coffee. I hadn't talked to Stephen in a couple of days and I hoped I'd find him there.

The restaurant was deserted. I grabbed a booth, the server brought a cup of coffee and I asked her if she had a spare pen and paper. I had some thoughts on my next Dana O'Brien novel, and wanted to use the time to record them. She ripped several sheets from her order pad and pulled a ballpoint pen from her apron. I was most intrigued with the China-India airlift during World War II. The Japanese had surrounded China, cutting them off from the sea. Their goal was to capture China. The U.S. needed to keep China in the fight, because, at the time, we weren't ready to start a direct assault on Japan. As long as China could conduct a war against Japan, it drained Japanese resources they could use to wage war against the

U.S.. China was under siege. In 1942, the U.S. launched a supply effort over the Burma Road between India and Kunming, China.

When the Japanese captured Burma and seized control of the Burma Road, it forced the U.S. to supply China by air. From bases constructed in northeastern India, the U.S. initiated air-service over the Himalayan Mountains otherwise known as the "Hump." The cargo planes and bombers used to ferry supplies and fuel to the Chinese were ill equipped to handle the treacherous, high altitude conditions. During the four years of the ferrying operation to keep China supplied, we lost 800 aircraft. Many of the planes crashed on the high mountain peaks or in the dense jungle surrounding them. Air-rescue operations were ineffectual. More than five-hundred planes and their crews were never found.

In my next novel, I wanted to tell the story of one of these crews and send Dana O'Brien on an expedition to the Himalayas to find a particular B-24 Liberator that had significant importance to military brass.

I was deep in thought, making notes on how I'd organize the story, when Stephen appeared.

"I'm not interrupting anything am I?"

"No, no. Sit. I was hoping I'd run into you."

Stephen slid into the booth, thanked the server for coffee, and said, "What're you working on?"

"Ah, just trying to get a start on my next novel. I'm behind schedule and I need to start putting some words on paper. What about you? What's the latest?"

The server came and took our orders. Stephen ordered a bagel sandwich and I ordered eggs and rye toast.

"Good news. Albert called me yesterday. He said the governor's office will offer me a job, but it will take a few days to jump through all their hoops. He knew I was short on resources, so they've arranged a short-term consulting contract that will help pay the rent on a small apartment I just rented until they figure out what they want me to do."

"That's great Stephen. What kind of a job do you think they'll offer you?"

"Albert was pretty vague about it. All he'd say was it will be a staff position working on the homeless taskforce. A couple of days ago, Albert sent me a stack of files by FEDEX. They were all related to various Florida cities and their own failed initiatives to fix the homeless problem. He wants me to bone up on it and be able to hit the ground running when the governor is ready to offer me something. He's also pushing me hard to study for the bar exam, but until I get the warrants resolved, I have a cloud hanging over my head. Besides, they don't give the exam until February."

"That's exciting, Stephen. I'm so pleased. Anything from Trimble Davis?"

"No, nothing. I'm not expecting anything for a few days. He did call to let me know they were going full-speed-ahead. But they had nothing to report yet."

"Did he give you any idea on time frame?"

"No. So, I'm in Limbo. But it's better than the street. At least I have a roof over my head."

We ate our breakfast, chatted about the memorial service for Jody's mom and about me adjusting to living in Key West.

I left Stephen and found Billie, sitting at the restaurant bar, which had become her makeshift office during construction. She hugged me with enthusiasm, and her face glowed with excitement.

"Today is the big day!" She couldn't contain her excitement.

"Big day?" I searched my brain for something important I'd forgotten.

"Baby day? Remember?"

"Yes, yes, of course. Is it today?

"Yep. The appointment is at four. Alex and I are leaving in an hour."

"In, Miami?"

"At the fertility clinic."

"Don't they do the procedure in the hospital?"

"Nope. Right there at the clinic."

"Jody and I should be with you, Billie."

"Jack, stop worrying. Alex will be there and the procedure is simple, nothing more vigorous than a pelvic exam. The whole thing will take less than an hour."

"And, then what?"

"We wait. I already bought some pregnancy tests. Maybe in a week or so we'll know whether it took or not."

"You sure you don't want us to come?"

"I'm sure. When we get home tonight, I'll call you to let you know how it went."

"Heard anything on the building?"

"They'll break ground any day now. I'm worried about how the construction will affect us."

"Why? You have a fence up screening their work."

"Noise and dust. In all my enthusiasm to get the process underway, I didn't think about all the noise this is going to create or the dust around the food trucks."

"Anything you can do to prevent it?"

"They can't do anything about the noise. But I think my patrons will cut me some slack on that. The dust is another matter. I'm supposed to meet with the contractor tomorrow before they break ground to talk about ways to keep it under control."

"You'll figure it out. How is business since you reopened?"

"Beyond any expectation I had. We're doing great!"

I told Billie I hoped her visit with her fertility doctor went well, and walked down Duval toward the Pier House. I wanted to go by Jody's gallery and see if she'd made it into work. The "open" sign hung in the window of the door, and the door was open. Inside, Jody was showing a customer some pottery. I got her attention and mouthed the words, "Call me." I backed out of the shop and walked to Jody's house.

It would be a week before we closed on our place on Whitehead Street and moved in, so opportunities of solitude and quiet to write were few. I seized the moment and spent the afternoon writing the first three chapters of the WWII story I had titled, *Left Behind.*

After Jody arrived home, and we enjoyed a light dinner and a bottle of Cabernet, Billie called to report the embryo implantation had gone without a hitch. She asked me to pray for her and Alex and the pregnancy. I told her I'd already been doing that.

# 31

The title insurance office, where they'd close the sale of the Whitehead Street house, was in a shopping center off US1 near Garrison Bight Marina. They were expecting us about ten a.m. Cynthia Pike had reviewed all the closing documents and had given her approval. We were to meet our Realtor at the house to do a final walk-through inspection before we closed. Pike said the sellers had already signed all the documents. All the title office required of us was the final inspection, our signatures, a cashier's check and we could begin moving in.

Jody wore a white sleeveless blouse and tan shorts anticipating the stifling heat of a typical August day. I wore a T-shirt, shorts and flip-flops, which was my standard uniform since becoming a born-again conch.

Jody said, "I'm going to miss this little place." She looked around, as she pulled her blond hair up into a ponytail.

I didn't respond. I didn't share her enthusiasm. I was ready for some room to spread out and for the seclusion of the guesthouse.

We walked the short distance to the Whitehead Street house. When we arrived, Florence Keen, our Realtor, handed us a list of repairs we'd requested when we'd made a final offer on the property. We'd hired a building inspector and they'd found a few items we wanted taken care of by the owners before we moved in. She escorted us through the house, taking inventory of the repairs and we confirmed they'd remedied everything to our satisfaction.

As we reacquainted ourselves with the house, the size of it overwhelmed me. After living in Jody's small conch house, it made this one feel like a palace. When I had first considered purchasing the house in Mount Dora, it had had the owner's belongings and furniture in it. The furnishings covered a lot of soiled walls, worn wallpaper, and signs of neglect. When I did the final inspection before closing, after the owner had removed their belongings, I was reluctant to close, I was so angry. But I held my tongue and closed the sale because of the house's spectacular setting on Lake Dora. Before Jody and I came here, I predicted we'd find the same thing and have buyer's remorse, or worse I'd find something that would delay the closing.

But that was not the case. Since we bought it furnished, I took special care to look behind furnishings and to check out areas I might have overlooked the first time we went through the house. Everything was immaculate. After spending an hour, re-inspecting the whole house, we found one or two inconsequential items that weren't worth mentioning. I loved the house. I could tell from the smiles I was getting from Jody she was in love with it, too.

The closing took less than a half-hour. We drove back to our new home through the Truman Annex, and used our new remote to open the garage door at the back of our new home. We repeated the walk-through we'd done earlier. This time we conducted our tour with unrestrained enthusiasm, shows of affection and marveling at our good fortune to have found the house.

Since Jody was going to rent her house as a vacation rental, all we moved from her place were our clothes and toiletries, which we accomplished with two trips in my SUV.

And while we bought a furnished house, the house was bare. We spent the afternoon at Walmart, buying sheets, linens and the essentials with which to cook. After a quick trip to Publix Supermarket, we had the makings for a small housewarming party that evening with Billie, Alex, Stephen, Cynthia Pike and Florence Keen who supplied the Champagne.

Early the next day, Jody and I rented a small truck and drove to Mount Dora. I was still undecided about what to do with the house. I could tell Jody felt a bit awkward in the home I'd shared with Emily. I decided, besides my personal effects and items pertaining to my writing, I didn't want anything else from the Mount Dora home. The furnishings there were reminders of my extended depression and the loss of my relationship with Emily. My life was on the right path now, and these items had no place in it.

As I looked out at the lake through the plate glass window of my studio, I knew I'd miss it; the calming affect the water had on my writing. We packed the rest of my clothes, personal effects and the equipment and files from my old studio and we returned to Key West arriving before midnight.

The next day, we used the truck to empty a storage space Jody had rented for household items that wouldn't fit into her small home and our occupation of the Whitehead Street house was complete. I organized the guesthouse with all my writing paraphernalia and I was anxious to give it a test drive.

Once we put everything away, Jody and I sat on the back porch with both outdoor paddle fans running full blast. The sun was setting, but it was still in the low nineties and humid. It was the first time we'd had to sit and relax. Jody, got up, walked into the house and returned with a bucket of ice, an opened bottle of Chardonnay and two-chilled, medium stem wine glasses.

She placed the glasses on a small table between two, double-wide rattan chaises, poured the glasses full, handed one to me and grabbed one for herself. I was sitting sideways on the chair, and she sat next to me, knocking me in the hip with hers to give her more room.

She held up her glass and said, "To our new home."

I returned her toast. "To our new home."

She swung her legs up and laid her back against the chaise. "I just love it." She looked around the landscaped back yard. "When I think back to us being kids on Hollywood Beach all those years ago, I prayed one day you and I would be together. But I never thought it would be like this. Not in my most ambitious dreams."

"And just think, in a few days, we will fill this porch with people and do something I wish we could have done years ago."

"We may have the ceremony," she said, "but I feel like we're already married. Being with you is like wearing soft flannel, Jack. I don't know that I've felt as close to another living soul."

"Me, too." I raised my glass and she touched my glass with hers.

"Barry and Clarissa arrive tomorrow. Everything is going to start getting a little crazy."

"How long has it been since you've seen your children?"

"Remember, when you went back to Mount Dora in April, I flew to Atlanta to see Barry and to Mobile to see Clare."

"Oh yeah, now I remember. I hope they're as excited as you are about the wedding."

"I think they are. They know how happy you make me." The chaise was wide enough for two and she pulled at me until I reclined alongside her. "You are going to tell me where we're going on our honeymoon, aren't you?"

"No. It's a surprise!"

"Come on, give me a hint."

"We won't ever get out of bed."

"Hmmm. I like the sound of that," she cooed. "Come on, Jack, just a hint."

"Okay, we will be surrounded by water."

"That's not much of a hint. Water surrounds Key West. That tells me nothing."

"Okay, one more and that's it. You won't need anything to wear but a swimsuit."

"Somewhere in the Caribbean?"

"You're warm, but that's all you're getting out of me."

"You're no fun," she said in a faux pouty voice.

I had found a sixty-foot yacht and crew who would take us from Key West to a private cove and beach off St. John in the Virgin Islands. Once there, we'll anchor, the crew will leave, and we will have four days of seclusion and privacy. At the conclusion of our stay, the crew will return and ferry us back to Key West. A dingy will carry us a half-mile to civilization, if needed. But the crew will lay in enough provisions for the vessel and, so, there would be no need.

I asked, "Have you made all the wedding preparations? You need any help?"

"All done. This is going to be simple. The wedding will be here on the patio. The reception in the yard," she pointed to the back yard in front of the guesthouse, "and a meal in the house for those who wish to stay. Billie is going to cater everything. A rental company will deliver all the tables and chairs for the reception in the morning. All we have to do is pray it doesn't rain."

This was a time of great happiness for everyone. Billie, Stephen, Alex, Jody and me, we were in a good place moving toward something better. I cherished these times. I knew I was allotted only so many of them. When the winds changed, and hardships came, I held onto those moments as the rare gems they were.

# 32

It was the day before the wedding. As I stood at the gate waiting for Lisa Catera to walk out of the jet-way, I reminisced about my long association with her. She'd just graduated from college when another author introduced us at a publisher's party in New York twenty-five years ago. She had interned at a literary agency during school and, although she had no clients, her energy impressed me. We were both in our early twenties and became instant friends. While there had been ebbs and flows to our relationship, hers was one of the enduring friendships in my life. Through my long depression, separation from Emily, and my firing from R&R, I'd taken her for granted.

During my long fight with depression, she endured many wine-laced, dark conversations where she never failed to try to encourage me. She applied constant pressure for me to seek out my psychologist-counselor, LuAnn Calder. The low point in our relationship came when R&R threatened to sue me for non-performance. I'd questioned Lisa's motives. She'd applied relentless pressure to get out of bed and start writing. At times, I thought she might be more concerned about her own financial losses than she was about me. She would have had to repay advanced royalties—and her commissions—a significant sum. Now as I waited for her to deplane, I regretted my lapse of faith in her.

While we'd talked on the phone about how I had treated her, we hadn't had any in-person, one-on-one time in which to bind the wounds of our relationship. I'd warned Jody I might take Lisa to the Chart Room at the Pier House for a drink, to convey my sorrow for the way I had treated her.

Lisa hadn't married and said she liked it that way. Her standard uniform was a pantsuit, a white blouse and Reebok tennis shoes. The uniform was a bow to the New York culture that imprisoned her. Her Reebok shoes were a sign that inside Lisa a rebel lurked. She was small in stature and had always been a little overweight. But, she was attractive, with a cherub face, freckles and thick, wiry, short brown hair—a boy cut, complete with pointed sideburns.

When Lisa came down the jet-way, I almost didn't recognize her. She was not wearing a pantsuit. She'd lost weight. Her hair was longer, with a softer cut. I always teased her about her white skin, which I called a New York tan. She'd dressed for the weather: white T-shirt, Bermuda shorts and sandals. She looked wonderful. She gave me a broad smile as she stepped into the gate area.

"What happened to you? No pantsuit?"

She dropped her carryon and we hugged one another.

"A guy happened to me."

"You look amazing, girl."

"Thanks. Call it the new me."

I picked up her carryon, and led her down the concourse toward baggage claim.

"Now all we need to do is get some color on your skin."

"I wish I could stay longer. But we're . . . I'm buried right now."

"I want to hear about this guy. I thought we could go get a drink at the Pier House and you can tell me all about him."

"Yeah, and I want to tell you about the movie deal before Barksdale arrives."

"Movie deal?  Which book?"

"*The Tainted Lady*."

"I thought that was just released. How did that happen so fast?"

"I'll tell you in a bit. I was so happy to hear about your nuptials. Are you excited?"

Before I could answer we arrived at the small baggage claim area, and she began to search for her bag.

The Chart Room was open but empty. It was eleven in the morning and there was only one patron sitting at the bar. Lisa and I slid into a booth opposite each other. The server took a Bloody Mary order from Lisa and draft beer from me.

"So tell me about this guy?"

"An attorney, can you believe it?"

"Do I know him?"

"Yes, Fred Simmons. He was here in April when we put the contract together with R&R."

"He's married, isn't he?"

"Divorced. His wife ran off with someone, took the kids out of state and filed for divorce."

"You've worked with him for a while, haven't you?"

"Over ten years. Never had a clue he cared about me. After their divorce was final, he asked me out."

"How long have you been seeing him?"

"Since May. Just over three months."

The server laid cork coasters on the table, set our drinks on them, asked if there was anything she could get us and went back to the bar to attend to two new patrons.

"Well, I like the effect he's had on you. You look ten years younger."

"I'd been single for so long, Jack, I just got to a place where I'd finally given up. Fred's confession of his longstanding interest in me swept me off my feet. All these years and I had no idea."

"I'm happy for you, Lisa."

"I'm happy for myself. But before we get too deep in the personal affairs, I just want to give you a heads up on the movie deal. You remember Uri Abrams?"

"Globe Pictures. They did the last Dana O'Brien film."

"Yep. As soon as we had *The Tainted Lady* ready for publication, I sent Abrams an advanced copy. He contacted me last week and expressed an interest in it, and one other book. He wants to combine the two stories into one movie."

"What're they offering?"

"We haven't gotten to that yet. But *Tainted* broke into the New York Times top ten bestseller list a month ago. And while it is riding high, and we can demand top dollar, we want to try to get this deal closed. "

Movie rights and television deals were the reasons R&R was willing to pay so much for my work. Barksdale, Lisa and I all made phenomenal money from them.

Lisa continued, "I want to make sure I have your authority to negotiate on your behalf."

During the contract negotiations with Barksdale in April, I'd interjected myself in the negotiation process, shoving Lisa aside. When R&R fired me, Lisa was certain my writing career was over and she lost faith in me. Emily made contacts with several publishers and secured lucrative proposals from them. When R&R got wind of their competitor's interest, Barksdale flew to Key West with a team of lawyers, expressed his mea culpa, and offered a better deal to re-sign.

I was still angry with Lisa for her lapse in confidence. But the tactic of pushing her out of the way hurt her in ways I hadn't anticipated. The reality is I'd lost my belief in her. She confronted me about it midway through the negotiations with R&R, and I backed out and let her finish the job. I was not disappointed in the results.

"I'm sorry, Lisa. I didn't handle that well."

"I've thought about what happened a lot these past few months. I didn't handle it well either. I only thought of myself. I let the business end of our relationship get ahead of twenty-five years of friendship. What you did hurt me. But I deserved it. When Emily shopped you around the industry and found solid interest, I realized I had dropped the ball. And I was angry about that, too. So, I'm sorry. I know we talked a little about it over the phone, but I just want to be sure where we stand and whether you want in on the negotiations with Abrams?"

"This past year hasn't been easy for either of us. I was angry with Barksdale for firing me. And I wanted to stick him in the eye. That was part of the reason for putting my nose in where it didn't belong. And I was angry at you. I don't feel that way any longer and your apology isn't necessary. Do I want to be in the negotiations? No. I have a lot of writing to do. And that's what I enjoy. I hate the business end of it. You and Nathan are more than capable."

"We're okay, then?"

"Yes, Lisa. More than okay."

I spent a few moments reporting the progress of my writing. Because of my past performance issues, Barksdale would grill her later about it. She liked my ideas and that I was writing again.

"What role will Jody have in your writing?" This was in reference to Emily's role as my editor and manager. The arrangement had been a burr in Lisa's saddle since Em and I first married. She endured it and adjusted to it, but I knew it cramped her style.

"She has no interest in my writing other than she appreciates it and supports me in it. She has an art gallery that consumes her attention. It's just you and me, Lisa."

She nodded. She didn't need to say anything. I knew this would please her.

She asked, "Have you interviewed Betty Worth?"

Betty Worth was the editor who used to work with R&R before she retired. She's the potential replacement for Emily.

"No. I called her and we meet after Jody and I get back from our honeymoon."

"Now tell me about Jody. Are you excited?"

"Lisa, I am. We're as compatible as two people could be. Soul mates is such a trite phrase anymore. Our relationship is so much more than that. Excited? I can't think of a time when I was in a better place."

"Me, too," she said. "To better places." She raised her glass, touched it to mine.

I repeated, "To better places."


We drove to the Whitehead Street house. Jody and I gave her the ten-cent tour of our new home, and I left the two of them in conversation. I ran to the airport to pick up Nathan Barksdale.

During Nathan's last trip to Key West, after we wrapped up the contract, he exchanged his formal attire for casual. I'd only seen Nathan in casual clothes the last time he was in Key West. His standard uniform was an expensive suit.

Nathan was a big, fleshy man, but as he labored down the jet-way, with his Hartman carryon trailing behind him on wheels, he was casually dressed and looked as relaxed as I'd ever seen him.

"Jack!" he said, extending a meaty hand for me to shake.

"Hi, Nathan. No suit?"

He looked down at himself. "Nope, when in Rome. Besides, I was so impressed with the Pier House I decided to come down for a few days. After the wedding, my daughter is flying down to spend a few days with me."

"Any bags to pick up?"

"No. I had my man pack for both Natalie and myself and had it shipped to the Pier House. All I have is this." He looked down at his rollaway bag.

"How is your daughter doing?"

He stopped in the middle of the concourse and turned to face me. His eyes were moist in his response. "Good. Wonderful in fact. She's benefiting from the counseling, medication, and she and I've spent a lot of time together, healing. What happened to her was a real wakeup call, Jack. I let my work consume me, while those who loved me suffered. I've backed off of work, delegated a lot of my duties to others and I'm determined to make up for lost time with Natalie."

I extended a hand to Nathan's shoulder and gave it a squeeze. "That's awesome news."

I showed him to my SUV parked in short-term parking, and I planned to drop him at the Pier House. I'd offered to put him up at our house, but now, with his daughter coming, I understood why he had declined.

As I pulled into the parking lot at the hotel, he said. "Can you have a drink with me? I've some news to share."

"I don't have much time Nathan. Jody and I have to pick up her children at the airport."

"This will take just a few minutes, I promise."

While Nathan checked in, I parked the SUV, met him in the bar that was bustling with patrons and our server took our drink order.

With his scotch, and my second beer of the day in hand, he said, "Global Pictures wants the rights to *The Tainted Lady*."

I tried my best to act surprised. He made no mention of the second book.

"I think it is your best work, Jack. It's still moving up the charts and it may exceed the single book sales record for anything you've written so far."

"Wow," I said. "That was one of my forty-five day wonders," referring to the two books I'd written in less than ninety days to avoid a lawsuit from Nathan.

"What're they offering?"

"Nothing yet. Lisa and I are still appraising what we think the rights are worth. But they definitely want the book. This could be a big pay day for you, buddy."

"And you, Nathan."

"And me."

He asked me to give him an update on the projects I was working on. I repeated what I'd said to Lisa not two hours earlier.

"We agreed on two, non-genre books in the first three years of the contract. I know what they'll be."

"Tell me about them."

I gave him a thumbnail of Jody's and Stephen's stories. I told him I would fictionalize them and thought he could promote them as "based on true stories."

He said, "Perfect. I didn't know what you had in mind for those books, but I like your ideas.

331

Let's proceed. But I'd like you to do another Dana O'Brien as fast as you can. With the movie deal, and the success of *Tainted Lady* I want to follow it up with another soon."

"I've already started on it." I explained the plot for the next book, but I knew I'd lost his attention once I assured him the next Dana O'Brien novel was a priority.

I offered him dinner at our house that evening, but he declined. I was all right with that since it would be chaotic at our house tonight, but I felt I needed to extend the invitation.

Nathan wanted to know the time of the wedding the next day. He ordered another scotch for himself and I said goodbye as I left to go back to the house to get Jody.

Clarissa had flown from Mobile to Atlanta and joined her brother Barry on a Delta flight from Atlanta to Orlando, Then they flew together on to Key West. We picked them up at the airport, brought them to the house. We gave them a quick tour, time to unpack and they joined us on the back patio for drinks before dinner. Lisa went shopping in town and she would return before the meal.

I'd never met either of Jody's children. Clarissa, Jody informed me, got her good looks from her father. But she looked just like Jody, down to the brown eyes, blond hair, olive skin and athletic stature. She even shared her mother's calm demeanor and gracious ways. Unlike her mother, she wore her hair short. Like her mother, she was outgoing, warm and, after a few moments in her company, I felt like I'd known her forever.

Barry looked nothing like Jody. He was tall, angular, with dark hair and features, and quiet. I got the impression Key West was the last place he wanted to be. I tried to engage him in conversation several times, but he wouldn't look at me. Before we gathered for happy-hour drinks, I asked Jody about it. She said to give it time. He'd come around.

I opened a bottle of Champagne and poured it into four fluted glasses Jody had set on the small patio bar. I passed a glass to Clarissa, Barry, and Jody. I offered a toast, welcoming Jody's children to our home and again, the attitude coming from Barry was palpable. Earlier I'd wanted to pull Barry aside to find out if I'd done something to offend him, but didn't. But I couldn't handle Barry's frosty demeanor any longer.

I reached for Barry's glass, set his and mine on the bar.

Bill Cronin

"Barry, come with me for a moment. I want to show you my new studio."

A puzzled look flashed on his face, but when I took a few steps down off the patio toward the guesthouse, he followed along.

Inside, I asked him to sit at one of two club chairs near my desk. I joined him in the other chair.

"Ever since we picked you and your sister up at the airport, I'm getting a clear signal you really don't want to be here."

Barry said nothing, only now we were making eye contact.

"I was wondering; have I done something to offend you? I'm marrying your mother tomorrow and I don't want to start my relationship with you on the wrong foot."

Still nothing. A dead stare.

"Look, I know you don't know me from Adam's housecat . . ."

"It's not you."

"I'm sorry?"

"It's not you." He said louder.

Sadness swept across his face replacing the stoic blank stare, as though someone had erased an image off an Etch-a-Sketch toy. I could see he was doing everything within his power to contain his emotions.

"Are you okay?" It was obvious he was not.

"I left work early today to come home and pack before meeting Clare at the airport. When I got home, my girlfriend had packed up and left."

"That's awful."

"She left a note on the kitchen counter."

"You haven't told your mom?"

"I haven't told anyone. I wasn't going to come. I was going to try to find Beth and try to work it out. But I knew mom was counting on me being here."

"I'm sure your mom would have understood. I would understand."

"My mom is over the moon about this wedding and you. She'd have understood, but she'd have been disappointed. I had to come."

That scored some points with me; his expressed care for his mother.

He continued, "Beth wanted a baby. And I wasn't ready. Hell, we aren't even married. We've been working through this for months. I guess she finally gave up."

"Did you try to call her?"

"She won't take my calls."

"I know you love her, or this wouldn't be bothering you so much."

He looked straight at me. "I do."

"Why do you object to a child?" This is one of the disappointments of my life, that I didn't father a child. My first wife couldn't have children, and Emily didn't want them.

"I've only been with Southern Power for a couple of years. We don't have a lot saved up, and I'd like to have a place of our own before we start a family."

"So this is financial?"

He stood up, towering over me. He paced back and forth in the small cottage almost having to duck to miss hitting his head on the ceiling fan. "For the most part. But being parents is a big responsibility."

I was hearing all the reasons why he didn't want children, but what I wasn't hearing was resolve. There was no power behind his words—no conviction.

"So let me ask the obvious question. Would you rather have Beth and a child in your life or no Beth in your life? It sounds like a child is important to her. It's a simple choice, unless there's something you're not telling me. I don't know whether your mom has told you our story. But we were childhood sweethearts . . ."

"Yes, she told me."

"We were in love, and she was taken from me. I regret we've missed so many years together. I'd do anything to have had the opportunity to have those years back. In the case of your mother and me, we didn't have a choice. Circumstances beyond our control separated us. But, you and Beth have a choice."

"You think I'm wrong?"

"This isn't a right or wrong decision. This is a decision of the heart. It's a decision of how important Beth is to you—how much you love her. A woman's need for a child is one of the most basic desires of the heart. There isn't anything more natural. To her, having a child, is a natural extension of her love for you. So this isn't about right and wrong."

Barry's face softened. He sat back down in the chair, his shoulders more relaxed. "I guess I've got some thinking to do."

"Barry, it seems Beth has agonized over this decision. And I don't know her. But, in many cases, when people make decisions and back it with drastic action, sometimes it's difficult for them to reverse course. Some people turn the page. If you love Beth, and want to pull this out of the fire, I'd act soon before it is too late. Perhaps you need to explain what's going on to your mom so she doesn't worry."

"I'll tell her after the ceremony. I don't want anything to spoil this for her." He paused a moment and said, "Thanks for this. It's becoming clear I've had my head up my ass."

"Barry, we all get stuck at times."

"For what it's worth, I see why my mom likes you so much. I hope I didn't offend you."

"Not at all."

"I'm happy for both of you." He stood up and extended a hand to me.

I shook it. "Thanks, Barry. I was hoping you'd feel that way."

Jody gave Barry an analyzing look as he and I walked up the steps to the back porch and walked through the screened door. Lisa arrived and we introduced her to Clare and Barry. We grilled hamburgers. Clare bartended and kept a steady stream of drinks coming. Still bothered by the events in his day, Barry made more of an effort and helped contribute to an enjoyable evening.

At about 9:00 p.m., Barry got a call on his cellphone and disappeared into the house, I assumed to talk to Beth. About thirty minutes later, Lisa was regaling us with stories from the early days of trying to sell my novels, when Barry appeared on the porch with good news written all over his face. He looked at me, gave me a thumbs up and he pulled a cold beer out of the bar on the porch. I looked at Jody. She gave me a puzzled look. It would be hard for me to beg off telling her of my discussion with Barry later. Barry tapped Jody on the shoulder, gestured for her to follow him and they disappeared into the house.

# 33

The wedding was a simple affair. We all crowded together on the back patio as we took our places before the notary public who performed the ceremony.

Despite the heat and humidity, Jody wore a sleeveless floor length dress with a single strand of pearls, and baby's breath woven into her hair.

It was too warm for a suit, but I still wore dress gray slacks and a white long sleeve shirt. Lisa produced a corsage for Jody and a boutonniere for me. Jody had hired a photographer who annoyed everyone with her commands to pose this way and that. Following the ceremony, everyone wanted to change into cooler clothing, but the photographer took her time taking pictures of Jody and me and pictures of the group.

Billie catered hors d' oeuvres at the reception in the back yard and steak and seafood in the dining room for dinner.

Barry and I didn't have an opportunity to talk in depth since our session in the studio the night before. He had excused himself from the dinner and returned dressed for travel. He hugged Jody, kissed her on the top of the head, made his way to me, and asked if he could speak with me for a moment.

I got up from the table and followed him through the house to the back porch.

"After we talked yesterday, I left a voice message on Beth's phone that I'd reconsidered having a child. I told her I loved her and that I was wrong. She called me last night and we had a long talk."

I'd already heard this from Jody last night as we were going to bed.

He continued, "She called me again this morning. She's still angry with me but she says she wants to work it out. So I booked an earlier flight."

"That's wonderful, Barry.

"You helped me, Jack. I needed that kick in the butt. Thank you."

We shook hands and Barry disappeared into the house and to a waiting cab out front on Whitehead Street.

Shortly thereafter, Nathan Barksdale bade Jody and I goodbye as he was on his way to pick up his daughter from the airport. During dinner, he'd talked about Marlin fishing. He said his daughter made him promise to take her on a deep-sea charter. I didn't know a thing about Nathan's daughter, but the last place I'd have expected Nathan to be was on a charter fishing boat.

As the party wound down, Jody kept pestering me to tell her where we were going on our honeymoon.

We were to leave first thing in the morning and the only thing I kept repeating was to 'pack light.' I kept telling her, "Where we're going you won't need any clothes."

# 34

I had expected we'd return home from our honeymoon, sunburned and ten pounds heavier. What began as a leisure cruise to St. John, ended up a mad sprint away from a developing tropical storm in the Lesser Antilles roaring toward the upper east coast of Florida. This shortened our ten-day trip to seven. The crew pulled anchor, reducing our time of privacy to two nights and one day.

The trip over to St. John was relaxing, and the two nights of seclusion were worth the trip. Even the threat of the tropical storm made the trip memorable.

When I returned to work in my studio, I'd left a sticky note on my computer screen reminding me of a pledge I'd made to Ruby before she passed away to find her adopted sister. In 1938, her half-sister Millicent had become pregnant by Awesome Banes, her mixed-race, half-brother. Millicent and Awesome were unaware at the time of their blood relationship. Millicent's father—Ruby's adopted father—John Barnes, had had an affair with a black woman, Lydia Banes when they were young. They had a son and agreed they'd hide their relationship from everyone, including Awesome.

Awesome was killed in a car racing accident, before his child was born. To avoid the bigotry their small town would have leveled against Millicent and her unborn child, Millicent agreed to be sent away to her father's sister in Michigan. She never returned to Florida. Ruby had lost touch with Millicent and, before her death, she asked me if I'd find her and make sure she was okay.

The only investigator I knew was Trimble Davis.

I called Davis and gave him all the information I had on Millicent Barnes. It wasn't much to go on, in fact, other than she went to Michigan, I had no idea where to direct him.

Davis said, "She'd be what, in her late seventies?"

"Yes, that would be about right."

"Any idea whether she had a boy or a girl?"

"None. You're not sounding optimistic."

"That's not true. I've found people with a lot less information than you've given me. More than likely, if she kept her child, and she didn't marry, her name would be on the birth certificate. We know the year the child was born, nineteen-thirty-eight or nine. And we know what state. If she had an abortion, that could be a road block."

"I don't think she'd have had an abortion. She went to Michigan to have the child. That wouldn't make sense to me."

"Well, let me look into it. What did you say the father's name was?"

"Awesome Banes. Why?"

"If she had a boy, it wouldn't be unusual for the mother to name the child after the father, in particular if the father was killed as you report."

"I hadn't thought about that."

"Just a thought. I'll get my folks started on this right away."

"How is Stephen's project coming?"

"I can't discuss the details with you. But I can tell you this. I wasn't wrong about John Baker. We haven't had to dig deep."

"How bad is it?"

"Again, Stephen is my client, so I can't get into specifics. But, when Stephen confronts the Bakers with what we have . . . well, Stephen will definitely have a strong hand. I wish I could tell you more, but until I talk to Stephen . . . ."

"I understand. Call me when you have something on Millicent."

"I'll be in Key West in a couple of days to go over what we've found for Stephen. I'll update you then."

"Call Stephen and at least give him an update. I'm sure you'll encourage him with what you told me."

"I'll call him now."

It had been a couple of weeks since I'd driven beyond Boca Chica Naval Air Station on the Overseas Highway toward Marathon. The sun blazed white in a clear blue sky and the aquamarine waters just off the thin strip of roadway made Lake Dora pale in comparison.

Near Sugarloaf Key, I noticed a tethered blimp-like balloon flying several hundred feet in the air. The conchs referred to it as Fat Albert. People told me it belonged to the Drug Enforcement Agency who used it to search for drug smugglers who use many of the secluded mangrove islands as drop points for drugs and marijuana.

At the north end of Sugarloaf, an RV resort was crowded up against the bridge connecting Sugarloaf to Cudjoe Key. Recreational vehicles of every description filled the campground and marina. Every time I passed this place, I had thought about making a road trip in an RV one day. My focus had been on my career, and I'd traveled little. As the campground whizzed by, I resolved to look into a motor home. I could write anywhere. I wondered how Jody might react to the idea.

Big Pine Key was the first key, from Key West that had a central business district. I followed directions Betty Worth had given me to her home and turned down a side street next to a shopping center. Halfway down the block, I encountered Key deer knotted together in the center of the road. Someone had thrown corn in the middle of the road, and the deer were oblivious to cars as they feasted away.

The Key deer were a third of the size of regular deer and unique to the Keys. Big Pine and No Name Keys are included in the Key Deer Wildlife Refuge. You're forbidden to feed these creatures, but the restriction in this case was ignored. I inched toward the deer. They moved out of the way just enough to get the car through and closed up again around the disappearing pile of corn. I'd read that Key deer are near extinction. They used to inhabit all the island keys, but now they were limited to Big Pine and a couple of smaller surrounding islands. Their population had dwindled to three-hundred. The outlook for their survival was not good.

Betty Worth's home sat on one of the many canals that fed into the waters around Big Pine Key. While her home was small, the fishing boat docked behind it dwarfed the house. When I parked at the street, the flying bridge of the boat stood a full story taller than the house.

I'd talked with Betty on occasion when R&R employed her to edit one of my novels, but I'd never met her in person. I knocked on her door, and a graying, tanned, athletic appearing woman greeted me in a wheelchair. Although her hair was almost white, her tanned face appeared to be young. I knew she'd retired, so I expected a woman in her sixties. If this was Betty Worth, she was only a couple of years older than me.

"Hi, Jack. I recognize you from your dustcover photos." Dustcover photos are always so deceiving. R&R continued to use headshots from fifteen years ago. If I'm still writing when I'm in my seventies, they're still going to be using the same photo of me.

"You must be Betty."

"You got it. Come in." She extended a hand, I shook it, she wheeled her sleek looking wheelchair around and I followed her into the house.

I looked around the small home. What struck me immediately was the openness of the house and the three sliding glass doors across the back wall. Even in the heat of the day, they were wide open and the breeze coming through them was refreshing. Beyond the sliders was an expansive deck and dock combination. It was obvious Betty and her husband spent most of their time on the deck.

The living room, dining area and kitchen were in one large room with a garage off to the left and bedrooms off to the right. While it was small, it appeared a professional had decorated it. Betty showed me to a Lazy Boy recliner and wheeled up next to me in her chair. She asked me if I wanted coffee or a soft drink, but I declined.

"I'm sorry you just missed Jim, my husband. He's out running some errands."

My natural curiosity wanted to ask about her disability, but I figured if she wanted to talk about it she would.

She said, "So Lisa said you need an editor."

"You've worked on my manuscripts, so I can't fake you out. I definitely need someone to keep me straight. Editing isn't one of my strong suits."

"When I talked with Lisa, she said R&R had agreed to do your editing. So I'm curious why you think you need my help?"

"Emily, my former wife and manager, used to do the cleanup work on my drafts, but she was more than that. She'd read my books for content, she would do the initial edits. She'd make suggestions and challenge my thinking on the plots."

"Lisa said you just got married again."

"Week and a half ago."

"Congratulations."

"Thanks."

"So how do you envision us working together?"

"I'd like to meet with you at the start of a project, give you my initial ideas and discuss them. I'd like your input. I'll write a detailed synopsis of the story, front to back and have you review it before I begin to write it. Once I complete the draft, I'd like you to read it for content and analyze what

I've written. If there are any rewrites to do, I'll do them then. Once we complete the draft, you'll edit it. I want to send a clean document to R&R.

"Alright. But my original question still stands. If R&R has agreed to pay for the editing costs, why not take advantage?"

"Personal pride, maybe. I'd like to retain control over my work. When I send an unfinished work to them, it gives them license to make wholesale changes. When I send a manuscript to them I don't want anything changed except for minor errors they'd find in a proofread."

"Okay, I understand. On the content editing, so much of it is personal opinion. How do you know you and I'll see eye to eye?"

"We won't know until we try."

"Well, for me, your timing couldn't have been better. We've been living here about a year. I'm finding as much as I enjoy fishing with Jim, I miss the work. And I'm going a little stir crazy here."

Without being specific, I asked her to tell me about herself. Her skiing accident, when she was thirty, was the defining moment in her life. A Queens, NY native, and an English major from NYU, Betty taught high school English until her spinal injury. She took leave following the accident to devote herself to physical therapy and to make the lifestyle adjustments of a paraplegic. She responded to an ad by R&R for copy/line editor, and she took the job because they allowed her to work from her home. She married Jim in her late-thirties. Jim was the personal injury attorney who handled her lawsuit against the ski-lodge where her accident occurred. She was ten years his junior, and when Jim retired, a year ago, they moved to the Keys.

We spent the rest of the time going over my ideas for novels based on Stephen and Jody's stories. We discussed the stories at length, and various strategies for getting the stories reduced to eighty-thousand words. I liked the way she thought. She was confident and expressed her opinions without trepidation. When I left Betty's home, we agreed to work three projects together and then reevaluate.

As I was leaving, I met Jim who said he loved my books, and invited Jody and I to go fishing with him anytime.

The Key deer were gone from the place I'd seen them. There was no trace of the corn on the road. I wondered to myself as I got back on US1 heading for home, how many species of wildlife had gone to extinction in Florida as the result of explosive growth and development, especially in the Keys. The string-of-islands was a national treasure. I felt, just like the Key deer, unchecked growth in the Keys would eventually squeeze its beauty out of existence.

# 35

It was a week later. Stephen had called to ask me to meet him and Trimble Davis at the Chart Room the next morning. He said Davis wouldn't discuss what he'd found on John Baker, but he said Trimble told him it was encouraging.

I met Stephen for breakfast and we speculated on what Davis had found, but neither of us had a clue. Each time I'd gotten together with Stephen he seemed stronger, more ebullient.

Davis waddled into the bar with Stephen in tow. I'd gotten there early, ordered a beer and found an open table. We exchanged greetings, we sat and Davis opened a briefcase, took out two files and set them on the table.

The server took our orders.

"After we finish with Stephen, Jack, I have something for you." He patted the two folders in front of him.

The server delivered drinks.

Davis started, "I've been doing this a long time. And I've investigated some pretty sleazy people, but your Mr. Baker is in a class all by himself." He opened the top manila file folder, and closed it again. "Before I show you this, let me lay a bit of a foundation. Are you both familiar with child prostitution?"

"No," I said.

Stephen said, "Isn't that where criminals abduct kids and sell them into the sex trade?"

Davis said, "That's part of it. There are many ways criminals exploit children and draw them into the sex trade. But what I want to talk about is something more secret, more sinister. There's a network of pedophiles who exploit their own children and swap them with other like-minded monsters. Sometimes money changes hands. At other times, the pedophile parents meet and exchange their children for sex."

"Like wife swapping?"

"Yes. These sick bastards handle all this through child porn clubs and now on the internet. They post pictures of their children on the internet like bait. Then they swap pictures of their children and make the connection."

Stephen asked, "Baker was into this?"

"Yes, still is. I know you and Melissa were married, so these first few pictures are going to be hard to see."

"Are you saying Melissa was involved?"

"Yes. As a child."

"I don't want to see them. Just tell me about them."

"Pedophiles have preferences. Some have fetishes about small children, while others prefer girls and boys arriving in their teens. John Baker was into girls aged ten through twelve."

"You're going to tell me he molested Melissa?"

"I wish it were that tame, Stephen. He was raping her. And when she grew out of his age preference, he offered his daughter up to others in exchange for their ten to twelve-year-old girls he fancied."

"How do you know this?"

"He made home movies and video tapes. I haven't had a lot of direct experience with child porn and pedophiles, but I know the retention of video tape isn't uncommon. These sick bastards tape this trash to use and reuse in the future."

I asked, "And you have tape of him having sex with his own daughter?"

"Yes, and he filmed others having sex with her, too."

"You'll have to excuse me." Stephen bolted from the table and headed down the hall towards the men's room.

"Sometimes I hate this job."

"How did you get access to these tapes?"

"I can't and won't discuss that. What I can say is these video tapes are in my possession."

Stephen returned. He was wiping his mouth with a wet paper towel and his face was white.

"There's more isn't there?" Stephen asked.

"Yes. Once Melissa was too old to have swap value, Baker went the more traditional route using child prostitutes. I have tape of it all."

"Does he know you have the tapes?" Stephen asked.

"No. He's, no doubt, by now discovered they're missing."

"How did you get them?" Stephen asked.

"I was just telling Jack I can't discuss that with you. I have them. That's all you need to know."

"Anything else?"

"Yes. My forensic accountants dug into Baker's finances just enough to confirm there's a paper trail connecting Baker to the extortion of your father and some other influential people. I had them stop, though. Had they gone further, it might have alerted Baker to our investigation. When we found the video tapes, I knew we had the leverage to meet your goals. But what we did find will be helpful to the FBI in launching a criminal investigation. I wanted to discuss it with you before we went any further."

"What do you think we should do?" Stephen asked.

"I think the child molestation tapes are all you need to threaten him. I'd wait on the rest. After you get what you need from Baker, you might think of turning the dogs loose on a criminal probe. What we've found will give the FBI a good head-start."

Stephen asked, "What about Baker?"

"You present Baker with the pictures in this folder, and I guarantee you he'll do what you want."

"I present?"

"I'm an investigator, Stephen. Not an attorney. Here's what I can do. I have possession of Baker's tapes. I'll hold them in safe-deposit-boxes. You should tell Baker someone will send these tapes to the *Atlanta Journal Constitution* if anything happens to you. My advice is I would not, under any circumstances, give up possession of those tapes."

"So you're suggesting I extract what I want from Baker in exchange for keeping the tapes quiet? What'll happen to all the perverts who're molesting these children? What'll happen to them?"

"Didn't you tell me Baker blackmailed your father, then, when your father quit-claimed the law firm to him, he released the compromising pictures of your father to the press?

"Yes."

"Well, do the same thing." Davis patted the file folder. "You're holding a strong hand, Stephen. Play that hand well. If you decide you want to go to the authorities with the extortion, let me know and I'll send you all the preliminary information we've collected."

Davis slid the top file over to Stephen. He moved the bottom file across the table to me. On the tab was the typed word "McNamara."

Davis asked, "Am I free to discuss this in front of Stephen?"

"Yes, of course."

"Millicent Barnes gave birth to Awesome Banes, Jr. on May 3, 1939, in Ann Arbor, Michigan. Millicent married in 1940, gave birth to a second child in 1941. Her husband was killed during the invasion of Normandy in World War II. She never remarried. She died from some form of cancer in 1956. Her son Awesome is in his late fifties, and owns several tire stores in Detroit, Ann Arbor and Lansing. His address is in the file, along with his sibling."

"That was quick."

"Not really. Since the father was killed before the child was born, there was a good chance, if it had been a boy, the mother would have given the child its father's name. Not rocket science. I searched that name first. It came up immediately. The rest of it came with an hour or so of research. Sometimes they're easy. If you need more information on the family, I could spend another hour on it?"

"No," I said. "This is fine."

"Well, gents. I have to be back in Atlanta for dinner."

"Do you need a ride to the airport?" I asked.

"No. It appears you two have a lot to talk about. I'll just catch a cab."

Stephen said, "Thanks, Trim. You did an excellent job."

"Good luck. Let me know if you need anything."

Davis labored up off the chair, collected his briefcase and shuffled out of the bar.

"You okay?" I asked, Stephen still looking pale and uncomfortable.

"No. I'm not okay. If I had Baker within my reach right now, I'd kill him."

"For what he did to your father?"

"That, too!"

"Melissa?"

He nodded his head. "What kind of man would do that to his own daughter?"

"And use her, to defraud you?"

"We must stop him, Jack."

"Are you ready to confront him? I don't know what's in that file, but if it shows what Davis said, it sounds like you have the leverage you need."

Stephen opened the file and took out the first picture. He slid it on the table to a point between us. It showed a young girl engaged in sex with an older man. The tagline on the picture read, "Melissa Baker age 11, with John Baker. TAPE 7." The next several pictures were similar. There were pictures of strangers with Melissa with the same type of tape reference numbers. The rest of the photos were of Baker with various eleven to twelve-year-old girls only the tape reference numbers were 247, 325, etc. Davis didn't say how many tapes there were, but it was obvious there were hundreds of them.

"Yeah, I'm ready to confront him. But I don't want to do it alone. Will you come with me?"

"To Atlanta?"

"I need your help, Jack."

"What you need is an attorney."

"In this meeting I'm going to blackmail Baker. An attorney is a sworn officer of the court. A reputable attorney would never agree to anything like that. They'd recommend taking what I have to the authorities and let them handle it."

"What's wrong with that?"

"My legal status and that of my father's law firm would be tied up for two to three years. I want to get on with my life. If I play this the right way, I can get what I want and have him put behind bars."

"How?"

"I need to think about that. But I don't want to meet with them alone."

"Them?"

"John and Melissa."

"Why both of them?"

"I don't know how much of this Melissa knows. I want her there when I present this filth to her father. I want to judge her reaction, and find out how complicit she was in all this."

"You think Albert Hall could be of help to you?"

"No. Not now. Maybe later. I don't want him to know a thing about this right now."

"When do you want to confront him?"

"I'm going to call and see if we can meet tomorrow." He paused a moment. "Will you come with me?"

"You sure about this, Stephen? What help could I be to you?"

"If it hadn't been for your concern and support, I'd still be on the street with no prospects. You started this journey with me, I want you to end this journey with me. Will you do it?"

"Alright. I'll do it. But I still think you need someone with more skill than me there."

"I'll call you as soon as I've made contact. Thanks once more, Jack."

I nodded without words.

Later that evening, Stephen called and said he had reached Baker. He said he told him we wanted to come to his office to work out the outstanding arrest warrant. That he wanted Melissa to be there since she'd have to okay any agreement. We're on at nine in the morning.

I'd already filled Jody in on all that had transpired, and, other than her fearing for my safety, she agreed I should help Stephen if I could.

I tried to sleep but it was useless. The horror story of John Baker's life haunted me. While I didn't have children, I could empathize with the children these sexual freaks had brutalized. What kind of emotional damage was done to a child raised under these heinous circumstances? What aberrant behavior had been created in Melissa Baker that she'd marry Stephen with the goal of co-swindling him out of his law firm and cause him financial harm? Was she a monster, too, or the victim of unspeakable crimes against her? While I was fearful of my role in this high-stakes drama—fearful of getting involved—I couldn't contain my natural curiosity.

# 36

Stephen was silent on the flight to Atlanta, no doubt thinking through how he'd conduct the meeting with the Bakers. Bumper-to-bumper traffic marred the cab ride from the airport to the law office. Stephen kept looking through the pictures Trimble Davis had given him, rearranging their order and rearranging them again.

When we stepped off the elevator the sign, "The Fitzgerald Law Firm," in silver, metal letters was attached to a stacked granite, stone wall. There was no office entryway. The law firm occupied the entire floor.

The receptionist whisked us past an all glass conference room reserved for their best clients and ushered us to a small conference room, marked "B," with a sliding sign on the wall next to the door which indicated it was "reserved."

A table with six chairs filled the small, windowless room. The receptionist showed us to our seats, said that Mr. Baker would be with us shortly and closed the door behind her. There was no offer of coffee, soft drinks or snacks.

I scanned the room for telltale signs of cameras, microphones or other devices. If they were there, they hid them well. The room was quiet except for a slight whistling of air from the vent in the ceiling.

Stephen seemed calm as he sat straight up in the chair, palms down on top of the file marked "John Baker." I turned to ask Stephen how he was doing and the door to the conference opened with a snap, and John and Melissa Baker filed into the room. Melissa sat across from me, but John Baker remained standing.

Baker was shorter than I had imagined, in his mid-fifties and heavy set. He was almost gray, had a full head of hair and dark brushy, low hanging eyebrows. Baker's most notable feature was dark, black eyes. Melissa was as attractive as Stephen described her. Well-endowed without being voluptuous, she had dark features, long dark brown hair and gray sultry eyes.

John Baker said, "Where have you been, Stephen?"

"You know where I've been. You sent your lawyers to the Keys to serve the warrant."

"You must have an angel watching over you, boy."

"You mean putting the warrant on hold?"

"Who's your friend?" He looked over to me.

"It doesn't matter who he is. What matters right now is what you did to my father."

"I've no idea what you're talking about, Stephen."

"You were blackmailing him. And after you sucked him dry, you humiliated him in the press. You drove him to suicide."

"Nothing of the sort. Your father was morally bankrupt and got what he deserved. The fact he didn't have the balls to face the music was a testament to his cowardice. You're a lot like him, Stephen, a coward. You couldn't face the music either so you ran. From what I've learned you've been living on the streets rather than face the realities of your own miserable little life."

I watched Melissa as she watched Stephen endure the humiliating remarks hurled at him by her father. There wasn't even a faint reaction on her face.

Stephen said, "Sit down, John. We have a lot to discuss."

John said, "We have nothing to discuss. You're in Georgia now. You're in my state. You can't hide behind extradition. There are two police officers in the lobby waiting for you. If you're not prepared to make Melissa whole on alimony, and turn over Melissa's stock to the law firm, they'll escort you to jail, and I assure you I'll see to it they prosecute you to the full extent of the law."

"Sit down, John!" Stephen raised his voice.

"Do you have the money and stock or not?"

"I've something more important to discuss."

"I didn't think so. Melissa?"

Melissa rose as she and her father moved toward the door.

"If you leave this room, I'll send this picture and all the tapes I have to the *Atlanta Journal Constitution*. Not only will you be finished in this town, your career will be over."

Melissa almost ran into the back of her father as he stopped short of the door.

"What picture?"

"Sit down."

"I'm not sitting down until you tell me what this is all about."

"Melissa. You need to sit too, because this involves you as well."

Melissa looked at her father for direction. She received none. She finally returned to her seat. I could see the mental wheels spinning in John Baker's eyes as the mystery of the photograph rolled over in his mind.

"If you don't sit down, I'll show this picture to Melissa first."

Stephen opened the flap of the envelope, slid the stack of photographs out and laid them face down on the table.

With hesitation, Baker eased himself down in the chair in front of Stephen.

Stephen said, "Before this day is over, you'll sign a quit claim to your shares of this law firm and assign them to me. You'll wire fifteen-million dollars into my account that will repay my father for the money you stole from him. And, Melissa, you'll sign a document releasing me from any further alimony and you'll drop your claim to any of the shares of this law firm."

John Baker bolted from his seat. Just as he was about to explode, Stephen turned over the first picture in the stack. It was a color photo of Baker engaged in sex with a pubescent black girl. Baker reached to snatch the picture out of Melissa's view, but Stephen had anticipated that and retrieved the picture. Stephen handed the picture to Melissa. Baker tried to grab the picture away from his daughter, but she stood and found a corner of the room and examined the picture.

I watched as the image in front of Melissa Baker found purchase and the horrified look that swept over her face.

"Where did you get that picture?" the red-faced Baker demanded.

"Pictures, John. Pictures. Many of them."

"Those are fake. I've never seen that girl in my life."

"What about these girls?" Stephen began to peel the pictures off his stack and lay them out like cards on the top of the table.

In a rage, Baker swept his hand across the table sending the photographs and the rest of Stephen's stack of pictures flying off the table. Most of them landing on the floor at Melissa's feet. One of the pictures caught Melissa's attention. She dropped the one in her hand, reached down to the floor, and picked up another. Judging by her reaction, she'd found one of the pictures of her and her father. Her hand began to shake, and tears leapt from her eyes dripping on the picture in her hand.

This time Melissa asked, "Where did you get these pictures?"

"Your father filmed you, and every other child he had sex with. I have hundreds of tapes of you and your father and other girls."

"You bastard," she said red-faced. At first, I didn't know who she hurled the insult at, her father or Stephen. Then she came across the room at full-throttle toward Stephen. I was able to stand, grab her around the waist and restrain her.

"Who the hell do you think you are? Those are personal. How dare you treat my father with such disrespect."

Baker stood, went around the table and restrained his daughter.

Incredulous, Stephen asked, "So you knew about all this?"

"Every great man has weaknesses. Look at your father."

That hit a nerve with Stephen. "Don't you dare compare my father's dalliances to this sick bastard." Stephen pointed an accusatory finger at John Baker.

John Baker asked, "What do you want?"

"I already told you what I want."

"And if I don't."

"As I said, I'll send the tapes to the *Journal*. Just so we understand one another, we've hidden the tapes in safety-deposit-boxes you'll never find. If anything happens to me, my representative will send all the tapes to the *Journal*."

"How did you get those tapes?" Baker seethed.

"How did you dig up the dirt you used against my father?"

"Tell him to screw himself, Dad."

"Shut up!" Baker shot a sideward glance at his daughter.

"I want those tapes." Baker said through clenched teeth.

"That's not going to happen," Stephen said.

"There will be no deal."

"Suit yourself. Come on, Jack. It's time to go."

"What assurances do I have you won't use those tapes against me?"

"None. There will be no agreements, no contracts, nothing in writing except the documents you sign to relinquish any claim to this law firm and of course, the money deposited into my account. And there's the alimony and stock your daughter was awarded."

"I'm not signing anything," Melissa spit the words out.

"Shut up. You'll do as I tell you." To me he said, "You took those tapes from me illegally. You'll never use them in a court of law."

From the same envelope containing the pictures, Stephen produced the legal documents he wanted John and Melissa Baker to sign. "They'll work fine in the court of public opinion. And that's where these videos will go if you don't sign these papers."

Red-faced, Melissa said, "How could you be so cruel?"

"You two destroyed my father and almost destroyed me. Cruel? I don't think I'm being cruel at all. I'm just righting a wrong, defending my father and putting my own life back together."

I looked at John Baker as he mentally scrambled trying to find a way out. "I need to think about this. I need some time."

I looked at Stephen, and I could see the beginning signs of victory on his lips as just the hint of a smile appeared.

"In the next ten minutes, if you haven't signed those documents and left the building, my next stop is to the *Journal* and a meeting with Benny Dayton on the metro desk.

"What about my things?"

"I'll have them sent to you."

"I have personal possessions in my office."

"I don't care."

"Don't do this, Dad. He's bluffing. We can figure something out," Melissa pleaded.

I remembered Stephen telling me he had pleaded with his father not to sign his ownership away to John Baker. Everything had come full circle.

"Jack, would you go out to the receptionist and tell her Mr. Baker needs two witnesses."

I did as he asked. When I returned to the room, Stephen had placed pens in front of the

Bakers. In a moment, two young staffers came in all smiles, eager to help the senior partner. John and Melissa Baker signed the forms in front of them and the witnesses signed under their signatures.

Stephen said, "Now the money." Stephen turned to one of the staffers and asked them to bring a laptop into the room. Both left and one returned with a computer. Stephen punched in the web address for Ameritrade, keyed in his account, and wrote down the wiring instructions needed to effect a wire transfer.

"Where do you have your brokerage account?"

"Morgan Stanley."

Stephen keyed in the web address. "Account number?"

"I don't know it."

"Social Security number, then."

"I can't …"

"Don't screw with me Baker."

Baker gave his number from memory.

"Don't do this, dammit," Melissa begged.

"Password."

Baker read off the letters and numbers.

Stephen found what he was looking for with ease. From his facial expression, I knew it had surprised him. I could see some large numbers just peering over his shoulder.

"I'm surprised you have so much in cash. I thought we might run into some problems with this." Stephen keyed in the amount of the withdrawal, the routing instructions and hit enter. He signed off the site, folded the laptop closed and slid it across the table to Baker.

"Now, both of you get out." Stephen stood up. "If you don't leave I'll have the police in the lobby, escort you out of the building."

"You little bastard!" Melissa spit in Stephen's face as she passed by him on the way out of the conference room. Stephen took a handkerchief from his pocket and wiped the spittle from his face as we watched them leave the room. We got up, walked into the hall and watched as they got on the elevator headed down to the lobby.

I followed Stephen to the receptionist. "Who's in charge of security these days?"

She told him.

"Ask him to meet me in conference room "B."

The older man entered the conference room and recognized Stephen immediately. Stephen explained the departure of the Bakers, and showed him the signed documents for verification. Stephen instructed the man to immediately remove the Bakers from access to any of the files of the company, to change elevator codes, door locks and security system passwords. He ordered the Bakers offices sealed except for their personal effects. He demanded all company credit cards, bank accounts, escrow accounts be immediately frozen. Stephen instructed the security chief to send notification to all the Fitzgerald Law Firm clients, effective immediately, the Bakers would no longer be associated with the firm, nor would the firm honor commitments the Bakers had made after the notice.

Stephen impressed me with the speed with which he seized control over the law firm. I hadn't seen this side of Stephen. He was confident, decisive and inspiring.

Stephen gathered all the senior partners into the glass enclosed conference room and explained the Bakers departure. He stopped short of revealing Baker's abuse of children, but spared no detail regarding Baker's blackmail and theft of the Fitzgerald Law Firm from his father. When he opened the meeting for questions, I had never experienced such an outpouring of support for what Stephen had done. For two hours, story after story of how the Bakers had destroyed the reputation of the firm and the relationship between the firm and its employees captivated me. They all expressed the hope that Stephen would return to take his father's place and to pull the firm out of its tailspin.

From what I gleaned from the comments, the law firm, under Stephen's father, provided legal services to corporations and state and city governments. Baker's firm was a personal injury law firm. When Baker merged the two, he 'milked' the corporate/governmental business to fund more high-risk personal injury cases. Baker also engaged in influence peddling, leveraging the firm's many contacts inside business and government for exorbitant retainer fees. He promised clients government contracts he rarely delivered, all the while lining his pockets.

The immense talent around that conference table fascinated me. Any one of the attorneys in the room would have made an excellent leader. But there was one woman with whom I was most impressed. Stephen addressed her as Sally. It was clear from the way she spoke with Stephen and the sway she had over the senior partners in the room, she was the natural leader of the firm. I had no idea what role she played, what her title was or her relationship with the others, but there was no question Sally had the systemic support of all her peers.

Following the session, which extended beyond our departure time at the airport, I asked Stephen who Sally was. All he'd say is, "soon to be the managing partner of this law firm."

Stephen told me he needed to stay in Atlanta for a few days and asked me if I wanted to remain. I declined and the firm's receptionist changed my ticket back to Key West for a later flight.

While Stephen attended to the pressing issue of cutting off the Bakers from any further access to the business or financial accounts, I waited in the lobby.

It was six-thirty before Stephen reappeared.

"You hungry?"

"Starving."

"My father loved a little restaurant up toward Roswell. He used to take me there for Steak Diane. You good with that?"

"I'd love to."

# 37

We took a cab up Roswell Rd to the Lark and the Dove restaurant.

The maître d escorted us to a private table. Stephen ordered for both of us. "I'm buying your dinner, Jack. Sally saved all my company credit cards. I'm now on an expense account." He pulled an American Express card out of his shirt pocket, held it between his finger and thumb and returned it to his pocket.

The wait staff and chef prepared the Caesar salad and the main course tableside. The service was showy, attentive and a treat for me. When we'd eaten our meal, and we were sipping after-dinner brandy, I asked Stephen to review the day with me.

"How did it feel to be back in the law firm again?"

"You know, I was so focused on how I'd deal with the Bakers I had never given a thought to being back in the office, with people I once worked with. I wasn't prepared for that."

"You did a marvelous job this morning, Stephen. You disheveled Baker with those pictures."

"The surprise for me was Melissa knew about the children her father was using for sex. I thought for sure, when she found out her father had taped their sexual encounters and his escapades with others she'd turn on him. At least that's what I wanted to believe."

"Are you still in love with her?"

"There was a moment there when she first looked at the pictures of her and her father together, I thought she might just be an unwilling victim in this. But when she came at me, railing against me that I'd exposed her father—if there were any feelings—she crushed them."

"And what're you going to do about the law firm? It sounds like they're in need of a leader."

"And they'll have one, it just won't be me."

"Why Stephen? It seems like a perfect fit, you stepping in to fill the shoes of your father. As a writer that would be the perfect ending to a rags-to-riches story; your story."

"I know it doesn't make any sense. I just don't want that responsibility or the headaches that go with it. The last three years on the street have taught me a lot about myself. I want to keep my life simple. The Fitzgerald Law Firm with several floors of attorneys is a giant ulcer I don't want."

"Couldn't you put someone in charge and become one of the staff attorneys and just work on cases that interest you. You just give the headaches to someone else?"

"As it stands now, I own a majority of the firm. If I worked there, there would be no way to isolate myself from the politics of the law practice. I'd be the person everyone would treat with kid gloves. I don't want that. At a minimum, I want to make Sally managing partner. At best, I'd like to hammer out an agreement where Sally and the rest of the partners buy the firm from me. That's why I need to stay for a few days, to iron that out. The other thing I want to do while I'm here is meet with the attorney general of Georgia and the FBI and go over what Trimble Davis found out about Baker extorting my father. Albert told me he could arrange a meeting with the Georgia AG. I want to see if I can interest them in launching a criminal investigation. I haven't gone through the files in Melissa and John Baker's offices. There may be something there that will add weight to what Davis has already found."

"Then what?"

"I like Key West. If I sell my stake in the law firm and combine it with what's in my bank account, I'd have plenty to buy a home there and start a law practice. But first, I need to pass the bar exam and get my law license. I thought I'd ask Cynthia Pike if she could make some room in her office for me. And I'm intrigued with the possibility of working for the governor. I'd have to be in Tallahassee a lot, but I think I can make a contribution to what he's trying to do."

"What about Baker? Do you think he'll try to reverse the wire transfer you made on his computer?"

"I hope he does. That would remove any hesitation I have about exposing his abuse of children. I have learned living on the street these past couple of years is I don't need a lot of money to survive. If it has taught me anything, it is I'm not afraid of failure. The trades I made earlier in his account wouldn't have been made until the close of business earlier today. That would have given him plenty of time to reverse the transaction, if he's going to do it. If I had been him, that's what I'd have done. I'd have left town and disappeared. He and Melissa both."

"I find it hard to believe Baker would have rolled over without a fight. If there are files in your office that could implicate him in your father's blackmail, or other cases of blackmail, don't you think he'll make an attempt to get into his office and retrieve that information?"

"While you were waiting in the lobby, I asked Sally to have everything in John Baker's office boxed and removed from the building and delivered to Trimble Davis for safekeeping. Ditto Melissa's office. I called Davis, filled him in on the meeting with Baker and asked him to go through everything from Baker's office to see if there was anything of value. I also asked Sally to post guards at the office for the next week as a precaution."

"Sounds like you covered all your bases. Are you going to send the tapes to the *Journal*?"

"Yes. First, I want to meet with the AG and talk with him about bringing a criminal case. Once that's underway, the tapes will surface. I will call Albert Hall, explain what happened today, and ask him to make the introduction for me."

"Good."

"Jack, none of this would have been possible without your help. Your willingness to stake me, and your constant encouragement and your friendship mean a great deal to me. I may be able to repay the money you, Jody and Billie have lent me, but I can't repay your emotional generosity. You stuck with me all the way through this. Thank you."

I caught a cab from the restaurant to the airport, and made it to the gate just as the agent was about to close the door to the jet way.

I tried but failed to clear the stressful events of the day from my thinking. But I continued to playback Stephen's masterful handling of the Bakers. From the guy on the street who was afraid to give people his real name, to the man who walked into that conference room in Atlanta and seized control of his father's law firm, I couldn't believe the transformation.

As the crew prepared for a landing in Key West, I thought about something Stephen said in the cab going to the restaurant. I asked him where he'd summoned the strength to do what he did earlier, confronting the Bakers. He said, "They humiliated my father, to the point he didn't want to live anymore. I couldn't let that stand." If there was a heaven, I hoped Stephen's father had been watching as his son defended his honor. I hoped his father was as proud of what he'd done as I was.

# 38

It was Thanksgiving. Billie had closed the restaurant and had invited a small gathering of family, friends and restaurant employees to dinner. Jody and I prepared to head to the restaurant.

In late August, Ransome Downes sent his lieutenant governor to Key West to offer Stephen a temporary cabinet-level position heading up the entire homeless initiative. Stephen had only expected a staff-level position. Stephen was honored by the job offer. He sold his share of his father's law firm to the other partners and purchased a modest home a few blocks from us. He shared office space with Cynthia Pike for a while, then found his own space two doors down from her. While he commuted often to Tallahassee, he did most of his work in Key West. Our friendship expanded and we settled into a routine of meeting two times a week for breakfast at The Marlin.

Stephen reported that John Baker's office at the law firm contained a treasure trove of evidence proving Baker had blackmailed Stephen's father as well as other high-ranking state officials and judges. With help from the Georgia AG, the FBI charged the Bakers and their cases awaited trial until they found them. They both disappeared following Stephen's confrontation. Stephen turned the tapes over to the FBI instead of the newspaper. It turned out John Baker had been part of a human trafficking ring, where they kidnapped under-aged children and forced them into prostitution. According to Stephen, from the tapes and information collected in John Baker's office, the FBI was on the verge of a multi-state bust of that ring.

Stephen was now a multi-millionaire, but he lived in simplicity and without pretense. I'd come to value his friendship.

I was already dressed and waiting for Jody on the back porch where she and I spent most of our time when I wasn't writing.

"You look nice," I said, when she appeared in the doorway to the house. She wore her blond hair down. Her tan from the summer sun was dark. She wore white shorts, a sleeveless navy blue blouse and white sandals.

"You don't look so bad yourself. I'm feeling guilty."

"About what?"

"We should have invited the kids down."

"It will be okay. We'll have them down for Christmas."

What I didn't tell her was I'd invited Clare and Barry. They'd flown in the night before. Barry had gotten back with his girlfriend, Beth, and they were planning on marriage soon. Clare, Barry and Beth were staying at Billie's to surprise Jody. They were moving to our house after dinner and would spend the rest of the weekend with us.

"It is such a nice day I was thinking we might walk."

I said, "I was thinking the same thing."

Jody and I walked past the "closed" sign hanging from the host stand at The Mangrove and made our way to the back of the courtyard where a long table had been set up. Molly Flynn was Billie's guest and it was unusual to see her at the restaurant in casual clothes. A pregnant Billie flitted back and forth between the food truck and the table making a fuss over everyone.

Barry, his girlfriend and Clare sat on the far right end of the table. Jody didn't immediately notice them. I got this sharp elbow into my ribs, "Why didn't you tell me they were coming?" Jody ran to her children as they stood to give and receive hugs.

I followed behind and joined in. Barry introduced Beth.

When Beth gave me a hug she said, "I hear I have you to thank for Barry's change of heart."

"I didn't do anything. Just freed him up to do what he wanted to do."

"Well thank you anyway. You know we're getting married."

"Yes. Barry was so excited he called Jody the day he proposed and you accepted. I'm so happy for you. When's the big event?"

"We haven't set a date yet, but maybe next year about this time. I want our wedding to be here, but when it is cooler of course and not so humid."

While Jody mingled with her family, I turned to Molly Flynn and said, "You have the day off, too?

"Wonders never cease. I told Billie she needed to conserve her strength, her being pregnant and all, but she wouldn't listen."

"You know, Billie."

"What do you think of the new building?"

"Oh you've just got to see it!" She grabbed me by the hand and dragged me through the gate in the fence. The two story building wasn't any larger than the old one, but taller. Much taller ceilings on both floors accounted for the increase in height. Contractors had completed the outside of the building except for landscaping which they couldn't do until Billie removed the food trucks.

As we walked through the main door there was an elevator door straight ahead, bathrooms to the right and to the left café doors into this huge kitchen. The dining area was gone.

"Okay, first the elevator leads to the second floor which has one large dining area, and office for Billie and two smaller private rooms we can use for either private meetings or parties. We can also convert them to expanded dining room space when we need it."

"And here is this incredible kitchen." She showed off the stainless steel and chrome as if she were Vanna White showing the jackpot gift on Wheel of Fortune. She gave me the tour of the expansive kitchen, the grille, the food prep areas, the massive walk-in refrigerator and automatic dishwasher. Walls and floors were all white tile, and everything gleamed. She stopped to explain each workstation and what they did at each. She'd had significant input into the design of the kitchen, so pride oozed from every word.

"So when will you be able to use it?"

"Another week or so. We have many little items on the "punch list" but we're hoping we can begin operations by December 5. That would be a Thursday. We'd have it operational for that weekend."

"Molly, it's beautiful."

"I know." She clapped her hands and looked around at the new facility a wide grin on her face. "I have your sister to thank for it. She's a marvelous woman, Jack. She's kind, generous and works so hard. I just love her."

She walked me back, to our group, and Stephen had arrived with Cynthia Pike.

I exchanged greetings with Cynthia and she headed down the table to greet Jody and her family.

Stephen moved close to me and said in low tones, "They found John Baker."

"You're kidding. The FBI?"

"Yep. The agent in charge called me ten minutes ago to tell me."

"Where did they find him?"

"Cudjoe Key! Can you believe it? They were monitoring his credit cards. He bought gas last night at a filling station with one of them. He must have gotten comfortable and thought no one was looking for him."

"That's less than-an-hour from here."

"Yeah, he'd rented a house under an assumed name. The Key isn't that big. Once they were on the island, they found his car in thirty minutes."

"They find Melissa, too?"

"No. Not yet. But they have him in custody. He's in the Monroe County jail here in Key West."

"That's an ironic twist, isn't it?"

I hadn't noticed Alex until she came up to me and, with concern, asked me if I'd seen Billie. I excused myself from Stephen and I followed Alex in her search for Billie. We found her in the refrigerated truck, sitting on a box and in much pain. Billie asked me to give Alex and her a moment.

I waited outside the truck until Alex popped her head out and asked me to get Jody. I ran to the courtyard and pulled Jody from her family, "It's Billie. She needs your help."

"What's going on?"

"I don't know."

We made it to the truck, and Jody went through the door and a moment later Alex appeared. "I'm sorry, Jack. I think Billie is miscarrying. She has intolerable, lower back pain and she's bleeding like a bad menstrual cycle. I'm headed for the house to get her some clean clothes and then we need to get her to the hospital."

In ten minutes, Alex came back with Billie's old, rusted Volvo. She went into the truck, and a moment later, Billie, Alex and Jody emerged.

Billie said, "I'm sorry Jack, about the dinner."

"Stop it," I said. "You're more important than a dinner."

Alex asked me, "Would you please explain to the others. I'll call from the hospital and let you know what's going on."

I did as she asked. Molly Flynn offered to finish the meal, but everyone had lost their appetite upon receiving the news of Billie. Those who remained, split into two cars and drove to the island's medical center. We huddled into the small waiting area in the emergency room hoping for word on her condition. Within the hour, Jody came out of the ER.

Stress devoured her face. "Billie lost one of the babies. They just gave her an ultrasound and the second child is doing fine. Her OB doctor is headed in right now."

"How is she doing?" I asked on-behalf of the awaiting group.

"She's okay. When they assured her the second child was doing fine, it raised her spirits. But she's still struggling."

Molly said, "What Billie needs to do is slow down and take it easy. There's no reason for her to work as hard as she does. I can handle it without her."

I asked, "How's Alex?"

"Alex is a rock, darlin'. Her first concern is for Billie. Her love for Billie is fierce. She's as protective as a momma bear over a cub."

"That's good. That's good."

"I want to get back in there."

"Tell her we're all praying for her."

"She knows."

A half hour later, Billie walked out of ER with Alex there to steady her.

"Well, I just got the ass-chewing of the century in there." Billie said.

Jody looked at me and with a glance confirmed what Billie had just said.

"Doc said she's not to be within a thousand feet of the restaurant unless she's eating there," Alex said more for Billie's benefit.

I asked, "What can she do?"

"As little as possible," Billie said.

Molly said, "Billie I got it. I can handle it."

"I know you can, sweetie. The problem is I love that place. It's going to kill me that I can't be there." To the rest of us she said, "I'm fine. Thanks for being here. It means a lot to me. But I'm exhausted and just want to crawl in bed."

Alex helped Billie into the Volvo and left. Molly offered to put an abbreviated dinner together for everyone and we all followed her back to The Mangrove and tried to make the best of a disappointing day. We all wished there were more we could do for Billie.

I prayed that nothing would happen to her surviving child. I knew how much this meant to her.

# Epilogue

A cold front had pushed through Key West, dropping daytime temperatures into the low seventies and drying out the humid air. Summer pushed its way into the Conch Republic, but the island fought it off. At this late stage of spring, perhaps the prettiest time of the year in the Keys, you welcomed these final blasts of cool air knowing they may be the last of the season. Soon, summer would smother the southern-most-point with oppressive air.

It had been three weeks since Billie and Alex lost their second baby. This was Billie's first day back at work. Jody and I had spent a lot of time with Billie and Alex bucking them up where we could. Alex took leave and had done everything she could to convince Billie not to go back to work for a while. But Billie said she needed to get out of the house and needed the work to take her mind off her disappointment. Molly Flynn had done a remarkable job of filling in for Billie in the last few months of her pregnancy and since the grand reopening of the restaurant in December, The Mangrove's business had doubled.

On my way from our house to the restaurant, I paused across the street from Hemingway's house. I reviewed the events that had happened since I'd stood there a year ago trying to decide if I wanted to live in Key West. So much had happened.

There was Stephen's triumph over the Bakers. He had settled in Key West, had passed his bar exam in February and was hard at work implementing the governor's homeless program. Within the past few days, Stephen called to tell me John and Melissa Baker's attorneys had settled out of court on federal charges of extortion, money laundering and conspiracy. John Baker would serve at least fifteen years and Melissa would serve five before they'd be eligible for parole. Charges were still pending for child prostitution and child porn against John. Stephen said prosecutors expected Baker to plead guilty on those charges to avoid a public trial.

Although I hesitated at first, I finally put my house on the market in Mount Dora. After Emily and Bob Decker had married, Emily had put a full-court-press on me to sell the home to her. When Jody and I moved into the Whitehead Street house, it was obvious to me, without a shred of doubt, Key West was where I belonged. I finally relented, called Emily and agreed to sell.

I thought I might miss the view of Lake Dora from my studio and that somehow it might affect my writing. But the guest house behind our new home was every bit the cocoon my studio in Mount Dora had been. I began work on *Left Behind*, a novel about a lost WWII bomber over the Himalayas in 1943, shortly after Jody and I returned from our honeymoon. I turned it over to my new editor Betty Worth just before Christmas. I had one more chapter left of *Joe and the Governor*, a fictionalized version of Stephen's story I'd written since the first of the year. So my new studio was a productive place. When I'd stood there, last year, ruminating about the need for a studio and a place to write, the Whitehead Street house fit the bill in every regard.

I'd been sitting on the information Trimble Davis had found about Millicent Barnes, and Awesome Banes, Jr. I had fulfilled my obligation to Aunt Ruby to find her adopted sister, but I still felt I needed to do more. I'd thought about traveling to Detroit, to make a connection with her adopted nephew, but I kept asking myself the question, 'For what purpose?' While I hadn't acted on it, I couldn't bring myself to take it off my bucket list. I felt like I needed to do it for Ruby.

Since spreading Helen Holland's ashes, Jody had plunged herself into making the Whitehead Street house her own. She also gave long overdue attention to her gallery, which she'd neglected during her mother's stay and illness. Since Helen's passing, she and Dr. Carnes talked weekly and Janis had become a frequent guest in our home. Helen's intervention into Jody's life was a godsend in my view. While there are no dramatic changes in her as a result, the thin veil of sadness the tragic loss of her family had produced had been lifted and she was happier, more engaged if that were possible. Jody was happy in every respect.

As I stood across the street, watching patrons queue up to get into Hemingway's, my thoughts turned to Billie. I couldn't help but think how hopeful she'd been about becoming pregnant. I considered how she waved off the disappointment of the miscarriage of the first embryo because they'd implanted two. Then, I explored the feelings the enormous loss of her baby at birth created in me. I wrestled with the reasons one person can go through life unmarred by tragedy of any kind, while someone like Billie suffered one disappointment after another. Billie would be an incredible mother and I had an impossible time finding words to comfort her. Only Jody could relate to the loss Billie felt. The two of them spent much time together as Billie faced her sadness and grief.

Billie's miscarriage and unsuccessful pregnancy stumped her doctors. They were encouraging her to try again. While I'd watched her and Alex try to get their emotional arms around another attempt, I hoped another failure wouldn't crush her. This time Alex led the charge for another try.

As I prepared to walk up Olivia Street to her restaurant, to find a way to lighten her load on her first day back to work, emotion overcame me about Billie. After a thirty-five-year separation, it had been a year and a half since Billie and I reconnected. In that time, I'd grown to admire, respect and love my half-sister. While she had experienced her unfair share of hardships, she had the strength of character to press ahead and succeed in spite of them. She was one of the most generous people I'd ever known, and had a head for business that had turned The Mangrove into a real success story. When she was about to lose her restaurant over a lease dispute with her old landlord, she confronted it head on and succeeded. When fire destroyed the main building at the restaurant, she bounced back and rose above it. Following all the abandonment she suffered as a child and into her adult life, she found Alex and made a life with her. During these past few weeks following the smothering loss of her baby, you could see her natural instinct to fight back, to rise up.

As I looked both ways, crossed the street, and walked along the crooked wall alongside Hemingway's on Olivia Street, I knew Billie would overcome. Whether she decided to have another try at a pregnancy or not, she'd be okay. She was a survivor. We were all survivors, Billie, Jody and me. Joined together, we could all face the challenges that came our way.

Bill Cronin

# The End

If you liked this Book.

Reviews are critical. Many paid promotional sites require a minimum number of "reviews" before they will allow an independent author to advertise. Without these sites, independent authors like me have little or no hope of gaining an audience for our work. If you liked this book, please leave a review. Eloquent words are not necessary. Even a simple, "I liked this book," would be helpful. If you feel compelled to say more, you have my gratitude.

## Contact Information

For more information on Bill Cronin's novels, visit his website at http://billcroninwrite.com. To receive updates and news on Bill Cronin's books, "like" his Facebook page at http://facebook.com/billcroninwrite. You can contact the author directly at: billcroninwrite@gmail.com

# Bill Cronin's Other Books

All books available on Amazon.

### ***Stand Alone Novels***

*Dial Tone, 2012*

*The Tainted Lady*, 2014

### ***Jack McNamara Chronicles***

*The Song of the Mockingbird*, Book 1, 2013

*Ruby's Story*, Book 2, 2014

*Letting Go*, Book 3, 2015

Bill Cronin